ONE GREEK SUMMER

KATE FROST

First published in Great Britain in 2022 by Boldwood Books Ltd.

Cover Design by Lexie Sims

Cover Photography: Shutterstock

A CIP catalogue record for this book is available from the British Library.

Paperback ISBN 978-1-80280-443-0

Large Print ISBN 978-1-80280-439-3

Hardback ISBN 978-1-80280-438-6

Ebook ISBN 978-1-80280-436-2

Kindle ISBN 978-1-80280-437-9

Audio CD ISBN 978-1-80280-444-7

MP3 CD ISBN 978-1-80280-441-6

Digital audio download ISBN 978-1-80280-435-5

Boldwood Books Ltd
23 Bowerdean Street
London SW6 3TN
www.boldwoodbooks.com

For Mum.

Thank you for your endless support and for always being there for me.

And in loving memory of my dad.

I'm so glad you knew this book with Boldwood was a possibility.

Dreams do come true.

1

WEEK ONE – FINAL WEEK OF PRE-PRODUCTION

The view of the tree-hugged island and sparkling blue sea was distorted by the sweat dribbling into Harlow's eyes. She wiped her face with a tissue and cursed both the unseasonable heatwave and the panic building as the ferry inched closer to Skopelos. A pine forest covered the hills behind Skopelos Town, a village of white-washed houses with rust-red roofs and Aegean blue shutters. The harbour glittered in the sunshine, with the masts of sailing boats clinking together in front of packed cafes and bars.

Harlow sighed, stuffed the damp tissue in the pocket of her skinny jeans and dropped her sunglasses over her eyes. She longed to get off the packed ferry and dive into the crystal-clear sea before sitting outside a cafe with one of those delicious frappés she'd been dreaming about, but she was here to work, and with a delayed flight in the UK meaning she'd missed her connection in Athens, she was already late.

It was the middle of June, but the cloud-free blue sky, sweltering heat and bustling harbourside made it feel like mid-August. As the ferry came to a stop, Harlow heaved her rucksack on to her back and, dragging her suitcase behind her, followed the stream of people in shorts and T-shirts off the ferry. She didn't have time to explore the town, and with the increasing intensity of the afternoon heat, the next best thing besides a swim in the sea followed by a cooling frappé would be the air-conditioned hotel.

The rush of people from the ferry dispersed into the town or to the rank of waiting taxis. Harlow was just in time to get the last one.

The bearded Greek driver stubbed out his cigarette and opened the boot as Harlow approached.

'*Yasas*,' he said, taking her suitcase from her.

'Hello.'

'Where are you going?'

'Hotel Eirene, please.'

'By Feggari Beach?' He closed the boot with a bang.

She had the hotel plumbed in to Google Maps on her phone, so she double-checked it and nodded. The last thing she wanted to do was give the taxi driver the wrong information and be even later.

Harlow slipped the rucksack off and slid on to the back seat. The engine was running, and upbeat Greek pop was playing on the radio. The air con was on too, a blissful relief from the stifling heat.

The driver turned down the music and drove away from the harbourside, navigating his way up through the narrow people-thronged streets.

'You are here on holiday?' he asked as they left the town and its whitewashed buildings for a winding road shaded by trees.

'No, working.'

'Ah, you with the film then, no?'

'Yep.'

'Let me guess, an actress.'

Harlow glanced away from the window and caught the taxi driver's grinning face in the rear-view mirror.

'No. I'm just an assistant to the location manager. Nothing at all glamorous.'

'You look like that actress, ah, what is her name... Kristen Stewart, that's it. My daughter's favourite.'

Harlow turned back to the window. He probably meant it as a compliment, but the assumption, as always, got her back up. She stared at herself in the glass. The sunlight made her cropped hair look darker, and her nose stud glinted.

She looked beyond her reflection. They'd climbed away from the sea and headed inland, the landscape zipping by in a blur of green. A forest of pine trees carpeted the hills on either side of the road, and despite the speed at which they were going, Harlow felt a sense of calm descending. The churning in her stomach that she'd felt as the ferry neared the island had momentarily been erased by the greenness and peace surrounding her.

'We're very proud our island got chosen again for a film,' the taxi driver continued, disturbing Harlow's peace. '*Mamma Mia!* gave Skopelos good business. Many tourists. We like it very much. What is the film you work on?'

'It's called *One Greek Summer* and it's a rom-com.' She caught his frown. 'A romantic comedy – think *Mamma Mia!* but with more sex and less singing.'

'Ah,' he said, laughing. 'My wife would like it, or maybe I do too.'

Harlow resumed looking out at the view, but she smiled. For an island of its size, it must be quite a win to have another big movie being filmed here.

The driver left her in peace for the remainder of the journey and the forest eventually thinned out, allowing a glimpse of blue sea up ahead. They rounded a corner and the sun streamed through the window.

'Is it always this hot?' Harlow asked as they turned into Hotel Eirene's car park.

'Not this early, no. One, two more days and it be normal till August, then we get much heatwave.' He stopped in a space at the rear of a whitewashed building which had splashes of purple bougainvillea and pink roses climbing the wall.

Harlow got out of the taxi and was met with a blast of heat and the high-pitched buzzing of cicadas. There was the delicious hint of salt in the air, mixed with the sweet scent of roses. She heaved her rucksack on to her shoulder.

The taxi driver lugged her suitcase out of the boot and she handed him twenty euros.

'Thank you,' she said, giving him a wave. She made her way to a paved path shaded by an olive tree.

It was cool inside the hotel reception. A smiling, tanned woman with black hair tied in a ponytail greeted her with a smile. '*Yasas.* Welcome to Hotel Eirene.'

'Hi there,' Harlow said, leaning on the cool surface of the marble counter. 'I'm late – I phoned ahead as I should have arrived and checked in yesterday evening. I'm with the film crew.'

'Ah okay, you are Harlow Sands?'

'Yes, that's me.'

The woman tapped in the information and looked at the screen. She handed Harlow a key card. 'You're in Villa Aegean, room six.'

'Thank you.'

'I'll get someone to show you there now.'

A tall, skinny guy who didn't look older than sixteen was called into the reception. He took Harlow's suitcase and she followed him back out into the searing afternoon heat.

A dozen or so white villas studded the gentle slope of the hillside. They were spaced apart to allow the ones set further back partial beach and sea views. They followed a paved path that meandered through landscaped gardens filled with olive and lemon trees, roses and lavender.

Villa Aegean was set back from the beach. They went into an entrance hall and up two flights of stairs. Harlow opened the door of room six. The boy left her suitcase just inside and she handed him a couple of euros.

She shrugged off her rucksack, kicked off her trainers and padded across the cool, tiled floor. She opened the doors to a decent sized balcony. It overlooked the pool and the paths that cut through the landscaped gardens and branched off to the other villas. Inside were pale grey walls, a white bedspread and splashes of colour in the paintings on the wall and the flowers on the dressing table.

She arranged the pillows and flopped down on the bed. From there she could see across the balcony to a patch of blue sky and the deeper blue of the sea. After what had felt like a never-ending journey, she was finally here. At best, she had three or four hours until the crew returned. She needed to unpack and have a much longed-for shower, but first she had to phone her mum.

She sighed and took her phone from the back pocket of her jeans. Where would her mum be right now? Harlow glanced at her watch: 3 p.m. Working, she was always working. As the producer of a big-budget movie filming on location for six weeks, she'd be working non-stop. It was the final week of pre-production; if it was a bad time, she just wouldn't answer. She let the phone ring.

'Harlow?'

'Hey, Mum, I'm here.'

'Harlow?'

'Can you hear me?'

'They're drilling something,' she shouted over the background noise. 'And we're testing out the wind machine too, thank God, 'cos it's hot enough to cook us alive today. Bloody noisy though. Let me move away.'

There was a crackle and silence, then the sound of chatter in the background.

'You've finally arrived then,' her mum Maeve said, her voice suddenly crystal clear.

'It's not my fault the flight was delayed.'

'I didn't say it was.'

'Anyway, I'm at the hotel.'

'I still don't understand why you won't stay with me.'

'Mum, you know perfectly well why.'

Maeve grunted. 'I have a private pool, a cinema room and an outside bar at my villa.'

'Good for you, but it's not like the crew are staying in some shitty hovel.' Harlow glanced around her spacious room. 'This place is lush. I'll be fine here.'

'Well, if you change your mind…'

'I won't.'

'If you say so. I'm needed back, but we'll have dinner together later.'

'And in the meantime…?'

'Do what you like. Get a bit of colour on that pale skin of yours. You do need to check in with Tyler though when he gets back. I'll see you later.' The phone cut out.

Harlow sighed again. The panic she'd felt on the ferry as she neared the island returned. Not only was she late getting to Skopelos, missing her first working day, but the two people she was worried about spending time with were the people she would end up seeing first.

She breathed deeply, left her phone on the bedside table and forced herself off the bed. After struggling out of skinny jeans which felt as though they'd melted to her legs, she showered and dressed in a short skirt and top. She grabbed an ice-cold Tango Lemon from the minibar, her copy of the *One Greek Summer* script, and sat outside on the balcony to finish reading through it.

By early evening, the crew had begun arriving back at the hotel in dribs and drabs. Everyone would be working flat out to get ready to start the shoot on time. She needed to make the most of this week, because once filming started, her day would be the longest. Along with hair and make-up and the production assistants, she'd be the first to arrive and the last to leave. Unlike her workaholic mum who seemed to thrive under pressure and weirdly love long days and little sleep, Harlow wasn't looking forward to that aspect of her job.

She didn't recognise anyone and as she couldn't see Tyler, she decided to ignore what her mum had said. Unless she happened to bump into him, she'd just wait until tomorrow when they'd be working together anyway.

* * *

Maeve sent a driver to pick Harlow up at half eight. Her stomach grumbled as they sped along dusky roads towards Glossa, the hill-side town where Maeve had been working for most of the day. The sun was melting into the horizon, sending a flood of pink and orange across the sea. Harlow had relaxed for a few hours and managed to avoid seeing Tyler, and despite the thought of spending an evening with her mum, she couldn't wait to tuck into dinner.

The driver dropped her off outside the hillside restaurant, Lefko. A waiter led her past blue-topped tables filled with people eating and drinking, candlelight flickering across their tanned faces. They went through open doors on to a spacious outside terrace that overlooked the bay. Harlow could only imagine how good the view would be in daylight. The sun had disappeared and darkness had taken over. Lamps and candles lit the outside space and vines were entwined around the large wooden pergola.

Maeve was sitting at a table on the edge of the terrace. She was pouring wine with one hand and had her mobile clamped to her ear with the other. Her hair was short and dyed blonde, her skin tanned. Large, hooped earrings dangled against her neck. Her dress had a colourful animal print pattern with flattering capped sleeves.

The waiter pulled out a chair as Harlow reached the table. Maeve glanced up and smiled, mouthing 'sorry' as Harlow sat down.

Harlow waved her hand, batting away the apology; she was used to it. The waiter poured her a glass of red wine from the carafe on the table and left with a nod. Harlow picked up the glass and took a sip, expecting a mellow red wine and instead being surprised by it being chilled and deliciously sweet.

The restaurant was packed. The background chatter was a mix of languages and Harlow could pick out a smattering of English and Greek. It was the kind of place her mum liked: popular and in a good location. Probably expensive. She couldn't fault its stunning position on the hill overlooking the moonlit Aegean.

Maeve's voice carried above the others; something to do with the logistics about the next day's set build during a heatwave. It was a sweltering evening without a hint of a breeze. The night-time heat seemed more intense because it felt as though the sun going down should have given a bit of respite.

Maeve finished her phone call and put her mobile on the table with a thump. 'It's been too long, Harlow.' She pointed to the glass clasped in Harlow's hand. 'Semi-sweet red wine. It's bloody lush.'

'It is,' Harlow said, taking another sip. 'But the reason we've not seen each other is you've been in LA for most of the year. It's not exactly easy to see you.'

'Which is why I keep telling you to come and live out there. I can get you far more opportunities in the US than the UK.'

'I don't want you to get me anything.' Harlow sighed. It was always like this, her mum trying to steer her in the direction she wanted.

'So, you're telling me you didn't want me to get you this job?' Maeve sat back in her seat, her glass in one hand, her other arm across her chest. She pursed her lips the way she did when she was annoyed.

'You didn't exactly give me much choice.'

'Joe breaks his leg ten days before we start shooting – I mean, any other job and we could have worked around it, but none of the locations are easy to reach, let alone on crutches. He wasn't able to drive. We needed to replace him fast; I chose you.'

'Did Tyler have a say?'

'You were available, Harlow. Be grateful. You've been floundering around all year doing goodness knows what.'

'I've taken some time out, that's all.'

'Still doesn't explain why on earth you've given up a promising career as a director to become an assistant location manager.' Her obvious displeasure was laced through her words.

Harlow bit her lip and stared out into the night.

Maeve sighed. 'And anyway, why are you worried what Tyler thinks?'

Harlow turned back and shrugged. Her mum took such little interest in Harlow's personal life that attempting to explain to her the awkwardness of working with Tyler, someone Harlow had a long and complicated history with, was something she didn't want to go into.

She was saved by the waiter returning with a tray. He placed half a dozen small dishes on the table between them.

'I took the liberty of ordering,' Maeve said as the waiter left.

Of course you did, Harlow thought, but followed her lead, taking a bit from each dish: beetroot and avocado salad, baked feta, chicken with lemon and oregano, octopus in red wine, grilled aubergine with garlic and olive oil, and a big bowl of Greek salad.

Maeve stabbed her fork into a piece of chicken. 'What were we talking about?'

'Tyler and the assistant job.'

'Tyler works for me. It's fine. Anyway, it's not like you don't know him.' Her mobile started buzzing and she picked it up, pressing the button to answer while continuing to look at Harlow. 'I'm sure he'll be delighted to spend time with you. Dan, hello. What's up?'

Harlow pushed the beetroot and avocado salad around her plate as Maeve listened to whatever Dan was saying. She didn't think she'd ever eaten a meal with her mum without her answering at least one phone call, certainly since being an adult, and probably in her teens too. Family mealtimes when she was a kid used to be just her and her dad during the week and she only remembered occasional Sunday lunches, usually at a pub, when the three of them ate together. Not that her mum would stay for long; she often left early, giving work as an excuse.

They never talked past everyday stuff. Her mum was usually frustrated with her about something, mainly to do with her career choices or lack of them. But then her mum didn't really know anything about her, as her comment about Tyler proved.

Maeve was doing all the talking now, running through a list of tasks for Dan to tackle. Harlow quietly studied her and chewed a mouthful of the chicken, deliciously seasoned with a generous amount of lemon, perfect for their surroundings.

'Sorry about that.' Maeve placed her phone back on the table. 'How's your dad?'

'Just peachy, Mum.'

Maeve tutted. 'Don't get sarky with me.'

'Why don't you phone him yourself?'

'You know I can't.'

'Why not? You've been divorced for twenty years. You're happy, he's happy. You're both living the lives you wanted – just not with each other. He'd be thrilled if you called.'

'Maybe so, but what would *she* think?'

'Gina would think at last you're being grown up about things and conversing like an adult with your ex-husband instead of via your daughter.'

'You really feel that way? It bothers you that I ask how your father is?'

Harlow shook her head and sipped her wine. 'No, it makes me happy that you actually think about asking after him.'

'I do care, I always have done. I wanted to see him happy after... well, you know.'

'You broke his heart.'

Maeve huffed and looked out at the glinting lights of Glossa decorating the hillside.

Harlow decided to change the subject. 'Where's the main location?'

'Not far from here. You'll go there tomorrow with Tyler and then it's down to him to coordinate you and the Greek location assistants. He's used to working with Joe – they've worked together on his last few projects. You'll need to get up to speed fast. You prove yourself on this shoot, the next job you get doesn't have to be just an assistant.' Maeve looked firmly at her across the candlelit table. 'Whatever you do, Harlow, don't let me or yourself down.'

2

Harlow perched on the white wall that surrounded the car park. The heat wasn't so bad at eight in the morning, but her stuffy head protested from too much wine and too little sleep. She'd got back to her room after dinner with her mum, had a quick shower and crashed into bed naked. She'd woken in the morning with goose-bumps, lying on top of the sheets with the air con blasting.

Tyler had messaged, telling her to meet him in the hotel car park at eight, so she'd arrived early, intent on not getting off to a bad start. Every fibre of her being wanted to prove to her mum too that she was more than capable of doing this job. She sighed and gazed beyond the tarmac to the trees covering the hillside, an oasis of green that made her want to put on hiking boots and go and explore.

'Only a day late.' Tyler's voice was loud in the stillness of the morning as he marched past her and over to a bronze-coloured Peugeot.

'Hello to you too.' Harlow stood up and walked over to him.

Even though she hadn't seen him for a couple of years, he was a familiar figure, with light brown hair, his freckles more pronounced in the sunshine and a few more tattoos visible on his arms. The sight of him took her right back to her late teens and early twenties and a time when they'd both been filled with so much creativity and optimism. At least, she had been.

He looked at her over the roof of the car, his blue eyes hidden behind sunglasses. 'I know your flight was delayed. Don't worry about it. Shit happens.'

The tension in her body abated. She hadn't really known how he was going to take it, being effectively forced to work with her, but at least it seemed like he was going to be relaxed and professional about it. They were here to work after all.

'I'm sorry about Joe breaking his leg.'

'Yeah, silly bugger. Slipped on the edge of the pool. That's all he did and managed to break his leg. He was gutted; I was too. We work well together.' He opened the driver's door. 'Come on, let's get going. Got lots to show you today.'

Harlow put on her sunglasses and slid on to the passenger seat.

Tyler started the engine and pulled out of the car park on to the road. 'I need you to drive the routes to the locations this week and prepare movement orders, so you can use this car when I don't need it.'

They went the same way as she'd been driven the evening before, except in daylight the view was apparent beyond the trees. The shimmering Aegean stretched endlessly and the island of Skiathos was hazy in the distance.

'The unit base is set up on the land next to the hotel.' Tyler put his foot down along a straight stretch of road. 'Most of the beaches we're going to be filming at, like Panormos and Kastani, aren't far away, but we also have the main location up the coast near Glossa, where we're finishing renovating an existing villa for the interior shots. Plus, we've got another location for some exterior shots on an olive farm up in the hills. The location we were going to use fell through last minute, which has been a complete nightmare. Joe found this new place and was liaising with the owner – I need you to continue with that, but if you don't feel comfortable taking it on then tell me now and I'll deal with it.'

'No, that's fine, I can do that. Is there anything in particular I should know?'

'The farmer's a bit grumpy and his English isn't the best, so we can get Dimitri – the Greek assistant – to negotiate the terms, but apart from that it should be okay. We just need to get the contract signed asap. As long as you're sure you can handle it?'

'Of course I can.' She wasn't thrilled with the idea of dealing with someone who sounded like they'd be a bit of a headache, but she wasn't going to admit that to Tyler. She had to prove to everyone, herself included, that she could to this; her mum had said as much.

* * *

The morning was spent at the location near Glossa, where a wraparound wooden veranda with breath-taking views was nearly finished being built on the side of a spacious villa. Tyler talked through all the locations and left Harlow to familiarise herself with the island while he made phone calls.

In many ways, it was tough to come on board just before shooting began and take over from someone who'd been so involved and had a long-standing and good working relationship with Tyler, but Harlow was determined to make the most of it.

They got back to the hotel just after lunch and Tyler showed Harlow the unit base on the land to the side of the hotel. The production offices and rest rooms for the stars of the movie – when they weren't at their luxury villas along the coast – were in a building that belonged to the hotel, while tables and chairs had been set up beneath the shade of the trees that edged the parched grass. A large marquee filled the rest of the space and housed air-conditioned hairdressing and make-up stations, costume-changing areas and workspaces, along with rest and dining areas.

The day flew by and the worries about working with Tyler began to ease as they settled into an almost comfortable rhythm, nowhere near as awkward as she'd anticipated. And so, at the end of the day, when Tyler suggested they got a bite to eat, she had little reason to say no.

Her mum had been right about one thing: she and Tyler knew each other. They had a history that stemmed back to when they started at the MetFilm School in London together. They had a foundation built on familiarity and now, at the age of thirty-one, were far more mature than when they'd first met at eighteen. Of course it was possible for them to be able to work well together; it wasn't as though they were going to be clamped to each other's side the whole time, as today had proved. Tyler expected her to use her initiative, and she would have responsibilities and a set of tasks each day. It would be fine.

With a lightness in her step and hope that this unexpected job would prove to be a good thing, Harlow followed Tyler to the bar on the edge of the beach. They were on the right side of the island to see the sunset. It was already low, casting a silvery-mauve wash across the horizon.

Tyler introduced her to a couple of the production assistants she'd be working alongside, and the first and second assistant directors, Jim and Dan, who were nursing glasses of ouzo up at the bar.

'It's good to have you on board.' Jim shook her hand and smiled warmly at her. 'We're all grateful you were able to drop everything and help out.'

If only you knew, Harlow thought. It was times like this when she was glad she didn't have the same surname as her mum; it always caused a *thing* when people realised who she was related to – not to mention the real reason why she was here. She wanted to feel like one of the crew and be embraced by them, not someone to be wary of or to suck up to because of her connections.

Harlow and Tyler sat at a table by the edge of the beach. They ate tender pork souvlaki, grilled to juicy perfection, served with chips and a refreshing horta salad of wild spinach, nettles and dandelion, drizzled with olive oil and lemon, all washed down with Mythos beer.

The sun disappeared into the sea and darkness took over. The heat was oppressive, the air still, the moon and stars blanketed by clouds. The bar glowed with lamplight, which spilled onto the small pebble beach. They chatted easily, but Harlow was aware they skirted certain topics, firmly keeping the conversation on the shoot, Skopelos and food.

More people arrived, lots of crew, but the place was open to everyone, so there were tourists too. As it became busier, Harlow and Tyler moved to stools up at the bar and ordered another drink.

Harlow stirred her gin and tonic. Tyler rested his elbows on the polished wooden bar and looked across the terrace. She studied him. He was familiar, achingly so. Many a time they'd sat together and poured their hearts out over a drink.

'You know, it really is good to see you,' she said after a while.

Tyler raised an eyebrow. 'Really? Considering I've called and messaged you over the past two years and heard nothing from you, that surprises me.'

'There's been a lot going on.'

'That's bullshit. We've both been busy; never stopped us staying in touch before.'

Harlow didn't know what to say. He was obviously oblivious to how much he'd hurt her two years ago. After a pleasant evening in each other's company eating delicious food in an idyllic setting, she didn't want to ruin it by being open and truthful about her feelings.

'I was beginning to think I might never see you again.' Tyler glanced at her, a serious look on his face. 'But then you're only here because...' He shook his head and looked away. 'Never mind.'

'Because what?'

'Nothing.' He sipped his beer and avoided meeting her eyes.

'Talk to me, Tyler. It's going to be a long old shoot if we can't be honest with each other.' She acknowledged the irony of her words when moments before she hadn't been able to bring herself to tell him the truth.

He swivelled on his stool to face her and ran his hand across his stubble. 'I was going to say, the only reason you're here is because your mum pulled strings.'

His words were like a slap in the face. 'And you have an issue with that because...?'

'She's the producer and you're her daughter.'

Harlow had wanted to remain calm, but he'd hit a nerve. 'Then why don't you complain to her about it?' She shook her head and held up her hands. 'Oh, that's right, because you don't have the guts.'

'I wouldn't put it past her firing me just to give you my job; I'm not stupid enough to get on the wrong side of her, but at the same time, I don't think she's stupid enough to put you in charge, not on a project she's heading up and there's a lot riding on.'

Harlow fought back the urge to say something, knowing she'd regret it. If she did, he'd only make her life a misery for the entire shoot. And it had all been going so well, until alcohol had loosened his tongue and an evening spent together had stirred up their history. She should have known that it would build up to this. She had been naïve to think they could spend the next few weeks working this closely without their past being dragged into it. It was bad enough that her mum had effectively given her no choice but to take the job – a job she knew so many other people would jump at the chance to have – but to have Tyler as her boss too...

She smiled sweetly. 'Just as well you're the one in charge then; it'll be your head that rolls if things go wrong.'

'You'd love that, wouldn't you?'

'No, I wouldn't.' Harlow frowned. 'Why would you think that? We've been friends for a long time... We used to be good friends.'

'The times we've got on best is when we're not actually talking...' He raised an eyebrow and gave her a knowing look.

Harlow's nostrils flared. It always came down to this. 'You're opinionated, that's the problem. You love to pick a fight with me.'

'You're easy to wind up.'

'Perhaps that's because you know me well enough to know which buttons to push.'

'I sometimes think I don't know you at all.' He sipped his drink and looked at her intently. 'I mean, what the hell are you doing working as an assistant location manager, anyway? Shouldn't you be a director by now? Isn't that what your mum wants for you?'

'You're being an arse.'

He shrugged.

Fourteen hours in each other's company and this was how it had ended. She should have seen it coming; today had been too good to be true. She'd been hopeful that the next few weeks would continue in harmony. Neither of them should have drunk anything this evening; it was like they'd reverted to being twenty-one again, but with the weight of their complicated history to muddy the waters. She'd have been better off having dinner with her mum.

Harlow put her nearly empty glass of gin and tonic back on the bar. 'The crazy thing is, you'd never dream of saying anything like this in front of her.'

'Of course not; I'm not going to risk my career taking down her precious daughter.'

'It's hard to believe we used to get on. We actually liked each other quite a bit if you remember. What the hell did I ever do to you?'

Tyler fake coughed into his fist. 'Nepotism.'

Harlow gritted her teeth. She leaned so close to him she could smell his aftershave; still the same one he'd worn since film school. 'You think I've had it easy, because of who my mum is? You have no idea.'

'Yes I do.' He held her gaze. 'You know I do.'

Harlow looked away, downed the rest of her gin and slid off the stool. 'It's late, I'm tired and you're drunk.'

'That's hardly fair – I can hold my drink.'

'Well then, you have no excuse for being such a dick.'

'You do realise I'm your boss…'

'I'm going to bed.' She grabbed her bag from the floor and marched across the bar and out on to the terrace. The moonlight cast a silver glimmer over the sea. Pockets of light spilt from the rooms, and lanterns edged the paths. Harlow got her bearings and headed away from the beachfront bar towards where she thought Villa Aegean was. All the villas looked the same, particularly at night and after a bit too much to drink. The swimming pools glowed a luminous blue, punctuating the landscaped spaces between the white buildings. She spied the sign for the villa and headed in that direction.

Footsteps sounded on the path behind her.

'I should have said I'd walk back with you.' Tyler caught up with her as she reached the door to the villa.

Harlow turned. 'You've got to be kidding. You're in this villa too?'

He had a gleam in his eyes like he was finding the situation amusing, which annoyed the hell out of her.

'Don't be pissed with me.' He brushed past her and pushed open the door. 'Remember, it wasn't supposed to be you being my assistant. Wasn't going to be an issue working with Joe.'

Harlow refused to rise to the bait and followed him in, her heart sinking as they reached the second floor and he took his key card from his pocket. He stopped by the door of the room next to hers.

'Fancy coming in?' He pushed open his bedroom door and winked at her. 'For old times' sake and all that...'

'Go to hell, Tyler.' Harlow stalked past him and fumbled in her bag for her key card.

'Suit yourself.' He disappeared into his room and closed the door.

Harlow resisted slamming her own door behind her. She stood in the darkness of her bedroom and scrunched her hands into fists. She was on a paradise island with a dream job, and here they were back to playing emotional games with each other – well, at least Tyler was. She wasn't going to let history repeat itself. But he'd hit a nerve when he'd suggested she should be a director by now. It was unsurprising that he was confused about her backtracking her career and starting off at the bottom with an assistant location manager role, and she knew her mum didn't understand either, but Harlow had her reasons, none of which she was willing to share with either of them.

3

Thunder crashed overhead. Harlow woke with a start. It felt as though the whole room was rattling with the impact. She'd left the patio door blinds open and rain was lashing the balcony, fat drops splashing on to the table and chairs. A silver-white flash of lightning lit the room, swiftly followed by another thunderous growl.

Harlow tucked her hands beneath her pillow, desperate to get back to sleep. She had no idea of the time, but it had been late when she'd got back from the bar with Tyler. She imagined him in the next room, lying in bed struggling to sleep too. Her head thumped and her heart raced. She was annoyed with herself for drinking too much, at letting her guard down with Tyler, for getting herself into a situation where she had to deal with him, her mum, and her own insecurities and uncertainties.

The thunderstorm must have eventually dissipated because Harlow woke at seven to her alarm beeping. She switched it off, staggered to the en suite and stood under the shower with the water at full blast. She emerged from the steam rubbing her hair dry and feeling less groggy.

Wrapped in a towel, she slid open the balcony doors and stood on the threshold between the cool air of her room and the gentle outside heat. It was hard to believe there'd been an almighty storm in the night. The rain had evaporated from everywhere the sun had already reached and the sky was pale blue and cloud-free. Tyler was sitting on his balcony, already dressed in shorts and a T-shirt, his bare feet resting on the table as he scrolled through his mobile. He met her eyes. She looked away and retreated inside to get dressed.

* * *

'Morning.'

Harlow looked up from her bowl of fruit and Greek yogurt as Tyler slid on to the seat opposite.

'Morning,' Harlow said calmly, wondering if he'd mention last night's conversation.

He yawned and rubbed his eyes, looking about as tired as she felt.

'Quite a storm last night.' He crunched a mouthful of toast. 'Feels a bit better today though, cleared the air and all that. Be a good day for you to work out the routes to the locations – I'm going to be here, so you can have the car.'

So that was that; they were moving on from last night and ignoring what had been said. It was probably for the best. Hopefully he'd got everything off his chest and maybe they could move on and behave like adults, professionally and emotionally. She was relieved that she could avoid him for much of the day, though, and she was pretty sure he felt the same way too.

* * *

After breakfast, Harlow went down to the beach bar. She spread the map out on a table and studied it. One of the bar staff brought over the frappé she'd ordered, and she sat for a moment with the ice-cold drink in her hand, gazing out at the half-moon bay and the glittering sea. She sipped the cooling, sweet coffee. This was what she'd wanted to do the moment she'd arrived on Skopelos.

A handful of people were already relaxing on sun loungers beneath umbrellas. Harlow imagined how blissful it would be to lie in the shade with nothing to do but listen to the waves roll in, but she had work to do. She took another sip and focused on the map. Tyler had marked the locations and one of the Greek location assistants had marked the routes. She now needed to spend the day driving to them and mapping them out, so, come the shoot, cast and crew would have clear and concise directions. She put the post-codes into Google Maps on her mobile. She was looking forward to a day spent on her own, driving across the island and perhaps discovering hidden gems along the way.

Panormos could be reached on foot from the unit base, so Harlow finished her frappé, folded the map, tucked it into her bag and reluctantly left the beach bar. The overnight thunderstorm had put an end to the heatwave. Although it was still hot, it was no longer oppressive. It was pleasant to walk along the narrow sandy path that led away from the hotel's grounds and disappeared beneath the dense pine trees that clustered the edge of the bay. It was shady, with pine needles carpeting the ground and a fresh sweet scent filling the air.

She emerged by a hotel to the view of a fine pebble beach sweeping round to another pine-clad hill on the far side of the bay. It was easily walkable from the base, but not for crew lugging equipment, so she needed to do the short drive there as well.

This was Harlow's favourite part of the job, being on location and working by herself. Admittedly this was an exceptional location and she reminded herself why she was here.

Your mum pulled strings. Tyler's words from the night before plagued her.

Harlow balled her hands and set off across the beach, intending to find the place where the crew would park before she moved on to the next location on her list.

* * *

The Olive Grove was set high on a hill above Glossa. It was the location that Joe had been dealing with. Even with the satnav on, Harlow had trouble finding the bumpy lane that led to its entrance. The importance of her job to map out directions was abundantly clear; she didn't want to send cast and crew on a wild goose chase on the day of the shoot. She knew what Tyler and her mum would say about that.

Harlow parked in a large shingle car park and walked the rest of the way along a wide paved path beneath a tunnel of vines laden with grapes. When Tyler had talked about meeting a grumpy farmer, she'd expected to arrive at an actual farm. She hadn't imagined she'd be blown away by the sight of a whitewashed restaurant on the hill. The brightness of the walls was broken up by pink roses and wild clematis, and the stone terrace was covered with more trailing vines. The wooden sign above the archway said, 'The Olive Grove'.

It was mid-afternoon and the restaurant terrace was empty, apart from a Dalmatian sleeping in the shade and the chef sitting at a table with one of the waitresses. Smoke curled into the air from the cigarette balanced on the ashtray between them. Harlow's senses were overloaded by birdsong and the sweet scent of the flowers.

She walked across the stone paving towards them.

The chef looked up. 'Sorry, we're closed till six.'

'Oh, that's okay.' Harlow stopped next to them. 'I'm actually working on *One Greek Summer* – the movie that's being filmed on the island. I've been told I need to speak to either Stephanos or Adonis. Are they around?'

'Stephanos, no. Adonis, *naí*. He's out there.' He gestured to another archway covered in climbing roses. 'Keep walking, you'll find him.'

Beyond the archway, another terrace dotted with tables and chairs looked out over the olive grove. The perfume of roses mingled with the freshness of citrus. Large potted lemon trees provided patches of shade. A low stone wall surrounded the terrace and a lizard was basking in the sun, its skin brown and wrinkled against the smooth cream-topped wall. Harlow stood for a moment, taking it all in. It really was the perfect location for the romantic dinner scene between the main characters.

There was no one in sight, so Harlow crossed the terrace and went down the steps. The long scratchy grass was dry, but despite that, there was an overwhelming sense of greenness and peace, the air fresher after the storm. She strolled beneath the olive trees. Their pale, grey twisted trunks reached up to an umbrella of slender grey-green leaves which cast patchy shade on the ground. Further up the hill were fig and plum trees and the deeper green of the pine forest beyond, covering the hillside. In the other direction it seemed as if the hillside dropped away. There was a sweeping view of treetops and, further down, the red roofs of white villas, then just sea, with Skiathos emerging in a green haze. It took Harlow's breath away. It was clear why this place had been chosen as a location; she'd already spotted a handful of places where the picnic scene could take place as well.

Bees buzzed beneath the trees and pale yellow butterflies

danced in the sunshine. There didn't seem to be anyone about until she spied movement right at the edge of the field where the olive grove seemed to meet the sky. She headed that way, glad to have paired her short-sleeved shirt dress with sensible white trainers.

The man was about thirty and shirtless, his hair dark and curly. His bronzed skin glistened with sweat, the muscles in his back tensing as he drove a spade into the hard earth. With no one else around, she assumed it was Adonis. He certainly lived up to his name.

Realising he couldn't see her, Harlow walked up the hill a little way and coughed. 'Excuse me.'

'*Ti malakía.*' He pressed his hand to his bare chest and looked up. His eyes rested on her.

'I'm so sorry,' Harlow said, swiping away a stray hair stuck to her hot face. 'I didn't mean to startle you.'

His eyes narrowed and his frown deepened.

'I, um... I'm with the film crew. I believe it was Joe or Dimitri who'd been talking to you – I was told to come and find you, or is it Stephanos I need to talk to... Is he your dad?' Harlow was getting more and more confused.

Adonis straightened up and wiped his brow with the back of his hand.

Harlow was having a hard job keeping her eyes fixed on his face. With a short, neat beard and dark eyes, he'd be as handsome as hell if he smiled, although the grumpy, brooding look was rather attractive too... She was getting distracted. 'Do you speak English?'

A flicker of something crossed his face. Was it annoyance? Anger? Or finally an understanding of what she was saying?

'*Oxi.*' He shrugged. '*Móno lígo.*' She wasn't sure of his meaning, but his tone bristled with anger.

Maybe it was Stephanos she should be speaking to. She didn't think she was going to get anywhere with Adonis apart from frustrated.

'It's okay,' she said. 'I'm sorry to bother you. I'll come back another time and speak to Stephanos...' She left it there, deciding she had enough to get on with for today. 'Thank you.'

She had no clue what she was actually thanking him for. So, without another word, Harlow turned and retraced her steps through the olive grove. She had the distinct feeling of being watched.

4

'What's happening with The Olive Grove location above Glossa?' Maeve stopped by the table Harlow and Tyler were sitting at having a coffee and looked between them. Large Gucci sunglasses shaded her eyes. She had her mobile clasped in her hand and a pile of papers tucked beneath her arm.

'I'm going back there tomorrow to meet the owner,' Harlow said. 'He wasn't there yesterday.'

Maeve looked over her sunglasses. 'We need the contract signed asap. I don't want another disaster to deal with.'

'It'll be fine. And it'll look incredible on film.'

'Then get it done, Harlow.'

Maeve walked away across the base to the air-conditioned production office. Harlow watched her until she disappeared inside.

She turned back. Tyler was looking at her with a smirk.

'What?' Harlow snapped. 'Is this why you gave the location to me to deal with?'

Tyler picked up his coffee and took a sip. 'Because it's a headache? Of course not.'

She wasn't convinced, but she would get it done. Dimitri had arranged for her to meet Stephanos. She had the paperwork ready to sign and the filming schedule printed off. She just needed to make sure he'd agree to it. She certainly wasn't going to ask Tyler for help.

The unit base was filled with activity. The principal actors had arrived, the costume department was busy doing final fittings, the first and second assistant directors were liaising with the director and the producers, production assistants were racing around doing last-minute jobs, and Maeve was micromanaging everything. It was no wonder she liked to escape back to her private villa at the end of the day.

'Did you know your mum's invited us for drinks at her place this evening?'

Harlow looked across the table at Tyler. 'She has?'

'She didn't mention it to you?'

'She probably thought I'd say no.'

'Well, I said yes.' He downed the rest of his coffee and stood up. 'There's no way Joe and I would have had an invite.'

'You don't know that.'

'Oh, but I do, Harlow. She probably figured asking me would ensure you'd come along too. I'll see you later.'

* * *

The day flew by, with Harlow finalising movement orders and fielding queries from locals to the Greek location assistants. Before she knew it, she was showered, dressed and sitting beside Tyler, driving inland along a winding and often steep road into the hills above Panormos. The idea of an evening spent in his company with her mum felt like hell. She was surprised Tyler had agreed to it, but she assumed it would be good entertainment for him to watch her struggle, and of course there was the added benefit of him getting additional airtime with her mum to help further his career.

It was only a ten-minute drive past dense forest to the villa, which was surrounded by nothing but pine and olive trees. They got out of the car to the sound of birdsong and rustling in the undergrowth. They'd left behind the noise of people, cars and mobiles back at the base.

They wandered along a path to the front of the whitewashed villa. Blue doors and shutters, plus a tiled roof, added colour, while the landscaped grounds stole Harlow's breath away. Three terraces were cut into the hillside: the first with an outdoor bar and barbecue area beneath the shade of an old oak; the second with a swimming pool glinting in the evening sun; and the smallest lower terrace with a table and chairs making the most of the view across the valley down to the mesmerising Aegean Sea.

'Tyler, Harlow.' Maeve emerged from the open doors of the villa wearing a flowing semi-sheer dress over a patterned swimsuit. She held a glass of fizz in one hand and her ever-faithful mobile in the other. 'There's prosecco inside, or you can grab a drink from the bar and join me by the pool.'

Tyler glanced at Harlow. 'You're driving back, right?' he asked, making a beeline for the outside bar.

'But of course,' Harlow said as sweetly as she could.

He grabbed a beer from the fridge behind the bar, handed her a bottle of Diet Coke and sauntered across the top terrace and down to the pool.

Harlow popped the lid off the bottle. This was her mum's reality. Yes, she worked hard; she worked long days and rarely took time off, but she got to live in places like this and her sprawling villa in the Hollywood Hills. At times, it was hard to believe they were related; their lives couldn't be more different.

Harlow would have happily stayed here, if it wasn't for the small issue of sharing the place with her mum. She managed to have enough influence over Harlow without them living together, plus, she didn't like how it would look to everyone else.

She wandered across the paved terrace. The oak cast much-needed shade over the villa and seating area. Olive trees edged the paving, their leaves dark green in the softening light.

She joined her mum and Tyler by the pool. Both were relaxing on sun loungers facing the view. Her mum's smooth, tanned legs were on display, gleaming in the sunshine, while Tyler had made himself comfortable, resting his bare feet on a rolled-up towel. Living in LA for most of the year, her mum worshipped the sun, but Harlow plonked herself on a lounger beneath an olive tree. The temperature was a little more manageable in the dappled shade.

Maeve wedged her sunglasses into her hair and looked at her daughter. 'We were just saying, I think Tyler's worked on almost as many projects of mine as you have, Harlow.'

'It's always a pleasure working with you, Maeve,' Tyler said smoothly.

Harlow resisted the urge to fake gag at him. This was why he'd never say anything to Maeve along the lines of what he'd said the other night; he was too much of an arse-licker. Not that she was surprised; Maeve had the power to make or break careers and Tyler wasn't stupid. But, as for her, she was practically the lowest of the low on this shoot; no wonder Tyler had commented about them being invited over for drinks. He'd be buzzing inside at getting the chance to socialise again with Maeve Fennimore-Bell, Oscar winning producer and a trailblazer in an industry dominated by men.

'I know just how good you are at your job, Tyler. That's why I want you to teach Harlow everything you know.'

Harlow wanted the ground to swallow her up.

'You want me to train my future competition?' Tyler winked.

'There'll be plenty of work for the both of you,' Maeve replied.

Another car pulled into the drive, and Harlow felt immense relief. The thought of continuing any kind of conversation with just her mum and Tyler filled her with dread. She could tell Tyler was enjoying himself, lapping up the praise Maeve was sending his way at her expense. It would be easier with other people there; perhaps her mum had thought so too, not wanting to spend another awkward evening with her daughter.

Assistant directors Jim and Dan, plus the director of photography and the assistant producer rocked up first, followed by the two stars of the film, bubbly blonde pop star turned actress Crystal, and Dominic Flynn, the UK's answer to Zac Efron. Harlow couldn't help but feel inadequate. Her only real reason for being there was because she was related to Maeve, but at least the attention had switched away from her and her failings. It also made her question why her mum was hiding away in a villa in the hills when she craved company and relished being the centre of attention. Was it because she liked to show off?

'Make sure everyone's drinks stay topped up, Harlow,' Maeve said on her way from the villa to the middle terrace.

Now it was clear the real reason why they'd been invited.

Harlow stood on the periphery for a moment, watching everyone interact. Tyler was doing his best to fit in, and her mum was being all touchy-feely, Hollywood-schmoozing with everyone as laughter and chatter filled the night air.

Harlow went and made herself a strong coffee; it was going to be a long night.

* * *

A sense of calm descended over Harlow as she bumped up the lane towards The Olive Grove the next day. There was something magical about the place. Whether it was because it felt off the beaten track, surrounded by countryside and the lush green of the pine-covered hills that Skopelos was famous for, Harlow didn't know. The restaurant glowed in the sunshine and the far-reaching views were a bonus.

The car park was full this time. The restaurant was open for lunch on a busy Saturday. Harlow parked, double-checked that she had all the paperwork in her bag and got out of the car. Chatter from the restaurant terrace mixed with the distant sound of goat bells. It was soothing to hear people enjoying themselves, their laughter sprinkling the sultry air.

The vine-covered walkway was dappled with shade. Apart from the grapes and the olive trees, she'd also spied fig and plum trees; it was a delicious and summery combination and the ideal location to set romantic scenes. She stopped dithering and marched on to meet Stephanos.

The courtyard was packed with people tucking into plates of souvlaki and Greek salad. There was a tang of lemon and grilling meat in the air, with the sweet scent of wild clematis.

One of the waiters greeted her.

'A table for...?'

'Oh, I'm here to meet Stephanos. He should be expecting me.'

The waiter nodded and ushered her through the archway on to the terrace, which was just as full as the courtyard.

'He's over there.' The waiter gestured to a table on the far side, next to the wall where she'd seen the sunbathing lizard.

Stephanos was drumming his fingers on the white tablecloth. He had a sour look on his face as he gazed out at the olive grove. He came across as grumpy as Adonis, who Dimitri had confirmed was Stephanos's son. There was a definite family resemblance. His hair was almost as thick too, but it was pure white, which accentuated his tanned, weather-beaten face. The frown lines looked permanent; the scowl, she assumed, was his usual resting face. He stood when she reached him and Harlow held out her hand. He shook it, his hand rough against hers.

'Thank you for meeting me.'

Stephanos grunted. 'You taken over from that other man?'

'From Joe, yes.'

He had a thick accent, but his English was decent enough, which made her wonder why his son didn't know much. Either way, it didn't matter; Stephanos was the owner and who Joe had been dealing with, so the conversation needed to be with him.

They sat and the waiter brought over a jug of iced water and a bottle of red wine.

'From our grapes,' Stephanos said, pouring them each a glassful.

'I'm driving...' Harlow started to say, but Stephanos handed her a glass.

'Try it.'

She took a sip. It was semi-sweet, like the wine she'd had the first night at dinner with her mum. 'It's really delicious.'

'You should try our olive oil. Sweet and fruity. The best.'

Harlow nodded. 'I'm sure it is.'

Stephanos sat back in his chair and surveyed her. 'So, you want to film on my land.'

'Yes please.'

'We get paid?'

'Of course, I assumed Joe and Dimitri had discussed it with you?'

Stephanos waved his hand in front of his face. 'Ah, they say lot of things. I only need to know the days and how much you pay. Keep it simple. I don't want to hear nothing about this amazing film and how good it is for Skopelos. We do okay. We have tourists. They buy meals and olive oil. That is what I do.'

With Stephanos listening intently and offering an occasional grunt, which Harlow took to mean an agreement, she went through the schedule and what filming at The Olive Grove would entail. She kept it brief but couldn't help but mention the considerable fee and the kudos The Olive Grove would gain from a movie to rival *Mamma Mia!* being filmed there.

She finished going through everything and he leaned back in his chair, looking happy enough without actually breaking into a smile.

Harlow sipped the iced water. 'You really do have a beautiful place.'

'It's been in my family long time.'

'You must be proud.'

He shrugged. 'Of course. But it is hard work.'

'Your son helps though?'

'He helps.' He tapped out a cigarette from the packet on the table and lit it. His fingers were rough, the nails stained with dirt. 'Is that all?'

'For now, yes, thank you.' She pushed the paperwork across the table and handed him a pen. 'I just need you to sign this. We'll film in the olive grove on the days outlined below and on the restaurant terrace on the day we've just discussed.'

Stephanos signed the papers. Relief flooded through Harlow as she gathered them together and put them back in her bag. At least that was sorted and would get Tyler and her mum off her back. They stood, and Harlow offered Stephanos her hand again. He grunted, shook it and sat back down to finish his cigarette.

'Is it okay if I walk through the olive grove?'

Stephanos shrugged, which she took as a yes.

She escaped from the terrace and on to the yellowed grass. Even with the restaurant full, the chatter of people and clink of cutlery ebbed away as she got further beneath the trees. The olive trees closest to the restaurant were larger, their thick trunks gnarled and twisted, while the younger ones were further down the hillside. She thought she'd found the spot where the two main characters could share their first kiss. The view from each angle was stunning; a backdrop of olive and fruit trees, with the forest-covered hill on one side and the view over Glossa to the Aegean in the other direction.

Satisfied, Harlow walked back up the gentle sloping hill towards the terrace and the car. Stephanos was still at the table, smoking another cigarette and drinking more wine, but Adonis had joined him. He had his back to her, his arm resting on the empty chair next to him, a T-shirt covering his muscles this time. Stephanos looked her way and nodded. She waved and smiled, just as Adonis turned and caught her eye.

5

WEEK TWO – FIRST WEEK OF FILMING

Harlow had got used to living in her mum's shadow and was perfectly comfortable not being the centre of attention. But the expectations her mum had about her career continued to haunt her. She was never good enough alongside her high-flying producer mum.

She gathered together the edges of the black bag and heaved it out of the bin. It was the third day of filming at the Glossa villa location, and she and Tyler had been the first to arrive, working non-stop to make sure everything ran smoothly. Harlow was now tackling the least glamorous part of her job – cleaning up and putting the set back to how it looked when they'd arrived.

Gripping the bin bag, she walked off the set and across the dusty ground to the bins out on the road. She lifted the hot metal lid of the container and chucked the bag in. With her back to the bustling film set, she paused for a moment and gazed out over Glossa. The sun glimmered, sending a hazy wash of light across the sea and giving the white-walled and red-roofed village below an almost mystical look in the early evening sunshine. Even as an assistant, this was the bit of the location manager job she loved, getting to be in a place like this; she relished the idea of scouting locations and finding the perfect spot to bring a scene to life, but that hadn't been the reality of her day.

She forced herself to walk back to the set. Her mum had been here all day, mostly behind the monitor, liaising with the director, being hands-on and practical like she always was – a domineering presence. She hadn't once spoken to Harlow, or even looked in her direction; it was a purely professional relationship, but it made Harlow feel small. The differences in their careers had never been more evident than on this shoot.

She put a new black bag in the bin she'd emptied.

A hand landed on her shoulder, warm against her skin.

'You finished?' Tyler asked. His hand remained on her shoulder as he unclipped his walkie-talkie with his free one. He pressed the button and spoke into it. 'Going off walkie.'

His casual touch made her tense. It was a relaxed and familiar gesture, one he'd made countless times before, but it was noticeable.

'Yep, all done.' She moved away from him and put the roll of bin bags in the cupboard. 'We're going back to the hotel?'

'Yeah, but I need to check a location on the way.'

Harlow put the walkie-talkies' batteries to charge and made sure everything was ready for the next day. She'd print off the following day's call sheets when they got back to the base.

'So, where are we going?' Harlow asked as she got into the passenger seat.

'Maeve's having second thoughts about Perivoliou – the beach location I secured for the heart-to-heart scene. She wants me to re-evaluate it with a view to possibly moving it to Kastani beach.'

'Won't that disrupt a lot of people?'

'Possibly, but it shouldn't be an issue if we tag it on to the end of the shoot we already have scheduled there. She's concerned Perivoliou will be too difficult.'

They skidded away from the dirt parking area and on to a narrow, bumpy lane. They took the road out of Glossa, in the opposite direction to the hotel. The winding tree-lined roads were becoming familiar, as were the hairpin bends and the occasional but breath-taking glimpse of endless blue sea.

Tyler turned down a narrow lane that cut beneath a tunnel of shady pines. A light breeze and the sweet smell of resin seeped in through the open windows. The uneven road turned into a track by the time they reached a parking area next to a taverna. There were only a couple of other cars parked, and once Tyler switched off the engine, it was blissfully quiet.

The taverna was perched on the hillside, with sweeping views over the sea sparkling in the soft evening light. A steep path, with steps cut into the stony hillside, led down to a narrow swathe of beach. It was almost empty apart from a handful of umbrellas and two families making the most of the last bit of sunshine. The stony ground was loose and slippery, so Harlow picked her way carefully down the steps, following Tyler. Soft green foliage clung to the edges of the rocky hillside that surrounded the beach. As they wound their way past heather-like bushes, she noticed the back of his neck was red. They reached the sand, a mix of pebbles and finer grains.

'You've burnt your neck,' Harlow said, feeling the intensity of the sun increase now they were lower down and out of the light breeze.

'Feels like it. You got any sunscreen?'

'Bit late for that, isn't it?' Harlow rummaged in her bag and retrieved a bottle.

'Better than nothing. Put some on, could you.'

They stood in the shade where the rocky cliff jutted into the bay. Harlow squeezed a blob of cold sunscreen on to her fingers and rubbed it in. His skin was hot beneath her touch.

An image flashed across her mind: gazing up at Tyler, her hands on his neck, tugging him down on top of her... Theirs was not a normal working relationship. Not that she had a problem actually putting the sunscreen on him, but she knew that he'd never have asked Joe to do something so intimate.

She finished smoothing in the cream and forced herself to erase the thought of Tyler in *that* way.

'This place is stunning,' she said, tucking the bottle back in her bag.

'I know; that's why I chose it.' He set off across the beach, down to the edge of the shore.

Harlow wandered after him. The sunshine warmed the chalky-coloured sand. The sea was shallow and the colour of a pale sapphire, twinkling with the gentle movement of the waves.

Tyler turned to her. 'What do you think about shooting here?'

'I mean, it's beautiful, it would look amazing.'

'But?'

'It's further away from the base than the Glossa locations. It'll be harder to get everyone here, not to mention getting cast, crew and equipment actually on to the beach.'

'That shouldn't put us off though, should it?'

'No, but...'

'Yeah, I know, I had my concerns when I first saw it, but I thought it would be worth it. I understand why your mum's worried.'

They spent the next hour walking the length of the beach and exploring the hidden bays tucked behind rocky outcrops. They took off their socks and trainers and splashed through the pebbly shallows, the warm water lapping at their bare legs. Tyler ran through the plan for the shoot and took more photos.

'The idea is to have a boat bobbing out there.' Tyler pointed at the calm horseshoe-shaped bay.

'That would be a good shot too; the scene from the sea.'

He glanced at her. 'Look at you with your creative director hat on.'

Harlow gave him a look. 'It's hard not to picture this place shot by shot.'

'Seriously, Harlow. Why are you here, working as an assistant?'

A mix of confusion and anger washed over her. 'I'm here because Mum made me. You know how good her skills of persuasion are. She knows exactly how to make me feel guilty, like it would be my fault, letting her and this shoot down, when I wasn't the one who went and broke my leg.' She glanced sideways at Tyler. 'Not that Joe should be blamed either.'

Tyler waded back to the beach and Harlow followed. The heat had mellowed a little, with a delicious breeze drifting in from the sea. The sun was beginning to disappear beyond the rocky cliff face.

'I get that about your mum. But why were you even available?'

'I was taking time out to re-evaluate everything.'

'Like what?'

'Like what I actually want to be doing with my life.' Harlow folded her arms, annoyed with his questioning. 'It's late; if you've finished we should go.'

'Let's grab some food before we head back.'

Harlow sighed and started up the steep path after him.

The taverna was almost as quiet as the beach and they were greeted with a smile but a curt, 'We close soon,' from the man behind the bar.

'Is there time for you to cook us whatever you have left?' Tyler asked.

The man wiped his hands on the towel over his shoulder and nodded. He gestured to a table right on the edge of the terrace.

One of the families from the beach was finishing their meal. The kids were squabbling over a phone and the parents were doing their best to ignore them and enjoy their wine. They looked Mediterranean: healthy and tanned from living outdoors. It crossed Harlow's mind how amazing it would be to live somewhere like this, a forest-covered island with hidden bays and sweeping beaches backed by cliffs and lush greenery.

Tyler was scrolling through the photos he'd taken on his phone. Harlow sat back and soaked up the view, happy to not be talking. The bay was perfect, but she could understand her mum's concerns. The waiter placed a white paper cloth on the table and pinned it down with clips. He set wine glasses and a carafe of wine between them.

She was annoyed that she was grateful that Tyler had included her in his re-evaluation of the location even if it meant them spending more time together. It was this part of the job that had been her reason for taking her career in a new direction and stepping back from the assistant director jobs she'd been working on over the last three years. She hoped working in the location management team would give her more freedom to explore, travel and be outdoors. Even back in the UK, she would love to scout for the perfect country cottage or a sixteenth-century mansion house.

The waiter returned with a tray and placed dishes on the table. The Greek salad was huge, with chunks of tomatoes, red onion and cucumber finished off with kalamata olives and a slab of feta drizzled with olive oil. It was summer in a bowl. The waiter added a basket of chunky white bread, another bowl filled with mussels in a tomato sauce and a plate of fried calamari.

'If this is just the leftovers, I can only imagine how good a meal here normally is.' Harlow speared her fork into the feta slab, crumbling a bit off and dipping it into the olive oil and juice. She popped it into her mouth with a chunk of tomato and red onion.

Tyler squeezed lemon over the calamari and looked across the table at her. 'Do you remember that meal we had at Sloanes at the end of our first year, the one your mum paid for?'

Harlow momentarily stopped chewing and nodded.

'This feels like another one of those memorable places.' He gestured around them. 'The view, the setting, the food. It was a night full of excitement and possibility. This whole shoot feels the same.'

Dusk had rapidly descended, with the sun setting on the other side of the island. Now the clear, dark sky was flecked with stars. Candlelight danced across Tyler's face as he watched her. Harlow took a ring of the calamari, tender and delicious, and chewed it thoughtfully.

Of course she remembered that night. Apart from her mum having paid for an all-expenses night out at a swanky and expensive restaurant in London for eight of them at the end of their first year at MetFilm School, it was later that night that her and Tyler's relationship went from friends to friends with benefits, or whatever else they could class it as. But why was he mentioning it now? Was he trying to remind her of their history, that casual sex and how her mum's influence had been twisted around them for over a decade?

* * *

They were both quiet on the drive back to the hotel. The tension that had been present the other evening had been replaced by a familiarity that felt comfortable and right. Harlow hated how much she'd slipped back into enjoying Tyler's company, particularly after everything he'd said in the beach bar. He seemed to be running hot and cold, between contempt for her and desire. Deep down, she knew he was no good for her, yet she kept getting drawn in. Perhaps if she'd met him for the first time now she would see him in a different light and have no interest, but with their shared history of happy times among the not so good, it was hard to not feel something for him. Theirs was a relationship built on the foundation of friendship and that was hard to let go.

They arrived at the hotel and she glanced at him. He met her eyes. She looked away and undid her seat belt. Why was she blushing?

They got out of the car and walked towards the villas. The lanterns glowed on to the bushes edging the path and the place was still and peaceful, with just the distant thrum of voices coming from the restaurant and the bar. It had been an insanely long day, only a few days into the first week of shooting and Harlow was ready to fall into bed, but she knew if she didn't get the paperwork sorted tonight, she'd have to be up even earlier in the morning.

They reached Villa Aegean, but she kept walking.

'Hey, you not coming up?' Tyler asked.

Harlow faltered. She knew that tone and the underlying suggestion. However much she'd enjoyed this evening, she needed to put a stop to it now before she did something she regretted.

'Not yet, no.' She turned to look at him. 'I'm going to go print the call sheets ready for tomorrow.'

She spun on her heel and walked away, but Tyler caught hold of her hand. He tugged her to him and brushed her cheek with a kiss. His stubble tickled and his aftershave smelt familiar, a warm woody citrus scent. As quickly as he'd grabbed her, he let her go and sauntered towards the villa.

'Don't work too late,' he said with a wave.

Harlow cursed herself even more for the physical feeling his kiss had evoked, her body betraying her head, which screamed, *Walk away, don't get involved, don't fall into the same old trap of ending up in bed with him*. Yet being around him always stirred something inside her. Whether it was actually more than a touch of lust, she had yet to figure out.

6

'Harlow Sands, as I live and breathe! I thought it was you.' A woman with wavy, bleached-blonde hair was striding across the base towards her with a beaming smile. 'I'd heard a rumour you were around.'

'Oh my goodness. Manda! I had no idea you were here.' Harlow embraced her.

'I arrived on the weekend and have pretty much been stuck in the make-up department ever since.'

'It's so good to see you. I'm so sorry I've not been in touch for ages.'

Manda waved her hand. 'Don't apologise, I've been the same. Life is just busy and we've not worked together for ages. I keep meaning to message you...'

'Well, we have time to catch up out here. I've got to go to location, but do you fancy dinner tonight?'

'I'm having dinner with the make-up girls tonight, but how about tomorrow?'

'It's a date.' Harlow kissed Manda's cheek and set off towards the car park with a wave. She hadn't realised how much she'd needed to see a friendly face. Spending so much time with Tyler and her mum – the work days plus two evenings in little more than a week when months would usually go by – had left her desperate to be around someone uncomplicated.

It was the last filming day of the first week and Harlow spent it at the Glossa set, ensuring the day ran smoothly. Once again she and Tyler managed not to talk about the evening before. It was easier that way, but at some point she knew they'd have to face up to their feelings. He was reeling her in one minute, pushing her away the next, much like he'd always done. Maybe she'd been no better, actively avoiding contacting him for the past two years. Friends with benefits summed them up perfectly, yet she was conscious that friends didn't treat or speak to each other in the way Tyler had done the other evening.

The sun was already beginning to set by the time they wrapped. Dominic and Crystal were driven back to the base, while the crew cleared away ready to begin again after the weekend. Tyler had left earlier with the car to make preparations for the following week, so Harlow needed to hitch a lift back. She looked around; there were still lots of people about tidying cables and packing up.

Olivia, one of the production assistants, was walking towards her.

'Maeve wants to talk to you,' she said, nodding in her direction as if Harlow didn't know who she was.

Harlow sighed and unclipped her walkie-talkie. 'I'll be over now.'

She took her time finishing clearing away, then wandered over to her mum, who was standing behind the monitors.

'What are you doing on Sunday?' Maeve asked the moment Harlow reached her.

'Nothing in particular.'

'Great, let's go to Skopelos Town and explore.'

Harlow realised too late she'd given her an opportunity to instigate a 'mother and daughter' day. It was something she did occasionally in an effort for them to bond, but Harlow was convinced it was more about her needing company when *she* wanted to do something.

'If you're finished,' Maeve continued, 'I'm leaving now so can drop you back.'

'I, er... You don't have to. I'll get a lift with one of the crew.'

Maeve folded her arms and looked at Harlow with pursed red lips. 'Seriously, I get that you don't want to stay with me for the entire shoot, but saying yes to a lift isn't going to kill you now, is it?'

Harlow couldn't argue with that. After all, she was going to have to spend the whole of Sunday with her. A twenty-minute drive to the hotel would be nothing compared to that.

* * *

Saturday started perfectly with a long lie-in. There was something so special about waking up to the sound of the sea. There was the sound of people too, laughter, voices and splashing coming from the pool in front of the villa, but with the sun streaming through the balcony doors and a whole day stretching ahead with no work or commitment of any kind, Harlow really didn't mind.

Before showering, she decided it was about time she went for a run. It was much later in the morning than she would normally go, but she felt the need to exercise and clear her head.

Harlow managed to leave Villa Aegean without bumping into Tyler. Someone was in the villa pool but she couldn't make out who. She imagined most of the crew were still in bed, at breakfast or perhaps on the beach ready to enjoy their day off. It was one of those beautiful days that seemed rare in the UK but were common on Skopelos, with a perfect temperature, a light breeze and endless blue sky without a wisp of cloud. The hotel complex sparkled in the sunshine. The villas were a brilliant white, the flowers a mixture of pink, scarlet and tangerine between fronds of green leaves, and the air was perfumed by roses.

She reached the edge of the grounds and broke into a steady run. She was already sweating by the time she reached the shady path beneath the trees. Running always gave her time to think. As her feet pounded the hard earth, her mind wandered to tomorrow and the reality of spending the whole day with her mum. It also reminded her that it had been too long since she'd spoken to her dad. She needed to rectify that.

* * *

By the time she'd showered and had breakfast, she felt relaxed and refreshed. Harlow wanted to sit outside on the balcony to phone her dad, but Tyler was already relaxing on his and she didn't fancy him listening in. She pocketed her mobile, grabbed the key card to her room and clattered down the stairs. She set off the way she'd run earlier, towards the inviting green of the forest that edged the grounds and hugged the coastline.

As soon as she was in the shade and the sound of chatter from the hotel bar was filtered out by the trees, Harlow called her dad. She padded along the soft pine-needle-strewn path as her mobile rang. She wondered where he'd be on a Saturday morning – probably acting as a taxi driver to one of her younger sisters, taking them to swimming or football, or maybe they were all on a family day out. It wasn't good to feel so out of touch with her dad and his family. *Her family*, she reminded herself.

'Harlow, how's it going?' Her dad's voice was full of joy, and as familiar and comforting as a hug.

Harlow scuffed the dried needles beneath her feet. 'Ah, you know.'

'That bad, eh?'

'Sorry, I don't mean to sound negative. It's all good, really.'

Even the sound of the sea was muffled by the screen of trees, so the clearness of her dad's voice made it seem as if he was walking the path with her.

'Have you got time to talk?' she asked as she wound her way past the slender trees and caught a glimpse of the sea splashing white foam on to the rocks edging the forest.

'Of course. I'm just waiting for Ellie to finish swimming. I've popped outside though. Hot and noisy in there.' She'd been right about her dad being out and about with one of her siblings.

Her half-sisters had sensible, traditional names: Abigail, Eleanor and Florence – or Abi, Ellie and Flo for short. The name Harlow had been her mum's choice, because it sounded like a film-star name. Abi, Ellie and Flo's mum, Gina, was as down-to-earth as their dad was. He'd come into his own now he was no longer being walked all over by Maeve. With a mum who was hardly around when Harlow was a child and her parents divorcing when she was only ten, growing up had been very different to the life her dad and his new family led in the country. She couldn't help but feel envious. The only thing they had in common was the Sands surname.

'Are you even listening, Harlow?'

'Sorry, yes,' she said, ducking under a branch and walking into the sunshine that was blazing across Panormos beach. 'I was just concentrating on where I was going.' She'd been in a complete daydream, so it was sort of true.

'You've started shooting?'

'Yes, beginning of the week.'

'And you're not staying with your mum?'

'God, no.'

Her dad laughed. 'You know anyone else besides your mum?'

'Tyler's here. He's the location manager, so my boss.'

'How's that working out?'

'Oh, you know, Tyler's being Tyler.'

'You two still, you know?' He did a funny whistle down the phone.

'*Dad*, no.' Harlow walked a little way along the beach and sat down on the pebbles. 'We've not seen each other for a couple of years.' She gazed out at the sea, its constant movement mesmerising. 'I mean, it's weird spending so much time with him again. He reminds me of the past. I don't know, I want to focus on the future and where I'm going from here. This job wasn't my choice and I kinda want to be figuring my own stuff out, but you know how Mum is.'

'You shouldn't let her bully you into these things.'

Harlow wrapped her arm around her knees. 'Really? You're preaching to me about that?'

'Yeah, yeah. I'm aware of how it sounds. But it's my prerogative to worry about you, even though you're plenty old enough to look after yourself. And I know your mum bullied me into things for years... maybe bully is too strong a word.'

'It's really not. It's what she does.'

'She's spent years negotiating and working her way up to a position of power in a man's world.'

'After all this time, you're still defending her behaviour.'

'She's your mum, Harlow. The boundary of work and family became blurred.'

'Dad, there is no boundary.'

'Yeah, well, let's not waste any more breath discussing your mum, eh.' He laughed. 'But honestly, you're okay, poppet?'

She loved how comforting it was, him still calling her that. 'Apart from being here with Mum and Tyler, it's fine. I promise. The island is stunning. I can recommend it for a holiday for you, Gina and the girls sometime.'

'Along with you of course.'

The sound of happiness filled the line; children laughing together. And then there was a familiar voice in the background.

'Who you talking to, Dad?'

'Only Harlow. Won't be long. Give me your swim things and go see your friends for a minute.'

'Hi, Harlow!' her sister yelled down the phone.

'Hi, Ellie!' she called back, knowing she'd already have scooted off to be with her friends. After swimming, she'd be ravenous, eager to get home to sit round the large kitchen table with Abi, Flo and their parents and tuck into a home-cooked meal. A blissful family scene. Harlow sighed. 'Sorry, Dad, I didn't hear what you said.'

'You should come on holiday with us.' Her dad's voice cut across the background noise. 'I know you can't this summer, but what about October half-term, or come to Yorkshire with us at Christmas. The girls would love to see you, as would Granny and Grandad, not to mention me and Gina.'

'I know it's long overdue, and I'd love to spend time with you all. Believe me, I really would, it's just I feel guilty about Mum, you know, being on her own, particularly at Christmas.'

'You shouldn't feel guilty, Harlow, not at your own expense. I know you're not happy in London. And you shouldn't have to do things for fear of upsetting your mum. It's of her own making. You do realise, she chooses to live alone and live far away from everyone. And she's not really alone is she, there's always some new bloke about. She's always welcome at ours if you want to invite her. But you have to think of yourself sometime.'

Harlow grunted a reply and swiftly moved the conversation on. They talked a little more about Harlow's sisters and said goodbye, her dad to spend the rest of the day with his family. It was the big happy noisy home he'd wanted for Harlow when she was growing up, but of course it had never happened.

Harlow remained sitting for a moment, staring out along the beach, her phone still clasped in her hand. Her dad and his life in the north Norfolk countryside seemed so far away, not just in distance but reality too. A wave of homesickness washed over her like the waves churning on to the shore. It wasn't because she was miles away on a Greek island for the summer; she realised she often felt like this even back in the UK – lonely, and disconnected from family especially. She had friends in London, went out and socialised plenty, but recently she'd let some friendships slip, like not staying in touch with Manda, someone she'd connected with on a job but wouldn't normally see on a daily basis. Home didn't feel permanent or truly lived in like she imagined a family home would, like their house had felt when she was growing up with her dad there. She lived in a beautiful flat in Bayswater, but it was owned by her mum, which left Harlow feeling as though she permanently owed her something. Her mum was happy to provide for her daughter financially, it was the emotional side that was missing. She shook the thought away.

The gentle heat caressed Harlow's skin and it felt good to just sit and soak up the sunshine and the view. She had a day to herself stretching ahead and no idea what to do with it. If Tyler wasn't using the car, she could go for a drive and explore the island beyond the filming locations. She picked up a hand-sized pebble, warm and smooth against her palm. There were a lot of crew back at the hotel, lots of people she could chat to. She'd happily go and introduce herself to people but that brought with it the inevitable questions, which led to people realising who she was related to and that changed everything. People would see her in a different light; people could try to use her connections to their advantage...

Harlow scrambled to her feet. Her shoulders were hot and

tingling; she needed to reapply sunscreen and retrieve her hat from her room. She couldn't hide away from everyone for the entire shoot. Things had gone well so far, and she should embrace the opportunity and get to know people. Life would be much better having more people to socialise with. At least she had dinner with Manda to look forward to that evening.

7

Harlow met Manda at dusk outside Villa Sporades, the villa Manda was staying in, set in the row behind the seafront villas. They walked the short distance together to the beach bar. Harlow was glad she'd booked a table; nearly every one was filled. The mouth-watering aroma of grilling fish mingled with the fresh sea air.

'I'm so glad you're here.' Harlow knocked her glass of wine against Manda's.

'Me too, because it's unexpected. I didn't realise you'd be here. I obviously know all the girls in make-up and most in the hair and costume departments, but it's good to have another familiar face around. It's strange being able to finally say yes to an opportunity like this.'

'Because Emma's left home?'

Manda put her hand to her chest. 'Breaks my heart. My baby. Don't give me that look, I know she's nineteen and it's been months and months since she went to uni, but me being abroad and not just a couple of hours away feels rather strange.'

'Good though too, right?'

'Oh definitely.' Manda grinned. 'It's just taken some getting used to, realising I can be choosier about what I work on and go for the jobs I've always wanted to do. I mean, what's not to like about spending a few weeks on a Greek island?'

Harlow fiddled with her bracelet. No one in their right mind would complain about spending time in a place like this, yet a part of her was doing exactly that. Manda was only twelve years older than Harlow, but their lives couldn't have been more different, with Manda married with a grown-up daughter and a career that she'd worked hard for alongside bringing up her family. Harlow was still trying to figure everything out.

'Anyway,' Manda continued, 'she's back from uni for the summer, although she's perfectly capable of looking after herself – it's her father I worry about more. Not sure he'll bother cooking anything with me gone; he'll probably live off cheese toasties and takeaways.' She shook her head.

'So, this is your time then.'

'It certainly is.'

They ordered a handful of dishes that felt just right for a balmy evening on a Greek island. They shared a bottle of the semi-sweet red wine that Harlow was now hooked on, and when the grilled fish, fresh crusty bread and little dishes of meze were brought to their table, they shared them too.

'How does your husband feel about you working away for weeks on end?' Harlow dipped her fork into a smoky aubergine dish and looked at Manda.

'He's fine about it; it's my turn. I've been used to him working away from home, admittedly only a couple of nights here and there, but he's made up for me getting this job.'

'You're lucky to have found someone so supportive.'

Manda nodded and chewed her food thoughtfully. 'Why the change in direction for you?'

Harlow looked up from her plate of mouth-wateringly tender fish. 'Don't you start.'

Manda held up her hands. 'Oh Harlow, I'm not having a go. If it's what you want to do, I think it's brilliant. I know how unhappy you were when we worked together last year. If working in that kind of pressurised environment wasn't for you, then it's good you got out. And I mean, that was a difficult and depressing shoot in the depths of winter in a muddy field. Lots of egos in front of the camera – and behind it too.' She raised an eyebrow. 'It's about time you were true to yourself. I'm just puzzled, that's all, why now, why start off at the bottom?'

Harlow shook her head and gazed out at the inky Aegean. Lights glinted in the distance from the villages lining the coast of Skiathos.

She turned back to Manda. 'Despite what everyone thinks – and by everyone, I mostly mean my mum and Tyler – I'm not really starting at the bottom. I mean, I'm here, on a big-budget movie, filming on a Greek island. What other assistant location manager would have got this job last minute with no relevant experience without having the connections I have?'

'Well, firstly, you have plenty of experience and I'm pretty sure you can already do the job with your eyes closed.' Manda sipped the dregs of her wine. 'And I know how much you hate the assumption your mum gets you th—'

'It's not an assumption when she does, though. Why do you think I'm here? I'm starting off as an assistant because *I* want to learn the ropes, *I* want to earn a location manager job and not have it given to me because of who I am – or, rather, who my mother is.'

'I get it, honestly I do. It's just you were a first assistant director. You have such vision and creativity, I imagined you'd be directing your own projects by now.'

Harlow sighed. 'What you said before, about being true to

myself, that's kinda what I'm trying to do. I still have a lot to figure out.'

Manda nodded but her creased forehead suggested that she didn't fully understand Harlow's reasons for turning her career on its head, and it was nothing Harlow wanted to verbalise, not when she was still figuring things out. Gradually, as she'd worked her way up the ladder over the last few years from third, to second, to first assistant director, her confidence had taken a nosedive and her happiness and excitement at her film career had diminished. It made her question why she was working in an industry she'd fallen out of love with – an industry that when she honestly thought about it she wasn't sure she would have gone into if it hadn't been for her mum. While it felt as though everyone around her thought she was sabotaging her career and her life – even her endlessly supportive dad had questioned her recent decisions – she strongly believed she was protecting her mental health.

A waiter cleared away their empty plates and took another drink order. The distraction gave them the chance to change the subject, neither of them wanting to press the issue further and end up in an argument. They talked about Skopelos instead and their longing to explore more of the island, which Harlow admitted, with a grimace, she'd be doing with her mum the following day.

Manda sighed and sat back in her chair with her hands resting on her stomach. 'That was delicious, but I always end up eating too much when I'm working.'

'Yeah, I went for a much-needed run this morning.'

'You have nothing to worry about.'

'Neither do you.'

'Apart from the dreaded middle-aged spread creeping up on me.'

Harlow shook her head. 'You look fabulous.'

'I'd feel even more fabulous with a G&T. Where are our drinks?' Manda looked around.

Harlow glanced behind her. Every table was filled and there was a handful of people sitting up at the bar too. She could only see two waiters, both busy with food orders.

Harlow turned back to Manda. 'I'll go ask. I need the loo anyway.'

She left the table and made her way to the ladies'. She washed her hands and caught sight of her reflection in the subtle light. Her skin already looked sun-kissed. Whatever her mum thought about her pale complexion, she preferred a natural tan to her mum's fake bronzed skin any day. Her cheeks were flushed from the heat, her eyes a little glazed from too much wine. She ran her hand through her short hair to give it volume and slicked on lip gloss. She needed to start running regularly again. It was a habit she'd got into back home, an early-morning run to clear her head. She stuffed her lip gloss back in her bag, left the ladies' and squeezed into an empty space at the bar next to a couple deep in conversation.

The woman behind the bar looked flustered and her tanned cheeks glowed with sweat. Two fans wafted the air at either end of the bar, but Harlow felt for her, having to work on such a humid night. From the perfect temperature during the day, the evening had turned still and sultry. She could feel her dress sticking to the small of her back.

The woman behind the bar caught Harlow's eye. 'A waiter will take your order at your table.'

'We've already ordered, about twenty minutes ago...'

'I'm so sorry,' the woman said. 'What did you order?'

'Two gin and tonics.'

'One minute and I make them now. Someone will bring them over.'

'Thank you, and it's no problem, I'll wait; save someone the trip.'

The woman gave Harlow a grateful nod.

Not wanting to watch her and make her even more flustered, Harlow turned, leant her elbows on the edge of the bar and gazed out. The sea was still and there wasn't even a hint of a breeze to take the edge off the humidity. The couple next to her were British tourists, but apart from an occasional word, she couldn't make out their whispered conversation over the Greek music and background chatter.

A few of the crew were dotted about, a couple of the supporting cast too. There was a good mix of tourists and locals, and she kept hearing snatches of Greek. She liked that it was a popular place and had a real buzz to it. She also liked it because it was the sort of place her mum wouldn't come to. Too relaxed for her taste.

The poor woman behind the bar was taking an age. Not that Harlow was in a rush, she quite liked people-watching. Manda gave her a smile. She seemed happy enough, relaxing back in her chair on the edge of the beach.

Harlow's eyes drifted across the bar. A young couple were gazing at each other longingly, their hands entwined together on the table. A tall lanky guy walked past them. He waved to the group of guys at a table not far from Harlow and they greeted him with a cheer. They'd been talking in Greek, but Harlow noticed that they switched to English as the new guy sat down. Harlow's attention shifted to the Greek with his back to her. He had dark curly hair and broad shoulders showcased by a white T-shirt. His arms were tanned and shapely. He had an accent, but Harlow caught bits of what he was saying, something about taking a boat out and exploring. He gestured out to the bay and turned enough for Harlow to see his profile. She might have only met him once, but he'd made quite an impression. He really was handsome when he smiled.

Without thinking it through, Harlow marched over to him. 'You do speak English then.'

The conversation at the table stopped and all eyes turned to her.

Harlow gazed down at Adonis.

He looked up at her, a flicker of recognition crossing his face. 'I, er—'

'So, you were just being a twat the first time I met you.'

Adonis frowned.

'If you don't know what twat means, look it up.' She realised too late that marching over and showing him up in front of his friends was probably a foolish thing to do. She glanced at the others; two dark-haired Greeks and the English guy who was looking bemused. 'I'm really sorry for disturbing your evening.'

She turned and paced back to the bar. She leant on it with her head in her hands this time, silently willing the woman to finish making the drinks.

'*You* thought I didn't know any English.' Adonis appeared next to her.

Heat rushed to her face as she looked at him. 'Only because you didn't say anything. And when you did, you spoke Greek. You looked confused and upset.'

'You assumed and I couldn't be bothered to put you right.'

She was aware of his friends watching them. 'Well, I'm sorry for the misunderstanding and for marching over just then.'

'I was angry.'

Harlow held his gaze. He was doing that sexy glowering look, the same as the first time, the difference was he was now fully clothed, the muscles she'd enjoyed an eyeful of in the olive grove hidden beneath a snug-fitting T-shirt.

'What were you angry about?' she asked.

'You wouldn't understand.'

'Try me.'

He shook his head. 'You're just some big shot from a movie.'

Harlow smirked. 'I'm really not.'

'All of you here, taking over our island.'

'I might have turned up unexpectedly that day,' she said calmly, 'but I was perfectly nice.'

His jaw clenched and he breathed deeply. He looked as if he was fighting back tears. She felt bad for overstepping and talking to him the way she had in front of his mates.

'Look, I didn't mean for us to get off to a bad start,' she said. 'There's no need for you to be involved if having a film crew around bothers you; I'll be dealing with your dad anyway.'

The woman behind the bar finally placed the glasses of gin and tonic in front of Harlow. She glanced between Harlow and Adonis. Harlow told the bar woman her room number and picked up the G&Ts. She turned back to Adonis.

'I really am sorry for disturbing your evening.' She walked away before he had the chance to say anything else.

Manda was watching her, a questioning look on her face.

'Who was that?'

Harlow sat down. 'Some arsehole of a bloke.'

'A mighty fine-looking arsehole if you ask me.'

Harlow gave her a wry smile. 'Story of my life.'

'So who is he?'

'The son of the farmer whose land we're filming on up in the hills above Glossa. By the sounds of it, he's not keen on a film crew descending on the island.'

'You'd think the locals would love the business.'

'I'm not sure what his problem is.'

Manda picked up one of the gins. 'Why were you talking to him anyway?'

'We kind of got off to a bad start when I first met him at The Olive Grove location. And I've just had a go at him for lying about understanding English, which I'm rapidly regretting.' She put her glass on the table with a thump. 'Shit. I don't know what I was thinking. That wine's gone right to my head. What the hell do I do if they don't allow us to film on their land now?' The thought of letting her mum and Tyler down made her break out in a cold sweat.

'I'm sure it won't come to that.'

Harlow shook her head. 'That was stupid of me.' She sipped her G&T. The barwoman had been generous with the gin after their wait. 'Hopefully The Olive Grove owner is more reasonable than his son.'

'His son really is quite something to look at, mind.'

'You're impossible. And very married.'

'Nothing wrong with looking.' She raised an eyebrow and stared past Harlow in Adonis's direction. 'I hope I get to go to this olive grove when filming starts. Knowing my luck, I'll be stuck at base all day.'

'I'd make the most of the view now then,' Harlow said with a wink.

8

Harlow met her mum in the hotel car park at nine the next morning. Not only was it an ungodly hour for a Sunday, but she wondered if she'd chosen this time because it was less likely anyone would see them together. Maybe she was being paranoid and unfair; her mum was not only a workaholic but rarely had more than five hours sleep a night and wasn't one for sleeping in even when she could.

There was a benefit to being up early – the heat wasn't as intense, and the road was quiet as they whizzed past the lush pine forest. When they reached Skopelos Town, they easily found a place to park.

It was peaceful too, early enough for it to feel as though people were only just beginning to emerge. A lazy Sunday morning in the Mediterranean. The air rang with the sound of church bells and was filled with the smell of strong Greek coffee. They passed white-washed churches squeezed between the shuttered houses. A tortoiseshell cat was curled up on a wall, basking in the sun as bees hummed around the flowers spilling from a window box.

'We had our eye on Skopelos Town as the main filming location.

One of the Greek team found a villa higher up on the hillside, but the Glossa villa has worked out for the best. This place though...' Maeve gestured ahead to the narrow lane lined on either side by the uniform white villas, their wooden doors and shutters painted mint green or the typical and instantly recognisable blue of the Greek islands.

They walked down through the narrow and confusing jumble of lanes, with Maeve attempting to follow directions on her phone.

'Where are we going?' Harlow asked as they turned into yet another lane.

Maeve stopped in front of a compact cafe with a handful of shiny blue tables and chairs outside, most of them already filled with people tucking into food.

'Apparently this is the best pie shop in Skopelos Town,' she said. 'Grab that table; I'll order.'

Maeve marched inside and Harlow sat down at the small table. The place was not her mum's style, but Harlow appreciated her embracing the local specialities, although she wasn't sure about eating pie for breakfast.

The cafe was tucked out of the way from the main tourist area of the seafront. A young Greek couple were sitting at the table next to her, their conversation loud and fast. Their coffee smelt divine and just what Harlow needed to perk herself up. A few people strolled by, gazing at the shop windows.

Maeve reappeared in a flurry of colour, her sundress pink and eye-catching. She sat down and wedged her sunglasses into her hair.

'I thought we should have a traditional Greek breakfast and then enjoy a late lunch after we've explored.'

A moment later, a man emerged from the shop with a tray and placed two Greek coffees on the table along with two huge breakfast pastries.

'The cream bougatsa.' He pointed at the pie sprinkled with a generous amount of icing sugar. 'And the cheese one. Enjoy.'

'My goodness, Mum. No wonder you suggested we have a late lunch.'

'When in Greece...' She let out a throaty chuckle, which made Harlow smile. 'I thought I'd get one of each; savoury and sweet. Tuck in.'

Harlow sliced into the cheese one. The filo crunched and flaked to reveal the white cheese inside. Harlow took a mouthful and raised her eyebrows.

'Good, huh?' Maeve said, taking a piece for herself.

Harlow chewed and nodded. Filled with warm feta, it was deliciously moreish. They sat in silence and ate, switching between the salty cheese pie and the creamy custard one with sips of the strong black coffee in between.

'Breakfast is my favourite time of day.' Maeve dabbed her red lipsticked mouth with a napkin. 'Particularly when I don't have an early start. I like the thinking time over a coffee. Sets me up nicely. Not that I could eat this every day; my personal trainer would kill me, but it's a nice treat.'

Harlow acknowledged the casual mention of her personal trainer. Harlow found it hard enough to get to the gym once a month. Running was more her thing, out in the fresh air – or the not so fresh air in London. But she understood her mum's desire to have time to herself; she felt that way about running, her legs pounding the ground while her head was free to think. She felt that way about being outside too, surrounded by the peace of the countryside, like yesterday, walking the forest path to Panormos.

'My and your dad's first holiday together was to a Greek island.'

'Oh? Which one?'

'Corfu. A couple of years before you were born.'

'You mean you actually took time off to go on holiday?'

Maeve flared her nostrils and focused on Harlow with a look she'd seen many times before, her blue eyes piercing beneath long, black lashes. 'I know family holidays when you were young were often interrupted...'

Harlow raised an eyebrow and took a last bite of the cream bougatsa. Interrupted was an understatement. Harlow couldn't remember a holiday with her parents which wasn't spoiled by her mum making phone calls or staying in their holiday cottage to work while Harlow and her dad would take a picnic and go for a walk or to the beach for the day. There'd been times when her mum had been too busy to even go on holiday with them in the first place, so just she and her dad went, often to her grandparents' farm in Yorkshire.

Maeve talked more about the Corfu holiday and Harlow listened with interest about a time when her parents had been together and happy. They left filo crumbs and a generous tip and set off towards the harbourside, Harlow matching her mum's pace. When Maeve got an idea about something, she went at it full steam ahead. A day exploring Skopelos Town would be just that; pounding the lanes, admiring hidden churches, drinking a frappé by the sea, and of course lots of shopping. And that's exactly what they did for the next couple of hours, looping along the harbourside and then zigzagging back up the hill, popping into shops to browse local ceramics and handmade jewellery. They discovered hidden lanes with magnificent views and escaped the heat of the early afternoon in the shady terrace of a coffee shop. What little time Harlow spent with her mum was like that too – there was an intensity about it, as if she was trying to soak up every second she had with her daughter by packing everything into a few short hours. Harlow had become used to it; she was resigned to time with her mum being brief and intense. That was one of the many reasons why she couldn't face living with her for the shoot. But whatever today was about, Harlow acknowledged it was better than nothing.

Although her immediate reaction had been to not want to spend the day with her, now she was, she wanted to enjoy it. Yet part of her felt that it was the perfect opportunity to talk to her on a deeper level rather than the superficial conversations they usually had.

'Do you wish you'd spent more time with me and dad when I was younger?' Harlow asked as they emerged from the coffee shop into the sunshine.

'What kind of question is that?'

'A perfectly reasonable one.'

'I don't regret anything. I made a choice to pursue my career and balance it with our family life. One day, Harlow, you might understand how difficult that is.'

They walked on in silence. Harlow didn't want to argue with her. They paused at the top of winding steps. The view was straight off a Greek island postcard, the stone steps edged with white leading to another of Skopelos Town's narrow lanes, with tourists, flowers and shutters blending together in a riot of colour.

* * *

By mid-afternoon even Maeve had had enough of exploring the town. She'd had the foresight to book a restaurant, and relief flooded through Harlow at the sight of the peaceful courtyard with a pomegranate tree providing much-needed shade.

'This is very nice.' Harlow ran her hands along the crisp white tablecloth and let her aching feet relax. She picked up the menu. 'Are you going to let me order for myself this time?'

'Of course.' Maeve opened her menu and scanned it. 'I've been told the pork in citrus sauce is rather special.'

'I think I fancy something traditional. I'm blinking starving after all that walking.'

They ordered food and the waiter brought a glass of red wine for Harlow and home-made lemonade for Maeve. He returned a little while later with the pork dish, a moussaka for Harlow and a Greek salad to share.

Maeve leaned forward and folded her hands on the table. 'Aren't you glad I got you this job?'

Harlow inwardly sighed, realising where the conversation was about to head. 'Yes, now I'm here and have settled in, I'm enjoying it.'

Maeve picked up her knife and fork and cut into the pork. 'You and Tyler seem to be working well together.'

'We're managing fine.'

'It must help that you know each other.'

'Uh-huh.' Harlow chewed a mouthful of moussaka and washed down the meaty richness with a swig of wine. She was now uncertain where her mum was trying to take the conversation.

'You used to talk about Tyler a lot, I remember; you seemed to be really close, then nothing. You've stopped mentioning him recently.'

'I'm amazed you noticed.'

'I do take an interest in your life, Harlow.' She stabbed her fork into an olive. 'So, did you and Tyler fall out over something?'

Harlow began to wonder if Tyler had said anything. 'We just drifted apart. You know how it is, we've naturally seen less of each other over the years as we've worked on different things.'

'It must be good to have the chance to spend so much time with him again then.'

Her mum really had no clue about her life. She asked token questions and she saw what she wanted to see. The same way she always focused on Harlow's flaws and never seemed proud. When they talked, it was about superficial stuff, never about their feelings or what was really going on in their lives. And it worked both ways, just as her mum didn't know about Harlow's long and complicated history with Tyler, Harlow really had no idea about her mum's relationships either. Most things about her mum's private life were gleaned through gossip. Harlow was as un-newsworthy as her mum was talked about.

The moussaka was delicious but filling and Harlow was glad of the salad and the wine to wash it down. After the best part of a day spent walking in the sun, it was a relief to sit in the shade. Even with the courtyard full of people, the setting was peaceful. Away from the bustling harbourside, it felt more relaxed and had a more traditional Greek vibe. The walls surrounding the courtyard were filled with pots of geraniums, the red, pink and purple splashes breaking up the sand-coloured stone.

They finished their meal and ordered coffee. The waiter brought a cafetière to the table and Maeve poured them each a mugful.

'What do you think about filming at Perivoliou, that quiet beach past Glossa, rather than moving it to Kastani?' she asked.

'I, er... You really want my opinion?'

'Of course I do.'

She wasn't sure Tyler would be best pleased if her mum took her advice over his, but she was asking and waiting for an answer.

'I think logistically it's a harder location, but it's a beautiful spot.'

'So is Kastani and we're already filming there; shouldn't be an issue adding on another two days.'

'True, but it has associations with *Mamma Mia!* – it's familiar and it's being used for other scenes. I guess it depends if you want the look of a beautiful, desolate beach despite it being a harder location to reach.'

'But do *you* think the extra effort to film there will be worth it?'

'I, er...' She was unsure how to respond; the last thing she wanted to do was step on anyone's toes, particularly Tyler's. 'That's really not my place to say. What has Tyler said?'

'It doesn't matter what he said; I'm asking you.'

'And I'm telling you, it should be his call if it's down to the logistics over the creative aspect.'

Maeve stirred milk into her coffee and looked across the table at Harlow, her eyes piercing and unflinching. 'This is your problem; your inability to make decisions and go with your gut. Deep down I know you have an answer to this, but I have no idea why you can't be sure of yourself. Is that why you shied away from a director role? You don't want to take responsibility? You can't bumble along as an assistant all your life. Show some bloody guts and determination.'

'Wow.' Harlow sat back and gripped the edges of the chair. 'You really are something else.'

Maeve's lips pursed. 'What's that supposed to mean?'

'So, because I'm not ruthlessly ambitious like you, you have to tear me down.'

'You don't have to be ruthless, just a touch of ambitious would do.'

Harlow's jaw clenched. She had an unbelievable desire to scream at her mum, but she couldn't, not surrounded by tables filled with people enjoying their meals. She focused less on the anger coursing through her and more on the thought that her mum was trying to provoke her. She wouldn't give her the satisfaction.

Harlow reached down and picked up her bag. She took out twenty euros and tucked it beneath the unused ashtray.

'Where are you going?' Maeve asked.

'For a walk. I'll make my own way back to the hotel. As always, it was a delight to spend time with you.'

She left, weaving her way across the courtyard between the

tables of happy tourists, down the steps and back out on to the narrow street.

Harlow walked in the direction where there were fewer people. She fought back tears as she strode along the paved lane. All she'd ever wanted was a proper relationship with her mum, one of love and understanding where they'd talk and share the ups and downs of their lives. A relationship like so many of her friends had with their mums, just like Manda and her daughter. She wanted with her mum what she had with her dad. She could talk to him about anything, and he listened too, properly listened and understood her. Maybe she needed to accept that her mum would never change and be thankful instead that she had a normal family in her dad and Gina. It was pointless to wish for a nurturing and loving relationship with a woman who was far from maternal.

9

WEEK THREE – SECOND WEEK OF FILMING

'Harlow, I need you at The Olive Grove location today to prep.' Tyler caught up with her on the path between the hotel villas and the unit base. 'Your mum's decided to stick with Perivoliou beach instead of Kastani, so I need to prepare for that. I also need you on set this morning and then again to wrap things up later, so you'll have to go to The Olive Grove over lunch.'

Tyler was flustered, which was exactly why Harlow hadn't wanted to shoulder the responsibility for saying yes to the awkward-to-reach, out-of-the-way beach rather than the easy-to-access one. Although it had been Maeve who'd wavered about its suitability in the first place. At least Tyler was getting paid to make those kinds of decisions. At the end of the day, the responsibility for bringing the film in on time and within budget fell to Maeve and the executive producers.

After an eventful weekend, Harlow had been relieved when Monday came and she could concentrate on work. She hadn't seen or heard from her mum since she'd left her at the restaurant. Harlow had blown off steam during her walk through the town. She'd felt calmer by the time she'd reached the harbourside. The bars and cafes had been packed with tourists tucking into plates of seafood or sipping cocktails as they enjoyed the late afternoon sun. She'd got a taxi back to the hotel and had gone straight to her room. After getting an early night, she hadn't seen anyone until that morning when a flustered Tyler had caught up with her.

As requested, she spent the morning at the Glossa set and organised for one of the Greek location assistants to cover for her while she went to The Olive Grove. It was only a short drive, but it gave her enough time to relive her ill-fated conversation with Adonis and worry about what problems she'd possibly encounter.

She parked the car and told herself to quit stressing about something that might not even end up being an issue. It was the tail end of lunch and there were still a few cars in the car park. She walked beneath the shady avenue of vines towards the restaurant. The place was as magical as she remembered it.

With much relief, she spotted Stephanos and saw no sign of Adonis in the restaurant courtyard. She headed over to him, past a handful of diners finishing off their lunch. Deep lines creased his tanned forehead. He acknowledged her with a nod.

'*Yasas*,' she said, not expecting her token word of Greek to impress him in the slightest.

It didn't. He grunted.

'Dimitri should have contacted you to say I'd pop here to prep for the filming, if that's okay?'

'Do what you have to do. It is no problem.' He waved his hand in the direction of the olive grove.

The knot of tension that had settled itself in her chest eased as she wandered down the terrace steps. Stephanos didn't seem to know anything about her run-in with his son, and even if he did, it hadn't caused a problem, for which she was immensely relieved. She needed to learn to bite her tongue in future.

As she walked through the long scratchy grass, she ran the

following day through in her head. She and Tyler would be the first to arrive and she was going to cordon off half of the car park for the film crew. To reach the olive grove, they could bypass the restaurant by following the grassy path that ran below it, and they'd be set up to film well before anybody arrived for lunch.

Harlow had chosen the perfect spot and the director, the director of photography and Maeve had already checked it out. She walked there now, halfway down the grove to an area where the trees were more spaced out. The trunk of the olive tree split into three, curling upwards to its canopy of leaves, a deep, dark green in the summer sun. The backdrop was more olives trees. Beyond was the orchard with its plum and fig trees and the deeper green of the pine forest further up. Harlow had no doubt the place would look incredible on film.

She sat down with her back to the tree trunk. It was the most romantic spot and ticked every box when it came to the brief for the scene. The storyboard had depicted a location just like this. Breathing in the warm air filled with the sun-dried scent of herbs, she picked out the freshness of oregano. She gazed into the branches above at the slender pointed leaves silhouetted against the bright blue sky. She could happily stay here forever soaking up the peace and beauty of the surrounding nature. But she had work to do.

Harlow got to her feet and dusted off flecks of dried grass from her linen trousers. She took a notebook and pen from her bag and cut between the trees to the low stone wall between the olive grove and the orchard. She perched on it with her notebook open. She could see past the olive trees to where the sky merged with the dark blue of the Aegean. Part of her didn't want to share the location with the whole crew tomorrow. She could understand Adonis's reluctance to have a movie descend on his peaceful slice of Skopelos. If she lived in a place this beautiful, she wasn't sure she'd want to share it either. She felt the pressure at having made the arrangements for the next day's shoot. She'd gone over things far more times than she'd needed to, but her mum's words of not letting her down played over and over like a stuck record.

It was good to sit in silence and contemplate. Back in London, there never seemed to be this quiet time, not that it was actually silent here, with birdsong, the bleat of a goat and tinkling bells. She was alone but surrounded by life, from the cicadas in the undergrowth and the ladybird crawling across the stone wall, to the butterflies carried on the gentle breeze. At home, she'd often go and sit in a park, desperate for leafy outside space that her flat with its compact balcony failed to provide, but she couldn't escape the noise: toddler meltdowns, dogs barking, screeching children, tinny ice-cream van tunes, sirens and the constant drone of traffic.

Harlow dragged her eyes away from the view and tried to focus on the open page of her notebook and the notes she'd started to make in preparation for the shoot. The actors' call time was six at the unit base for costume, hair and make-up, ready for a seven thirty start at The Olive Grove. Harlow was planning on being on location with Tyler at least an hour before anyone else. She needed to get the call sheets and signage done to ensure everyone knew what they were doing and where they were going. It would be an early start and a long day, which she was used to, but the pressure reminded her of her old job as an assistant director, but with less pay and less respect.

A shadow fell over the bright white page.

Startled, Harlow looked up.

Adonis loomed over her, his features distorted by the glare of the sun behind him.

'Baba said you were down here.' His voice was deep, but it seemed softer than when they'd last spoken. Less angry. 'I'm sorry about the other night in the bar. I was having a bad day. Actually both times. Then and when we first met.'

Harlow shrugged. 'You and me both.'

A dog padded past him, the Dalmatian Harlow had first seen in the restaurant.

'This is Sam,' Adonis said as the dog nuzzled his wet nose into Harlow's lap. 'I didn't mean to take my frustration out on you in the bar. You took me by surprise.'

'Yeah, I'm sorry about that,' she said, stroking Sam's soft fur. 'I'm not sure what came over me. I heard you speaking English, *perfectly*,' she stressed, 'and stupidly decided to say something. I think too much wine and sun had gone to my head.'

He gestured to the space on the wall next to her. 'Can I?'

'Knock yourself out.'

A brief frown crossed Adonis's face, but he sat down regardless. Harlow waited for him to say something else. As the silence between them grew, she found it harder to know what to say either.

'Baba said you film in the olive grove for the next two days?'

'Yes,' Harlow said, relieved that the silence had been broken. 'It's perfect for the scene we're doing.'

'The film is a romance?'

'It is indeed.'

Sam settled down in the shade by their feet. Great tits swooped between the branches of the trees, their distinctive song battling against the constant chirping of the cicadas.

'That's an Eleonora's Falcon.' Adonis pointed to a large bird gliding gracefully, its long wings and tail silhouetted against the clear sky. 'The longer you stay here, the more you see.'

It only confirmed her earlier feeling of how amazing the place was. She really could sit here all day and soak up the sights, sounds and the fragrant and natural scent of herbs, trees and the earth.

'How come you were at the bar the other night?' Harlow asked, breaking the peace. 'It's a little way from Glossa.'

'It's our usual place when it's not overrun with film people.' He raised an eyebrow and gave her a sly smile. 'My aunt owns the hotel. Not much to do up here in the hills.'

'I really hope I didn't offend your friends.'

'They found it funny. Jack in particular. He's from the UK and works on a boat over the summer, but is based on Skiathos, so I don't see him often.'

Harlow realised he was the tall lanky guy who'd joined Adonis and his friends.

'When I told Baba what happened, he was worried I'd offended you and you'd not film on our land.'

'That makes two of us. I was worried I'd messed things up and we wouldn't be able to shoot here. So we're all good, yeah?'

'All good. Baba comes across like he couldn't care less if a film crew was here, but he's proud of this place.'

'He should be; it's stunning.'

'Plus he'd never say no to the money.'

'It's decent money.'

Adonis stood up and shoved his hands into the pockets of his shorts. There was none of the moodiness that there'd been the first two times they'd met, but he had a quiet reserve and looked serious.

'I'll let you get on,' he said.

Harlow nodded. 'Thanks, and maybe see you again tomorrow.'

She watched him walk back up between the trees, Sam padding behind him. She did wonder if his dad had asked him to talk to her, worried about losing a lucrative deal, but she was relieved that they'd cleared the air before the whole film crew descended on the place.

Harlow finished writing in her notebook and closed it. Adonis intrigued her.

10

Harlow slept fitfully, the worry of the next day stopping her from getting a restful night. The responsibility that her mum had pulled her up on the other afternoon, that Harlow knew she shied away from, sat heavy on her shoulders. The harshness of her mum's words twisted and jabbed at her insides until she felt a physical tightness.

She was awake well before her alarm. She threw off the sheet and locked herself in the en suite. A torrent of warm water pummelled her shoulders and began to work away at the tension.

She packed her bag and left the villa. She was so early, they weren't even serving breakfast, so she made herself an instant coffee at the base and went to the production office to print out that day's paperwork.

By six, the place was alive with voices and bustling with people as the costume, hair and make-up departments became busy. Harlow caught sight of her mum hotfooting it from the rest area in the marquee to the production office, a coffee cup in her hand and sunglasses wedged in her blonde hair.

Harlow handed out the call sheets and movement orders and found Manda in the make-up area of the marquee wiping down her workstation.

'Morning,' Harlow said, tapping her friend on the shoulder. 'I'm about to head to location, just wondered what you're up to?'

Manda made a face. 'I got the short straw; I'll be here all day. You go have fun. Maybe you'll see that handsome, brooding Greek again.'

'He found me in the olive grove yesterday and apologised for getting arsey the other night.'

'I really wouldn't mind him getting arsey with me...' Manda grinned.

'What are you like?' Harlow shook her head. 'I had some apologising to do too.'

'You kissed and made up, huh.' Manda winked.

'Hardly.'

'You wish, eh!'

'You deserve to be stuck here all day.'

Voices made them turn. Crystal swept into the make-up area, with her assistant hot on her heels.

'Morning,' she said breezily. She plonked herself in Manda's make-up chair and her assistant handed her a coffee cup.

'Morning, Crystal,' Manda said, smiling. 'You look bright and fresh-faced as usual.' She turned back to Harlow and said under her breath, 'Go have a great day – without me.'

Tyler was already waiting by the car when Harlow rounded the corner of the hotel.

'You weren't at breakfast so I got you a bacon sarnie, grilled to crispy goodness, just as you like it.' He handed the wrapped sandwich to her.

'Thank you.'

'I'll drive.' He dropped his sunglasses over his eyes and got in the car.

There were times when Tyler seemed to know her better than she knew herself. She couldn't think of anything better than a bacon sarnie to fuel her for the long day ahead. She'd relished eating the local cuisine for breakfast, lunch and dinner, but this felt like a real treat and a slice of home. Working with him wasn't all bad.

* * *

Harlow and Tyler arrived at The Olive Grove at six thirty. Harlow felt as though she'd already been up for hours. All the location signs were in place and the area of the car park the film crew were using cordoned off. Harlow was going to direct the cast and crew to where they were filming, but for good measure she put a sign up that pointed to the side of the restaurant and the path leading to the grove. The last thing she wanted was for crew to be traipsing across the restaurant terrace.

Maeve was the first to arrive and picked her way across the shingle car park in heeled sandals. She had a large bag slung over her shoulder and clasped her phone, while her assistant followed behind clutching a notebook and a tablet.

'Morning, Harlow,' Maeve said as she reached her. 'All set up? The crew aren't far behind. Tyler down at the location?'

'Yes, follow the path round that way and it's halfway down the hill.'

Maeve set off with her PA. Harlow didn't point out that heeled, open-toed sandals and bare legs in a mid-length dress were probably not the best choice, but then Harlow had been clear about the location details: hard, uneven ground and long, scratchy grass. Her mum had the same information as everyone else. Harlow was comfortable in trainers, cropped trousers and a vest top. She had sunscreen lathered everywhere, a hat shading her face and sunglasses for good measure. She was ready for a day working outside in the Greek heat.

Harlow didn't see either Adonis or Stephanos; she assumed they were staying well out of the way. Harlow directed all the vehicles, and once everyone had arrived, she followed on down and set up a drink station, then made three more trips with drinks and snacks for the cast and crew.

While the sun beat down, Crystal and Dominic lounged on a chequered picnic blanket beneath the shade of the olive tree. Dappled sunlight filtered onto the grass surrounding them, and butterflies fluttered in the light. It was exactly as Harlow had imagined from the storyboard. The olive grove fell silent for the first take, the only sound the actors' voices and the ever-present chatter of insects and the occasional sigh of the wind through the leaves.

The morning raced by, a repetitive cycle of action, reset and the next take. By late morning, the scene was to be shot from another angle, so while Crystal and Dominic took a break, the director and the director of photography discussed the next part of the shoot.

Harlow stood in the shade by the drink station, her shoulders aching from leaning against a tree all morning.

Tyler walked over and grabbed a bottle of water. 'I need you to talk to the owner about removing a branch from the olive tree.'

'Why do they need to do that?'

'It'll be visually more pleasing,' Tyler said. 'It's not up for discussion; Jim's just asked. We need to get this done asap.'

Harlow traipsed up the olive grove, diverting off the grassy path at the top and on to the empty terrace. Diners would soon be arriving for lunch. Beyond the restaurant, a path skirted the orchard, leading to a whitewashed villa and various outbuildings.

Adonis's Dalmatian Sam was lying in the sun. He lifted his head as she walked past and flopped back down again.

The villa's blue-painted front door was wedged open.

Harlow knocked. 'Hello?'

Slow thudding footsteps sounded and eventually an elderly woman with white hair, a black dress and leaning on a walking stick thumped her way along the hallway.

'*Naí*?' she said brusquely.

'I, um... Is Stephanos or Adonis around?'

The lines on the woman's weather-worn face became starker as she frowned.

'*O Stéphanos échei páei stin póli. O Adonis eínai sto ergastírio. Ekeí káto. Ekeí, ekeí*,' she said, waving her hand and indicating towards the outbuildings.

'Okay,' Harlow said slowly, trying to make sense of the woman's meaning. 'Thank you. *Efharistó*.'

She backed away, turned and walked along the top of the orchard in the direction the old woman had vigorously pointed.

The view was even more incredible from this high up. Harlow could see past the fruit and olive trees to the sea. The chatter from the film crew drifted up, reminding Harlow that she needed to get permission for them to remove a branch fast otherwise the shoot would be held up.

She passed a series of outbuildings, some in better shape than others. The sound of scraping came from the one at the end where the forest bordered the olive farm.

Large barn doors opened onto a paved area with weeds poking between the stones. Harlow stood in the doorway and let her eyes adjust from the bright sunshine to the gloom inside.

Adonis was standing at a workbench, running a hand plane over a piece of wood. Curls of pale wood floated to the sawdust-covered floor. He caught sight of her and stopped.

'Sorry to disturb you, but the lady at the house sent me down this way. She's your grandma?'

'My yiayia, yes.'

'You do woodwork then?' Harlow admired the carved pieces of wood stacked against the wall.

'When I get the chance. Like today, because of the filming, I'm not in the fields.'

The barn smelt of fresh sawdust and the sun streaming through the large open doors caught the dust dancing in the light.

'The pieces are beautiful.'

Adonis nodded. 'Do you need something?'

Harlow stopped looking around and focused on him. 'The shoot's going well, but there's a branch in the way of the scene we want to shoot next and we were hoping you wouldn't mind removing it, please.'

'You want to cut down a tree?'

'Not a tree, no. Just a branch.'

Adonis sighed, his face morphing into a scowl. He took a saw from a rack of tools hanging on the back wall. 'Show me.'

He muttered something in Greek as they left the barn and stalked ahead, cutting straight through the orchard towards the olive grove. The moody version of Adonis had returned. She partly understood why she might have pissed him off; it must seem such a trivial thing, them wanting a branch removed purely for the aesthetics, while his job was all about nurturing. Ripe plums hung heavy, gleaming invitingly as they ducked beneath branches. Harlow had a job keeping up with him.

The crew were still setting up to reshoot the scene from the opposite angle. Her mum was behind the monitor, deep in discussion with Jim and the director; Dominic was talking loudly on his phone; while Crystal was sitting in the shade beneath another olive tree having her make-up reapplied. Tyler caught sight of them and walked over.

'Hey, you're Adonis, right?' Tyler said as he reached him.

Adonis gave a curt nod. Harlow could see how pissed off he was from the tension in his shoulders. If he gripped the saw any tighter, it might have looked as if he was about to attack someone...

'What do you want cut?' Adonis asked Tyler.

Adonis's words from the other night rang in her ears; the film crew 'taking over the island' was not going to be helped by them demanding the removal of a branch.

Harlow let Tyler explain what he wanted doing, and without a word Adonis set about sawing off the branch. It came away, large and packed with green-grey leaves.

Adonis turned to Tyler. 'Is that everything?'

'Yes, thank you.'

Adonis set off back up the hill, the branch and saw clutched in his hand.

Tyler shook his head and looked at Harlow. 'What's his problem?'

'I'm not sure he particularly likes us invading.'

'It's not like they had to say yes. Cutting that branch is not much to ask. And what kind of dickhead name is Adonis?' he scoffed.

'It's a perfectly normal Greek name.'

Harlow watched Adonis until he disappeared beneath the trees in the orchard. She didn't like feeling responsible for upsetting him, not after his apology and their chat which had cleared the air. Harlow sighed. While her mum seemed to thrive on conflict and making difficult decisions, not caring if she pissed people off, Harlow didn't like it. She never had done, ever since hearing the constant arguments between her parents as a child. Either her mum didn't care about upsetting someone, or over the years she'd developed a thick enough skin for it to no longer bother her. For Harlow it left her feeling decidedly uncomfortable.

'First positions, everyone!' Jim called, and the shoot continued, with Dominic and Crystal resuming their positions lounging on the picnic blanket, and any crew like Harlow and Tyler removing themselves from shot.

* * *

At lunchtime, Stephanos wandered down to see what was going on. He said a brief hello to Harlow, grunted his approval and returned to the restaurant. Harlow positioned herself by the restaurant terrace to field questions about what was going on and to ensure inquisitive diners didn't take it upon themselves to wander into the olive grove and into the back of the shot.

The aroma of grilled pork, along with the sight of sesame and honey-drizzled fried cheese and huge bowls of Greek salad made Harlow's stomach rumble. The actors and a handful of the crew were driven back to the unit base for lunch, while a production assistant handed out paper bags of picnic lunches to everyone who remained.

Harlow sat beneath a tree to eat hers, with the restaurant terrace just behind her. She took out an apple, a bag of oregano-flavoured crisps and two generous slices of spanakopita. The filo crumbled as she bit into it. She brushed away the flakes from her cropped trousers. The pie was moist and tangy with the feta and spinach; it reminded her of breakfast in Skopelos Town with her mum before things had inevitably taken a downward turn. Her mum was still here, sitting behind the monitor watching the morning's rushes. Harlow hadn't seen her eat anything; she had a tendency to focus on work and ignore everything else when she was in the zone.

'Are you working on the movie?' A deep voice with an American twang made Harlow jump.

She glanced behind.

'Apologies for creeping up on you.' The man was short and stocky with a flushed face and a neat moustache. A woman joined him and tucked her arm in his.

'You're with the movie?' she asked.

'I am,' Harlow said, swallowing a mouthful of spanakopita.

'Oh my goodness, you are so lucky.' The woman took off her sunglasses and shielded her eyes from the sun as she gazed down the olive grove.

'I'm just an assistant.'

'Oh, don't you "just assistant" me,' she said, laughing. 'You're working on a movie! That sure is something to show off about. I would.'

'Trust me, she would.' The man raised an eyebrow and grinned.

'We've been watching what's been going on while having lunch, haven't we, Doug? Got more than we bargained for – a sensational meal and we gotta watch a movie being made.'

'Hopefully we haven't disturbed you?' Harlow said.

'Oh my, no, you've made our day.'

'You're on holiday from the US?'

'Texas born and bred, but we live in California now,' the woman replied and the man nodded.

'You should be used to all this then.'

'Oh, we're from a small town,' Doug said. 'Although Sylvie would move to LA in a heartbeat, wouldn't you?'

'I'd give anything to live in a city like LA.' She nodded towards the olive grove set. 'Ain't that Maeve Fennimore-Bell?'

Harlow looked at her mum, who was now standing and talking to Jim. She looked every inch a glamorous Hollywood movie producer, with her blonde hair, red lips, tanned skin and her bright, attention-seeking, completely unsuitable dress.

Harlow turned back to the couple. 'Yes, it is.'

'Oh, this is super exciting. Just wait till we get back and I tell Jayne that I've seen Maeve Fennimore-Bell in the flesh. I am so jealous you get to work with her.'

'Well I don't work directly with her – she's way up here,' Harlow indicated above her head, 'and I'm way down there.' She pointed to her feet.

'She looks even more glamorous in real life. If only I could look half as good as she does...' Sylvie sighed.

'If you had her money, you probably would.' Doug grinned at his wife.

'Mind you, having an affair with a gorgeous actor a good few years younger probably helps.' She raised an eyebrow at her husband. 'That'd keep anyone young.'

Harlow looked sharply at the woman. 'An affair?'

Doug shook his head. 'Sylvie lives for gossip.'

'Ooh, it's been quite the scandal. I'm surprised you haven't heard about it.'

'I don't tend to keep track of things like that,' Harlow said, gazing down the hill. *Particularly when the gossip is about my mum*, she thought. She turned back to the couple and smiled. 'You should go down there and ask for her autograph.'

'Oh we couldn't,' Sylvie said, wide-eyed. 'Could we?'

'We're on a break from filming at the moment. It won't be a problem. I'm sure Maeve will be thrilled to chat with you. Tell her Harlow sent you.'

Harlow watched Doug and Sylvie pick their way across the olive grove. They reached her mum. Sylvie was doing all the talking, flinging her arms around excitedly and gesturing back up the hill towards Harlow. Her mum looked in her direction and met her eyes. Harlow smiled and waved. Her mum turned back to Sylvie and gave her biggest Hollywood smile.

If what Sylvie said was true, Maeve was up to her usual tricks again. Perhaps it was about time Harlow asked some pertinent questions. She certainly wasn't going to trawl through gossip blogs to get the dirt on her mum, but at the same time, she didn't like finding things out by chance through people like Doug and Sylvie.

11

Day one of the shoot at The Olive Grove wrapped on time and before the light began to fade. The restaurant had been busy for lunch and then quietened down in the afternoon when filming resumed for the picnic scene. Harlow was busy for the rest of the afternoon, particularly when people started to arrive for an early dinner. Her lunch seemed a long time ago and her stomach rumbled at the delicious smells wafting from the restaurant. She didn't catch sight of Adonis for the rest of the day, but every so often Stephanos appeared on the edge of the terrace to check what was going on.

They wrapped twelve hours after Harlow had arrived. Dominic and Crystal were chauffeured back to the base, with the hair and make-up assistants following a little later. The crew began to pack up, clearing away the cables and lugging equipment back to the vehicles in the car park. Harlow folded the picnic blanket and scoured the area beneath the trees to make sure nothing had been left behind. She picked up a discarded apple core and a paper bag with the leftovers of someone's lunch. Apart from the missing olive branch and the places the grass had been trampled on by dozens of feet, it looked the same as when they'd arrived.

The lights of Glossa weren't yet glowing, but the sun was making its journey to the horizon. The white villas dotting the hillside below gleamed and life hummed around her, moths emerging from the undergrowth now the crew had dispersed. It smelt fresh and fragrant, a magical combination of grass and earth. Harlow stood for a moment soaking up the peace after a day filled with constant chatter. She took one final look around and, satisfied that she was done, reluctantly started to make her way to the car. She'd be back first thing in the morning. Tyler had caught a lift earlier and only her mum and Jim were left, chatting together a little further up.

Maeve put her hand on Jim's arm. 'I'll see you later. Harlow, a word.' She folded her arms and waited until Jim had walked away. 'What was all that about earlier, sending that couple over?'

'The woman seemed to be your biggest fan and was keen to meet you. Was it a problem?'

'No, of course not,' she said with an edge to her voice which made Harlow certain it was anything but okay. 'She asked personal questions, that was all.'

'What do you expect, Mum, when apparently your life is out there for all to see?'

'You wanted to show me up; that was what it was all about?'

'No, I—'

Maeve marched ahead, not waiting to hear Harlow's answer. She went at quite a pace considering she was wearing such impractical footwear.

Harlow faltered before following. Is that why she'd sent them over, knowing it would piss her mum off? Maybe. Perhaps Harlow liked pressing her mum's buttons as much as her mum did hers.

* * *

'How was your day?' Manda joined her at a table on the terrace of the hotel's restaurant.

'Long.'

The sun had set, lights twinkled in the distance and the place was buzzing. Harlow was ravenous after spending the day surrounded by the delicious smells drifting across from The Olive Grove terrace.

'Did you get to see the Greek God?'

Harlow laughed. 'Is that what you're calling him now?'

'His name even means "extremely good-looking" – I looked it up. So, was he there?'

'Yeah, but I think I upset him again.'

'Oh, Harlow, what have you gone and done now?'

'I asked him – politely – to cut down a branch of an olive tree. Honestly, his reaction was like I'd asked him to cut down every tree in the place.' Harlow sighed. 'Mind you, I think I have a tendency to piss people off.'

'You don't piss me off.'

'And you know why? Because you're a friendly, happy, uncomplicated person. I understand you. Adonis is... I don't know, moody, intriguing, interesting...'

'Sexy...'

Harlow shrugged. 'There is that too. Maybe that's what makes him so intriguing. When I went there to prep for the shoot, he was lovely. He was talking about the birds in the olive grove. He had this quiet, sensitive side... I don't know. Today he was back to moody and glowering.'

'He sounds utterly swoonworthy to me. Even the moodiness is attractive.'

A waiter stopped at their table and placed plates of chicken souvlaki and fries in front of them, along with a bowl of salad with sun-dried tomatoes, green leaves and curled shavings of cheese.

'Oh, this is the best thing I've seen all day,' Harlow said, sliding a piece of chicken off the skewer.

Manda snorted. 'If you say so!'

Harlow resisted rolling her eyes at her.

Manda pulled the tender, grilled chicken onto her plate. 'Do you know what me and my husband talk about when I'm home; whose turn it is to take the dog for a walk, what we're going to have for dinner and is it going to rain. I'm oversimplifying things, but a guy who can talk about stuff, you know, interesting stuff, other than football, sounds a dream.'

'You might be right.'

'It's why it's so good me being away for a while, we'll actually have something proper to talk about when I get home. And it's crazy because we talk more on the phone or over Zoom than we do when we're actually together.'

'You've obviously needed this time to do something for yourself.'

'My goodness, yes. I totally underestimated how not focusing on me for so long would leave me like a shadow of my former self. I know that sounds dramatic, but until Emma turned eighteen and went off to uni, I was always known as Em's mum. And it's like with Rob, he has a normal nine-to-five job and I've always had to try to work around him and figure out babysitting when I have a job that's anything but nine to five. You know how it is.'

'I do... I mean, I know what the job is like, not how to juggle it with a family.'

'Is that something you'd like one day?'

'A family?' Harlow skewered a chip. 'That's so far from anything I'm thinking about at the moment. But working in this industry has its restrictions. Its freedoms too, I guess, being able to jump at last-minute opportunities and work abroad, but I imagine the long hours and unpredictability of the work would play havoc with a relationship.'

'That's why I compromised. I didn't want it to impact my family.'

'And that's because you're a kind, thoughtful and loving person. Your daughter is lucky to have you.'

'Not the same for you growing up then with your mum?'

'Hardly. I didn't see her a lot of the time. She had no qualms about taking off to work on a project – long days, overnight stays. Sometimes she was away for weeks at a time, and when she was back, her life revolved around work and socialising. She'd turn up to an occasional school play and then, of course, that was a whole thing because movie producer Maeve Fennimore-Bell was watching and everyone would try their hardest to impress her, because you never know, she might have spotted a future star at my secondary-school production of *Our Town*.'

'You sound bitter.'

Harlow sighed. 'Yeah, I do, don't I. That's probably why I have a habit of pissing her off. I've never forgiven her.'

'Oh goodness, you are having a bad day, aren't you.' Manda smiled at her warmly. 'Think we need a G&T on the beach after we've finished.'

'That sounds good.' Harlow picked up her nearly empty glass of wine, leaned back in her chair and looked across the table at Manda. 'Do you know much about my mum?'

'What do you mean?' Manda concentrated on cutting up the chicken on her plate.

'Do you read the stuff written about her, you know, online, in gossip mags?'

'Not intentionally, no.'

'But you do read stuff?'

'It's hard not to.'

'Huh.'

Manda looked up from her plate. 'You don't?'

Harlow shook her head and sipped her wine. 'No. I've always avoided looking at websites or magazines that she's in. I think it stems from being a teenager and knowing *way* more about my mum than I wanted to from friends who did read those kinds of things. I met an American woman today and it was just something she said about Mum having an affair...'

Manda nodded slowly. 'I assumed you knew.'

'I know very little, it seems. I mean, I'm actually glad she's having some fun and not just working all the time. I don't care if they're younger than her, but married...' Harlow shook her head. 'That just screams trouble.'

'Why don't you talk to her? I mean properly talk. I get why you avoid reading that kind of trash journalism, because, hey, we all know lots isn't true. Your mum's a target for gossip – she's a powerful, single woman. She can make or break an actor's career – hell, anybody's career to be honest. Don't you think it's time you talked to her about how you feel?'

Harlow flared her nostrils. Her mum had never been one to discuss feelings and Harlow didn't much like the idea of bringing up the subject. Although when she thought about it, her mum was quite happy to stick her nose in Harlow's life, at least when it came to her career. Personal stuff, not so much.

Manda popped the last piece of chicken in her mouth and placed her knife and fork on her plate. 'I expect she doesn't know that much about you either.'

'That's true, but then I don't have my life splashed all over the internet, so the only way for her to find out anything is to ask and be interested, which she never has been.'

'Maybe it's time that changed.'

'Maybe.' Harlow gripped the stem of her wine glass tighter and gazed out over the still, moonlit sea. She turned back to Manda. 'How about that G&T?'

* * *

Day two of filming at The Olive Grove was like déjà vu for Harlow, minus a run-in with Adonis. He seemed to have made himself scarce. Dominic and Crystal nailed the scene and they wrapped earlier than the day before. Standing on the side-lines, Harlow was certain the scene would look spectacular on screen, with the young, photogenic actors looking perfect against the fresh greens of the olive grove and the backdrop of blue sky.

After doing her end-of-day checks and ensuring the signage and cordons in the car park were removed after the last of the crew had left, Harlow made her way to the restaurant. It was before customers started to arrive for dinner and it was quiet except for the waiters laying the tables. Glass candle holders were lined up on the wall and Harlow imagined the flickering candlelight later and the view across the dusk-tinged olive grove to the lights of Glossa.

Stephanos was sitting at a table in the inner courtyard. It was warm and sheltered, and the scent of roses was almost overpowering. He looked up from his newspaper.

'Finished?' he asked gruffly.

'Yes, thank you for the last couple of days.'

'It is nothing.' He folded the paper. He pointed to his half-finished frappé. 'You like a drink?'

'Oh, no thank you, that's kind, but I need to get back. Everything's cleared away. We'll be back on the 19th to film the restaurant scene, but I'll be in touch before then to arrange a time for our heads of department to visit.'

'Of course.'

Harlow made to go, but she felt bad about how things had been left with Adonis. Perhaps she was being oversensitive, but still... She turned back. 'Um, is Adonis around?'

Stephanos looked at her intently, his permanent frown lines furrowing a little more. 'No, he went to meet a buyer. About our olive oil,' he added as if he needed to explain the reason for his absence.

'No worries then,' Harlow said, but faltered. 'Tell him thank you and that I say hi.'

Stephanos gave a curt nod. 'My son, he finds it... *dýskolo*... er, difficult. He finds it difficult.' He shook his head and waved his hand. 'Ah, I say too much. We see you later in July.'

Harlow left, confused by not only what Stephanos had said but why he'd said it. What did Adonis find difficult – them filming here? There hadn't been anger in his voice, just concern and also that he felt as though he was sharing too much. She'd just been doing her job yesterday and if that had annoyed Adonis, there was little she could do about it now. But it upset her that she'd upset him. Her mum was right; she wasn't cut out for a role where difficult decisions needed to be made, not when she reacted sensitively to such a little thing. She was glad they wouldn't be returning to The Olive Grove for a couple of weeks. Tomorrow would be spent at the Glossa set in the morning and Panormos in the afternoon, so at least she wouldn't feel as though they were invading at either location.

12

The morning at the Glossa set flew by. The pressure had eased now Harlow was at a location that she wasn't in charge of. After lunch, the shoot was moving to Panormos for the afternoon, but Tyler wanted to prep another location up in the hills on the way, so they took a longer route along one of the winding interior roads.

Tyler was driving and Harlow was enjoying the rush of air through the open window as they sped along the quiet road. They rounded a sharp bend on to another straight bit of road with trees on either side. She saw the pothole but realised too late that Tyler was heading right for it to avoid a van coming towards them in the middle of the road. The front tyre hit the hole and made a bang like an explosion, followed by a thrump thrump, thud thud, thrump thrump as the split tyre smacked the tarmac.

Tyler swore, rammed his foot on the brake and turned the car on to the grassy verge. They rumbled to a stop and he switched off the engine.

Harlow went round to the driver's side and looked in dismay at the shredded tyre, while Tyler opened the boot.

'You have got to be kidding me! The spare's flat.' He slammed the boot shut and took his phone from his pocket.

Harlow sighed. They weren't going anywhere any time soon. 'Who you phoning?' she asked.

'One of the PAs.' He held the phone to his ear and waited.

In the stillness of the forest-edged road, she could hear the phone ringing. Someone answered.

'Hey, Olivia. We've got a puncture. I'll send you our location, but we're somewhere between Glossa and the hotel. Can you call a garage to come and change the tyre?'

Olivia said something on the other end of the line that Harlow couldn't hear.

'Of course I thought of that, but the spare's flat.' Tyler listened and rubbed his creased forehead. 'I don't know, Olivia. They need to have a spare tyre for a Peugeot. We're a bit more than ten minutes from the hotel. They can't miss us; we're the ones broken down on the side of the road in the sweltering heat.' He ended the call and stuffed the phone in his back pocket. 'Let's see how long this takes.'

'You didn't have to be quite so arsey with her.'

'I wanted her to understand she needs to pull her finger out and get something sorted. Maeve will be on the warpath if the shoot at Panormos is without a location manager.' He glanced at her. 'Or even an assistant.'

'Then let's get someone to pick us up and we'll leave the car here and sort it out later. Or you go ahead and I'll wait with the car.'

She could tell he was annoyed that he hadn't thought of that first. 'We'll give it ten minutes and if we hear nothing, I'll get Olivia to drive up and get me.'

Harlow didn't relish the idea of being stuck up in the hills in the baking sun for goodness knew how long, but it was probably better being on her own than with an annoyed Tyler.

'And while we wait, what could we possibly do to pass the time...' He winked at her. He actually winked.

'Are you serious?'

'It's pretty sheltered beneath the trees.' He nodded towards the forest.

Harlow shook her head. 'You're officially mental, you realise that, right?'

'I'm messing with you. See, I was right about you being easy to wind up.'

'I'm not sure you are joking – I don't think Grace in costume would be too happy, or is it Olivia or one of the other PAs you've got your eye on?'

Tyler shoved his hands in his shorts pockets and looked at her with a sly grin. 'We've always done this, Harlow. You're single, I'm single; I can't see the problem. No strings attached.'

'Not up against a tree in the middle of the day. There's a definite problem with that.'

'Ah, but you're not saying no, just not outdoors in public.'

She couldn't hide her annoyance. 'I'm not saying anything. It's inappropriate, Tyler.'

'What, because I'm your boss?'

'There is that, and the way you spoke to me that first night.'

'I'd had a bit to drink, that was all.'

'You were adamant you weren't drunk.'

'Come on, you know I didn't mean anything by it.' He walked over, slid his arm round her waist and knocked his shoulder against hers in a playful way. 'We're friends. We're more than friends.'

Harlow manoeuvred away from him. 'You obviously don't remember the last thing you said to me two years ago, the last time we were together "acting on it".'

Tyler shrugged. 'Which was?'

He had no understanding the impact his words had had on her

and she had a hard job trying to verbalise it now. It's not that she wanted a relationship with Tyler – something more than them occasionally falling into bed with each other – because deep down she knew that she didn't. Not any longer. What hurt was that they both felt the same about it being a casual thing, yet he felt the need to define what they were and put barriers up, making it seem as though she was the one needing him and desperate for more, while he was happy to have all the benefits without emotions being involved.

Harlow gritted her teeth. 'You said, "I can see us having sex till we're ancient, but we're never going to be together, not in a serious way", or something along those lines.'

'And you have a problem with that because...'

'It didn't need to be spelt out. We both know what this is; what it was. It's been happening since we were nineteen. We didn't need to define it and you certainly didn't need to try to take the upper hand and make it seem like you were the one in control and it was only me who had any kind of feelings. It's been a relationship of convenience for both of us.'

Harlow scrunched her hands into fists and walked away. She leant against a tree trunk, relishing the shade. The trees were dense, the air still. Tyler was standing where she'd left him, his T-shirt sleeves rolled right up, revealing his tattoos that gleamed black in the sunlight. He wandered over.

'So you're saying what? You don't want to have sex with me ever again?' He stopped right in front of her, his blue eyes unflinching. 'Is that why you've been ghosting me?'

'I'm just telling you what happened two years ago. How do you think that made me feel?'

He shrugged.

'Exactly. You have no idea. What we need to work on is how to behave as friends again, and that certainly doesn't include you propositioning me in the middle of nowhere. You need to learn to respect me. You never used to talk to me the way you have done here.'

'Well, things change, don't they?'

'What does that mean?'

Tyler's phone started ringing. He whipped it out of his pocket, obviously eager to avoid answering the question. 'Olivia, please tell me you've managed to sort something out.' Tyler walked back over to the car. 'How long's it going to take?' He rubbed his forehead. 'Really, that long? You need to come pick me up then and take me to Panormos. Yes, now. Harlow will stay and wait for the mechanic.'

Tyler ended the call, opened the car and grabbed their bags. He walked over and handed her a bottle of water, her bag and the car keys.

'You sure you're okay to stay? Maybe I should, instead of you on your own out here.'

'Oh, now there's concern. Don't worry about me. You know where I am. It's daytime. A garage has been called. I have mobile reception, plenty of battery and water. I'll be fine.'

They waited in silence, both focusing on their phones and doing their best to ignore each other. Olivia arrived less than twenty minutes later. Harlow reckoned she'd floored it from Glossa after the way Tyler had spoken to her. She disliked the way production assistants were often treated as the lowest of the low, when they were an integral part of keeping a shoot running smoothly. She was glad to see the back of Tyler, his concern at leaving her grating on her nerves. She waved them off, just resisting sticking a finger up at the back of the car before it disappeared round the corner.

A fallen tree trunk lay on the pine-sprinkled ground, its bark dry and flaky. It was beneath the trees and in the shade. Harlow sat down with her rucksack at her feet. She opened the bottle of warm water. Despite being on her own, Harlow felt more relaxed now

Tyler was gone. It wasn't as if it was desolate up here either. The island was relatively small and there were lots of tourists about. A few cars had already passed by. She stretched her legs out, leant her hand on the rough bark and breathed in the pine forest scent. It took her right back to her childhood and the den she'd made beneath the large and imposing fir tree at the bottom of her grandparents' garden. The branches drooped so low that they'd formed a circular space inside littered with dried pine needles. She'd spend hours down there making tools from branches and furniture out of logs. The tree was so heavy with needles that even when it rained the area beneath remained dry. She had to be dragged inside when dusk descended and made to wash the mud off her hands before dinner. She wondered if Abi, Ellie and Flo had ever turned it into a den. She couldn't remember if she'd even told them about it. It felt like a lifetime ago, but sitting beneath the trees now took her right back to simpler times.

A car rounded the corner and slowed down. Harlow watched from behind her sunglasses and gripped her mobile tighter. It definitely wasn't the mechanic. The driver stopped and wound down his window. He was middle-aged with a deep tan and a dark beard flecked with grey. Harlow held her breath for a moment.

'*Éste kalá*?'

'Sorry, I, er, don't speak Greek.'

'Are you okay?' he said with a thick accent.

Harlow nodded. 'Yes, thank you. I'm waiting for the mechanic – someone's coming from the garage to look at the car.'

He nodded, wound his window back up and drove off.

Harlow breathed freely again and glanced at her watch. She'd been here for nearly an hour. Tyler would be down on Panormos beach by now, quite the location to be managing and a rather pleasant place to spend time even while working. Everywhere was idyllic here and Harlow loved the greenness, so different to her impression of a Greek island. It had the typical Greek island views, but it was also a naturally beautiful place and she loved that. It was everything she'd craved for so long – minus her mum, Tyler, and being forced to take on a project when she was taking time out, but the place itself...

Another vehicle was approaching and slowing down. A pickup truck; perhaps this was the mechanic... With the sun high overhead, the driver was shadowed. The truck pulled up behind the hire car and it was only when the driver emerged into the sunshine that Harlow recognised him.

'You okay?' Adonis asked, slamming the truck door shut and walking over.

'Yes, thank you. Well, apart from being stuck on the side of the road waiting for the car to be fixed.'

Adonis frowned. 'You're on your own?'

'I am now. Tyler got picked up as he was needed on the shoot.'

'He left you?'

'It was my idea; I insisted. I'm waiting for the mechanic.'

'You wait a long time. You have no spare?'

'It's flat.'

'I've got one in the truck; I'll see if it's the right size.'

Harlow followed after him into the blazing heat of the early afternoon.

'Are you sure you've got time to do this?' She was concerned that he was going to be even more annoyed with her than when she'd asked him to remove the olive branch.

He looked at her like she was mad. 'Of course. I'm not going to leave you alone up here.'

'Thank you.'

He shrugged. 'It's nothing.'

He tucked a wrench into the pocket of his jeans, heaved the spare tyre out of the flatbed of the truck, rolled it over to the hire car and checked it against the tyre size carved into the rubber of the punctured tyre. He pushed the sleeves of his T-shirt right up to his shoulders.

'You have the key lock?'

Harlow went to the other side of the car and hunted about in the glove compartment for it. She handed it to him. 'Is there anything I can do to help?'

'I also need the... I don't know the name in English. To lift the car up.'

'The jack.' She opened the boot and passed him the jack and anything else she thought he'd need. 'English is a complicated language. I think you speak it brilliantly.'

'My mama was half Greek, quarter Italian and quarter English,' he said, as he started to loosen the nuts with the wrench. 'She was fluent in all three languages and taught me Italian and English too. We learn English at school from very young, and of course we have lots of British tourists to the island.'

'You put me to shame. I only learnt French at school and I was rubbish at it.'

'Everyone is different. I found learning languages easy, but I was no good at school. I was much better at practical subjects and never liked sitting still for long.'

Harlow crouched next to him and watched him work. His bicep tensed as he fought with the wrench to loosen the last nut. It was obvious from his physique that he liked doing practical things and she imagined he spent most of his time outside. He obviously had a mum who'd spent time with him and was keen to pass on her knowledge; she liked that. She'd also noticed the softening of his voice as he'd talked about her, and the way he used the past tense. She didn't question further; it wasn't the right time or place.

The car was parked in the open and she could feel the sun sizzling on her skin as Adonis wound the jack up until the wheel began to lift off the hard, parched earth. He hadn't even broken a sweat. If the hire car's spare tyre hadn't been flat, she could only imagine what a hot mess she and Tyler would have been trying to change it.

With the flat tyre lifted high enough, Adonis removed the first nut.

'You've done this before, then?' Harlow asked, as he handed it to her and she placed it carefully on the ground.

'Many times. Baba is self-sufficient. He never likes to get anyone to help unless it's an emergency. We do most things ourselves: cars, plumbing, electrics, building work. He's practical and has taught me a lot.'

With the nuts off, Adonis grabbed each side of the wheel and lifted it away from the hub. Harlow rolled it out of the way while Adonis took the spare and slid it on. Harlow handed him the nuts and he tightened them one by one. He sat back on his heels to admire his handy work.

'It looks good,' Harlow said. 'Goodness knows how long I'd have waited if you hadn't been passing.'

Adonis started lowering the car until it touched the ground. He removed the jack and gave it to her. 'Was it the garage in Skopelos Town?'

'I think so.' Harlow put away the tools in the back of the car.

'I'll phone them, let them know they don't need to come out now.' He got to his feet and brushed the dirt off the back of his jeans. His cream T-shirt was smeared with oil from the tyre. He wiped his hands on a cloth.

'Thank you so much. I'll return the tyre once I get a replacement.'

He waved away her thanks. 'Glad I could help. You need to get to work, yes?'

'Yes, I do. But I owe you a drink sometime to say thank you at the very least.'

Adonis placed the punctured tyre in the boot of the hire car and turned to her. 'How about tonight? I was planning on coming to the hotel anyway...'

'It's a date. Well, not a date...' She felt her cheeks flush hot.

Adonis laughed, his smile lighting up his handsome face. 'I understand what you mean. I'll see you at the beach bar later. Nine okay?'

'Yes, absolutely. See you later.' She got into the car and started the engine. She pulled out on to the road and drove past Adonis with a wave and a giddiness that made her heart flutter.

13

After spending two hours in the heat at the side of the mountain road, followed by the rest of the afternoon working on the beach, Harlow was desperate for a cool shower by the time she got back to her room.

She had just stepped out of the shower when there was a thundering knock. She wrapped a towel around her middle and padded across her room. She swung the door open knowing it would be Tyler. Even his knock annoyed her.

'Hey,' he said. 'A few of us are going to walk to Panormos for a drink. Fancy joining us?'

'Um, no thanks. I'm going to stay here.'

Tyler's eyes drifted downwards and lingered. 'You can invite Manda too if you want.'

'I'm good, thanks.' She was ready to slam the door in his face. He'd seemingly forgotten their earlier conversation on the mountain road. First he'd propositioned her, and when she'd eventually made it to the beach, his only concern was about her getting a replacement tyre sorted with the car hire company.

'Suit yourself.'

He sauntered away. He was wearing skinny jeans and a short-sleeved chequered shirt, the same style he'd had for the last ten years.

Harlow closed the door firmly. She was glad that he wouldn't be around this evening. She was only having a drink with Adonis to say thank you for helping her, but she knew how it would look to Tyler. And the more she thought about it, the more she realised having a drink with Adonis surrounded by the people she worked with was probably not such a good idea, but it was too late now. She needed to quit worrying about other people and what they thought. She was her own person and could make her own decisions, see who she liked. Not that she was 'seeing' Adonis.

Harlow breathed deeply, slipped on her underwear and hung the towel in the bathroom. She riffled through the wardrobe, agonising over what to wear, eventually deciding on a blue and grey leopard-print playsuit that reached the middle of her thighs and had capped sleeves and a deep V-neck. She felt dressed up. Was she trying to impress? Manda would think so. Scratch that, Manda would encourage her to do so.

Harlow slicked on a nude-coloured lipstick and stared at herself in the mirror. Having been a tomboy growing up, she liked the natural look, even though she'd embraced her more feminine side as she'd got older. She still loved lounging about in a pair of dungarees on the weekend, or putting on hiking boots and heading out of London for a stomp which would leave her hot, sweaty and exhausted. Her hair had been short since her early teens, but it was styled now, its shape and chocolate tones framing her high cheekbones and showcasing her long black eyelashes. There was no doubt that she had inherited her mum's good genes, although with their differing styles no one would think they were related.

Her mobile buzzed. Manda.

Fancy a drink in the restaurant? Going with the girls. M x

Harlow started thumbing a reply. Manda was going to have a field day with this.

Can't tonight, sorry. Having a drink with Adonis to thank him for saving me after the car broke down earlier.

Manda's reply came back within seconds.

OMG, how do I not know any of this?! You're going on a date with the Greek God!!!!!

This reaction is exactly the reason you don't know anything!

You're killing me!

Will tell you about it tomorrow.

Too right. You're going to tell me EVERYTHING in the morning. First thing over breakfast. Xx

Harlow took one more look at herself in the bathroom mirror and switched off the light. Her mobile buzzed again.

Have a fabulous evening and don't behave yourself ;-) xx

Harlow smiled and shook her head but acknowledged the weird feeling in the pit of her stomach. Was it nerves about having a drink with someone she'd had more run-ins with than polite conversation, or did it mean something else?

* * *

Adonis was already at the bar chatting to one of the waiters. He didn't need to be more dressed up than slim-fitting jeans and a T-shirt to look hot, but he was wearing a short-sleeved cream shirt with the top couple of buttons undone. Harlow noticed the admiring looks he was getting. He caught sight of her and said something to the waiter, who winked and patted him on the shoulder.

Adonis gave her a warm smile. She'd only seen this side of him a couple of times and she liked it. She was determined not to do or say anything that would upset him this evening.

His hands were warm on her bare arms as he kissed her on each cheek.

'Evening,' she said, smiling.

'I have a table.'

She followed him, saying hello to a couple of the film crew on the way. They sat down at a table in the centre. Candlelight flickered between them. Animated chatter pulsed across the terrace, mingled with laughter. The beach bar was beginning to feel familiar, but it was strange to be with someone other than Manda or Tyler, although it was certainly refreshing to have Adonis's company.

'*Yasas*.' A smiling waitress arrived at their table and looked between them. She recognised her as the woman who'd checked her in when she'd first arrived. '*Ti kánis*, Adoni?'

Harlow listened as Adonis chatted with the waitress, the Greek flying between them and going right over her head.

Their conversation finished and Adonis turned to her.

'Harlow, this is my cousin, Thalia.'

Harlow smiled up at her. 'Hi there, don't you usually work in reception?'

'Yes, but we are very busy and short-staffed. I help out where I can. Is the filming going well?'

'Yes, it is, thank you.'

'Adonis say you film at his place.' She grinned at Harlow. 'It is very exciting to have another movie filmed here. I could talk to you all night about it, but...' She motioned at the packed tables. 'What can I get you to drink?'

They ordered and Thalia squeezed Adonis's shoulder and left them with a smile.

'It's a proper family business,' Harlow said. 'And successful too by the looks of it.'

Adonis nodded. 'Ereni, my aunt, has always been business-minded. The land has been in our family for a long time. Ereni has this, my baba The Olive Grove. They both work hard. Ereni is good with people, Baba less so.'

'Well, both places seem hugely successful. Your family should be proud. By the way, this evening is on me to say thank you for earlier. Honestly, you saved me so much time.'

'It was nothing.'

'You didn't have to stop and help, so it was something.' Harlow fiddled with the edge of the tablecloth. 'Particularly when I pissed you off when we were filming.' She met his eyes and held his gaze. 'It was a shitty thing of us to ask and I'm really sorry I did. The place means a lot to you, huh?'

'It does.' It sounded as though he was choking back the words.

Thalia returned with a tray and placed two bottles of lager, a bowl of crisps and the bill tucked inside a glass on the table. She smiled and was off to take another order.

Apart from the well-timed interruption by Thalia, Adonis obviously didn't want to talk about his reaction at The Olive Grove and she wasn't going to press him. Harlow understood his tone and moved the conversation on to the hotel and how Adonis's uncle and aunt had come to own it.

When Harlow took the last sip of her cold, refreshing lager, the place was still heaving and Thalia and the other waiters were run off their feet.

Adonis downed the rest of his bottle. 'Have you worked on a big movie like this before?'

'A few times, in a different capacity though.'

Adonis's eyes narrowed. 'What do you mean?'

'This is only the second film I've worked on as part of the location team.'

'What were you before?'

'A first assistant director.'

'That sounds like a more important job than what you're doing now?' His voice was slow and steady as if he wasn't too sure whether he should be asking.

'It is.'

'Sorry, I didn't mean to make that sound bad.'

'It's okay, it's the truth.' She suddenly felt hot and hemmed in sitting in the middle of the bar's terrace surrounded by people. 'Do you fancy a wander along the beach?'

'Sure.' Adonis stood and reached for his wallet.

Harlow tucked ten euros in the glass with the bill. 'My treat, remember.'

14

Harlow's heart pounded. She expected her reasons for changing direction in her career to be questioned by her mum or Tyler, but she wasn't prepared for anyone else to. She hated the way she felt she had to defend her decision. Adonis knew little about the film industry, but even he understood that she'd backtracked her career. Why would anyone give up the opportunity to direct their own projects to start off at the bottom again? Less pay, less respect, less everything; that was the reality.

Harlow shoved her hands in the pockets of her playsuit as they picked their way across the pebble beach. It was a small bay and they quickly reached the edge of it, where the headland, clustered with trees, met the Aegean.

'I didn't mean to sound like I, um, what's the word... questioned your choice to be an assistant location manager. If it's your dream, then I'm happy for you.'

Harlow stared at the waves lapping the stones, sending white foamy bubbles almost to their feet.

'Is it your dream, what you're doing now?' Adonis asked.

Harlow walked up the beach a little way and sat down on the

end of a sun lounger. Adonis joined her on the one next to it. The beat of music and rumble of chatter seeped on to the beach from the bar behind. The air was still, the starlit sky cloud-free and the warmth was all-encompassing. Harlow enjoyed not having to wear layers, not having to think about bringing a coat, a cardigan or an umbrella out with her in the evening.

She kicked off her slip-on trainers and rested her bare feet on the cool stones. She turned to Adonis. His profile was lit by the moonlight.

'I thought it might be.'

'But it's not?'

'I don't know yet. I don't think I've had enough time to make up my mind. This is the first big project I've worked on in this role, and it's complicated why I'm here and who I'm here with.'

Adonis was watching her intently.

'My mum is here too. She's the producer and the whole reason I got the job. We have a difficult relationship – that's the simplest way to describe it.'

'So your mum is like the big boss? And you don't get on?'

'Exactly.'

'I'm sorry.'

'Don't be; it's always been like this.'

There was a gap between the sun loungers, enough for it to be too far to comfortably reach out and take his hand, which was exactly what she wanted to do. It felt easy talking to Adonis and she wondered what it would feel like to shuffle closer and rest her shoulder against his. She watched the waves splash on to the pebbles instead and stopped herself thinking those kinds of thoughts. It was Manda's fault for putting the idea into her head that a drink with Adonis could lead to more.

Harlow allowed a glance at Adonis. He looked thoughtful as he stared out to sea. Was he thinking the same thing as she'd been thinking?

She made herself focus on the moment, rather than the what ifs. 'It was my dad who raised me. He kinda had the role of being my mum and dad. He was the one who dropped me off at breakfast club and picked me up from after-school club, took me swimming and to Brownies. All my happy childhood memories are tied up with him; I'm not even sure I have any good ones of just me and my mum, and the memories I do have are of her arriving back with last-minute airport gifts from wherever she'd been working. My memories are filled with other people – *her* friends, *her* colleagues – the glitz and glamour that as a tomboy I was so not interested in.'

'A tomboy?'

'I was into stuff that boys typically liked – I dressed like a boy most of the time. I liked playing football and digging in the garden, getting filthy, which my mum despaired about. One of my favourite things when I was younger was going on long walks with my dad. Like proper hikes in all weathers.'

'You like walking?' Adonis asked.

'Love it. Walking is still one of my favourite things.'

'The same for me.'

'Really?'

'That freedom... At least it feels like I'm free... I didn't imagine you would like doing that.'

'Why not?'

He shrugged. 'You don't look like someone who goes hiking.'

Harlow laughed. 'And what does someone who goes hiking look like?'

'Not as pretty.'

Harlow laughed even harder. 'Oh Adonis, so pretty people don't walk?'

He smiled at her sheepishly. 'I made an impression of you, that's all. And you're beautiful, not just pretty.'

Harlow focused again on the waves lapping the shingle. Her heart was thudding, her hands sweaty. She didn't dare look at him. This is what Manda had meant about Harlow *not* behaving herself this evening. How easy would it be to lean over and kiss him...

'I really do love walking,' she said instead, deciding the urge to do something that seemed rather forward wasn't a good enough reason, not when they were getting to know each other. 'I used to do a lot more. Dad and I would go camping in Scotland or Wales, loads of beautiful places. We'd take a picnic and walk all day, then come back to our tent and cook sausages and beans on the camping stove. They were the best times. And my grandparents live on a farm so are surrounded by countryside.'

'But you live in a city?'

'Yes, in London, because of work rather than choice. I go walking there a lot – admittedly, it's different walking in Richmond Park than hiking up Snowdon, but it's something. Do you go walking here?'

'There are lots of walking trails across the island, all through the hills. They're my place to go when I want peace or to be on my own.'

The melancholy was back again, lacing his words with a quiet reserve, which made Harlow want to reach out and hug him.

'I'll take you next weekend. If you're free?' He stood up abruptly. 'Have you ever eaten loukoumades?'

The question seemed to have come out of nowhere.

'No. What are they?'

'They are delicious, that's what they are. Thalia said my aunt's making some tonight. Come.' He reached out his hand and pulled Harlow to her feet.

She slipped her trainers back on and followed Adonis across the beach, away from the laughter and light spilling from the bar. It looked warm and inviting, with candles flickering on each table. The main restaurant was still full of people too, set further back and overlooking the largest pool on the complex. Shadowy palm trees loomed in the moonlight, and as they walked by, Harlow could see some of the make-up and costume girls enjoying a late-night drink. Manda was sitting with her back to Harlow so she slipped by without being spotted.

They walked together up through the grounds, past the villas and the pools glowing turquoise in the darkness. They went past the path that led to Villa Aegean and carried on up to the hotel's reception.

'My aunt and uncle live above.' Adonis pushed open the door to the side of the reception and they clattered up the tiled steps. They reached the top and entered an apartment. 'Ereni?'

'*Eímai stin kouzína*!' a voice called back.

Harlow followed Adonis into a large open-plan living area with a kitchen on the far side. They were greeted by a deliciously sweet smell of honey and something frying.

A woman was standing over a fryer. Next to her was a plate piled high with what looked like very small round doughnuts.

The woman glanced around and beamed. 'Adoni! *Írthes gia tous gnostoús mou loukoumádes*!'

'They are indeed famous, Ereni. The best ones I've ever tasted. Thalia said you were making them.'

Ereni nodded and smiled at Harlow. 'She better finish on time if she want some.'

Ereni was a happier, younger, female version of Stephanos. She had a healthy tan and laughter lines rather than the frown lines of her brother.

'Who's your friend, Adoni?'

'This is Harlow. Harlow, my aunt, Ereni. My uncle is asleep on the sofa.'

Harlow looked behind her.

Ereni snorted. 'Even the smell of loukoumades don't wake him.'

A man with a round, tanned face was lying on the sofa, his hands resting on his stomach, his mouth gaping open. Harlow smiled; she hadn't noticed him when they'd walked in. The large L-shaped sofa defined the space between the living area and the kitchen-diner. The place was cool, comfortable and homely with a fireplace in the far corner.

'Harlow's working on the movie...' Adonis was still talking to his aunt.

Harlow turned back.

'You've given us good business this year. It is a big thing having the film based at our hotel.' Ereni switched off the fryer and sprinkled cinnamon over the mountain of sticky loukoumades.

'You have an incredible place – this hotel, the setting...'

'We are very lucky.' She picked up the plate. 'Come, let's eat.'

'Shall I wake him?' Adonis looked over at his uncle.

Ereni shook her head. 'Let him sleep. I have you two for company now.' Holding the plate of loukoumades, she walked towards the balcony calling back over her shoulder, '*Ta piáta, ta piroúnia kai to pagotó*.'

Adonis got a tub of ice cream from the freezer and handed Harlow plates and forks. They went through the wide doors and joined Ereni on a balcony that ran the length of the villa. Even in the dark, Harlow could see that it had a view over the other villas to the sea. Lights twinkled in the darkness and the sound of people chatting and laughing together mixed with the rush of waves folding on to the shore.

Ereni dished half a dozen loukoumades on to each plate and topped them with a generous scoop of the vanilla ice cream.

'How you know Adonis then?' she asked, handing them each a plate.

'Through the filming we've been doing at The Olive Grove.'

'You're an actress?'

'Goodness, no.'

'You look like you should be.' Ereni waved her fork in Harlow's direction. 'It is a compliment.'

'Well, thank you,' Harlow said, deciding to be gracious and take it as one. 'I work within the location team. I've always been a behind-the-scenes person. I prefer it.'

'I know someone else like that.' She raised an eyebrow and unsubtly nodded in Adonis's direction. 'Shying away from fame.'

'Oh?'

Adonis shook his head. 'Ereni, *óhi tóra*.'

'Adoni, you are too sensitive. What's the word in English... when you not like to show off.'

'Modest,' Harlow said.

'Adonis is too modest.' She stuck her fork in a loukoumades and motioned for Harlow to do the same. 'Please, eat.'

Harlow speared one of the loukoumades with her fork; honeyed syrup oozed out of it.

'Adonis was talent-spotted by a producer on holiday on the island,' Ereni continued.

Adonis, his face impassive, picked up the ice cream tub. 'I'll put this back in the freezer.'

Ereni waited until he'd gone inside. 'He don't like to talk about it. I don't know if it is because he wanted to do it but couldn't or is embarrassed to be asked.'

Harlow frowned. 'Asked to do what?'

'It was a producer of *The Batchelor*, the Greek version. You know the TV programme. She was on holiday here and saw him on a walking trail to one of the beaches. She wanted him to be on the show. She followed up with emails. She was serious about it, but he said no. Ah, it is in the past now.' Ereni pointed to Harlow's plate. 'You like them?'

Harlow finished chewing her mouthful of deliciously sweet loukoumades. 'Absolutely delicious.' She took a sip of water and wiped her sticky mouth with a napkin.

'Have you finished talking about me?' Adonis reappeared in the doorway.

'Tsch, Adoni.' Ereni batted her hand at him. 'It is good story, I like talking about it. Our very own bachelor.' She winked at Harlow. 'See, he is too modest.'

An image of the first time Harlow had laid eyes on Adonis, bare-chested in the olive grove, popped into her head. She wondered what his reason for turning it down really was; from the little she knew of him, being thrust into the limelight because of the way he looked didn't seem to be something he'd be comfortable with. She liked that about him, even if it was an assumption.

'But now we have another movie on our island and this time our family's land is part of it,' Ereni said as Adonis sat back down.

'It's the perfect place for the scenes we're shooting there. You're very lucky to have such a beautiful place in the family, and the hotel, of course.'

'My brother was always going to run The Olive Grove and stay there. It was always my dream to run a hotel on the island. With my husband, we made it our dream come true. It has grown over the years. But I have a husband, three daughters and a son who all work in the family business, so I do okay. It is my life.'

'Family business is what we do.' There was an edge to Adonis's voice.

'Tsch,' Ereni scolded, shaking her head at her nephew.

'It's just you though?' Harlow asked Adonis. 'No brothers or sisters?'

'No, just me.'

She caught the look between Ereni and Adonis and didn't question further. There was a lot about Adonis she didn't know. The way he could be so sweet and endearing and then moody and angry in an instant. Yet it didn't feel as though his anger was directed at her; she sensed there was more of an internal battle going on. If he wanted to share more, he would.

Adonis's aunt was as warm and chatty as her brother was gloomy and succinct. Adonis seemed relaxed in her presence and Harlow was sad when the evening naturally drew to a close and they took their empty plates inside.

'You must take some back for Stephanos.' Ereni filled a small box with the sweet and sticky loukoumades and handed it to Adonis. 'But tell him not to eat them all at once.'

'I'll try.'

Ereni turned to Harlow. 'It was lovely to meet you. I hope we see you again. Maybe my husband will be awake next time.' She rolled her eyes at the sofa where he was still lying prostrate and snoring.

Harlow and Adonis made their way downstairs and back out into the night. It was gone midnight and voices still drifted up from the beach bar and restaurant. The air was perfumed from the roses entwined in the trellis next to the door, but Harlow also got a waft of a stronger spicier scent of Adonis's cologne.

'I'm just down there,' Harlow said, pointing along the path towards Villa Aegean. 'Not far.' She gestured towards the car park. 'Will you be okay driving back?'

'Of course. I'm used to it.'

She'd noticed he'd only had the one bottle of lager and then he'd drunk water at his aunt's. It must be the nature of living up in the hills and having to drive somewhere for a night out.

'Well, thank you for a lovely evening. It was really special to meet your aunt, and those loukoumades...'

Adonis grinned at her.

'Did I pronounce that right?'

'You said it perfectly. And I meant it earlier, about taking you on one of the walking trails next weekend.'

'I'd love that.'

They swapped numbers. Adonis leaned closer and held her arms. He kissed her gently on both cheeks. His beard tickled her skin and sent a frisson of excitement through her. '*Kalinychta*.'

'Night,' Harlow said quietly. She watched him walk to his pick-up truck, the box of loukoumades for his dad tucked beneath his arm. He gave her a wave and drove off.

Harlow sighed and walked towards Villa Aegean, his kisses still imprinted on her skin.

15

Tyler was staggering along the path up ahead. Harlow was hoping she could avoid him, but he was right on the edge of the path that led to their villa.

Her heart sank as she got closer.

'Oh my god, Tyler, how much have you had to drink?'

He swayed in front of her, his eyes tiny slits as he tried to focus on her.

'Harlow.' He smiled weakly, gagged and was sick into a rose bush.

'For goodness' sake.' Harlow put her hand on his back. 'Let's get you to your room.'

He managed to get himself upright, and with his arm heavy around her shoulder, she guided him along the path towards the villa entrance. The security light over the door switched on and Tyler groaned.

The stairs might as well have been a mountain. Slow step after slow stumbling step, Harlow somehow managed to get him up the first flight.

'Who on earth did you go out with?' she asked as they started up the final flight of stairs to their rooms.

'Jim... The other ADs...'

They reached the top and he toppled. Harlow grabbed him more tightly and grimaced as her hand got squashed between his shoulder and the wall. She shoved him along the landing and released her hand.

'Olivia was there too. She's hot... Bit young, but hot...'

'You really need to stop talking.' They reached the door to his room. 'Where's your key card?'

He shrugged.

Harlow sighed. She was rapidly regretting stopping to help. He was leaning against the wall looking completely out of it. She wasn't going to get any sense out of him. She felt in his pockets and slipped his wallet from the back of his jeans. He still had his bank cards and money but no key card. She put it back in his pocket and ignored his sly smile. Now she was really regretting helping him. It was late and she could hardly faff about trying to get a new key card for his room when he looked like he was about to collapse.

'I feel sick.'

Harlow swore under her breath and opened the door to her room. She guided Tyler straight into the bathroom.

'Jim's banging your mum,' he said, chuckling and burping at the same time. 'Did you know that?' His eyes were barely open.

Harlow wrinkled her nose. 'You're talking nonsense, Tyler.'

He dry-retched and she made him lean over the toilet. She left him alone. Her clothes were still strewn on the bed from earlier. She tidied them away and pulled back the cover. This wasn't the first time she'd looked after Tyler when he was out of it, but it was the last thing she'd imagined she'd be doing tonight.

It had all gone quiet in the bathroom. With trepidation, she went back in. Tyler was leaning on the sink with the tap running. Harlow flushed the toilet and took a towel off the shelf.

'You're the best.' His words were slurred, his voice gravelly as if he'd been shouting over loud music all evening.

Harlow filled a glass with water. 'Drink this.' She waited patiently while he drank it, then wiped his face with a damp towel. 'You done being sick?'

He nodded slowly.

'Let's get you to bed then.'

She draped his arm across her shoulder and he leant into her. His breath stank, and the aroma of alcohol and worse in the confines of the bathroom made her long for the sweet smell of loukoumades that she'd been enjoying only a little earlier.

She managed to manoeuvre him to the bed and sit him down.

He looked up at her. 'I love you, Harlow.'

She shook her head and ignored him. His shirt was splattered with goodness knew what.

'You're so going to regret this in the morning.' She started undoing the buttons on his shirt. She was glad he was too out of it to make a comment about her undressing him. Her fingers brushed the black tribal tattoos etched on his chest as she wriggled the shirt off him and dropped it on the floor. She pushed him gently back on the bed until he was lying down. She took off his trainers and dragged him over until he was on his side.

'I really do love you, Harlow Sands...' A guttural snore took over.

Harlow emptied the bin and put it next to the bed, just in case. She sat on the sofa and watched Tyler half naked and snoring.

It had been such a good evening. Despite her reservations about him, Adonis's company was easy and she'd enjoyed spending time with him. She felt there were layers to peel away, but he probably felt the same about her. She knew she was holding back things until she got to know him better. Yet, here she was ending the night with Tyler passed out on her bed and thoughts of what he'd said about Jim and her mum tumbling round her head. Could they be true?

She braved the bathroom again to wash her face and clean her teeth. With Tyler dead to the world, she slipped out of her playsuit and into her pyjama shorts and vest top. She left the air con off, grabbed a pillow from the bed and curled up on the sofa, Tyler's rumbling snore in her ears, while the memory of Adonis kissing her cheeks played over as she fell asleep.

* * *

'What the fuck happened?'

Harlow woke with a start. Her phone alarm was beeping and sunshine was streaming through the balcony doors across the tiled floor to the bed. Tyler was sitting propped against the pillows looking washed out, his eyebrows furrowed, squinting in the bright light.

Harlow hit the snooze button and manoeuvred herself so she was leaning on her elbow facing the bed. 'You don't remember anything?'

'Why are you sleeping on the sofa?'

'Because you were puking your guts up and I didn't fancy risking sleeping next to you.'

'We didn't, you know...?'

'*No*, we didn't.' She resisted rolling her eyes in despair. 'Tyler, you were out of it. If I hadn't come across you, you'd probably have passed out in a bush.'

He looked around. 'Are we in your room?'

'Oh my god, Tyler. I think you need to go back to sleep.'

'I need coffee.'

Harlow dragged herself off the sofa and switched on the kettle.

'You didn't join us then last night?' Tyler asked, still looking confused. 'It was a good night – the bits I remember.' He propped himself further up on the pillows and folded his arms across his bare chest. 'It's hot in here. Shit does my head hurt.'

Harlow switched on the air con.

'Why am I not in my room?'

'Because you seem to have lost your key card.' Harlow stood at the end of the bed and looked at him. 'Tyler, it's really simple. You were drunk and stumbling about outside. I helped you up here, couldn't find your key, couldn't leave you alone to pass out on the landing, so I decided you'd be better off crashing in here.'

'Sorry if I ruined your night.'

'You didn't ruin it, my night was finished and I was heading back here to sleep.' She made the coffee and handed him the cup. 'You really don't remember anything?'

'Not after leaving the bar in Panormos. I sort of remember walking back through the trees.' He cupped the mug in his hands and looked at her, his frown deepening. 'Why, what did I say?'

'Not much, drunken gibberish mainly.' Her anger at him from the day before had dissipated. He was hungover and looking sorry for himself. 'I'm supposed to be having breakfast with Manda in half an hour. You're welcome to use my room until you get a new key card.' She wrinkled her nose. 'You need a shower. You can have one after me.'

She grabbed clean underwear and a skirt and top from the wardrobe and left Tyler drinking his coffee in her bed. She locked herself in the bathroom and enjoyed a refreshing shower, although the whole time she was thinking there was only a thin wall between her and Tyler. Somehow taking care of him when he was drunk and vulnerable seemed incredibly intimate and what he'd said sounded honest. Alcohol had erased his inhibitions last night, almost as though he'd taken a truth pill. And the thing about Jim and her mum...

Harlow lathered on sunscreen, got dressed and finished off with a slick of mascara and bronzer. Tyler wasn't in bed when she came out of the bathroom. Her heart thudded when she realised he was standing drinking coffee on her balcony dressed only in his jeans for anyone wandering the hotel grounds to see. She hovered in the open doorway.

'I'll see if I can sort out a new key card for you before I go for breakfast. And you need to soak your shirt – it's not pretty.'

Tyler wrinkled his nose and gave her an apologetic look. 'Sorry for being a drunken nightmare.' He reached out and touched her arm. 'And thank you. I owe you one.'

Harlow was relieved to get out of her room and into the fresh, sunny Saturday morning. She was pretty certain that Adonis wouldn't have had this kind of shit to deal with when he got home.

The hotel reception was quiet. Harlow explained the situation to the receptionist and waited while she sorted out a replacement key card.

'*Kaliméra*, Harlow.' Ereni took Harlow by surprise as she came into the reception area.

'Morning.'

'You're up early.'

'I'm meeting a friend for breakfast but had to sort something out first.'

'You lost your key card?' Ereni asked as the receptionist handed Harlow a new one.

'Not me, a colleague – he managed to lose his and lock himself out.'

Why on earth did she feel guilty? Nothing had happened last night with Tyler, yet she felt as if something had, all because he'd spent the night in her room and was still there the morning after. She knew she didn't want anyone to get the wrong idea, least of all Adonis's aunt. Not that anything had happened between her and Adonis either, apart from them spending an enjoyable evening in each other's company. She was getting stressed over nothing, but when she thought about it, this was exactly the reason she'd had reservations about working on a project that would involve spending a huge amount of time with Tyler.

Harlow forced her worries away and thanked the receptionist for the key card. She said goodbye to Ereni and returned to Villa Aegean. Her phone pinged. Manda.

On my way to the restaurant for breakfast. See you there in 5? I want to know all the goss! Xx

The gossip Manda was hoping for wasn't anything like how Harlow's night had played out.

Harlow pushed open the door to her room. Tyler was perched on the end of her bed with a towel wrapped around his middle.

'Your key card,' Harlow said, placing it on the desk.

'You're a star.' He stood up and before she could react, he took her in his arms. 'I really meant it before when I said thank you.'

He smelt a hell of a lot better than the night before. Harlow realised she was hugging him back. Being wrapped in his arms was such a familiar feeling and not an unpleasant one, but she was also aware of how little he was wearing, with just a damp towel between them.

'No problem.' She let go of him. 'That's what friends are for.'

* * *

Manda was sitting in almost the exact same place as the night before when Harlow had walked past with Adonis and spotted her with the make-up girls. They helped themselves to the buffet breakfast and returned to their table. People were already lying on the sun loungers that surrounded the main pool in front of the beach. A boat was anchored a little way out and the hills on either side of the bay jutted out in a forest of green.

'So, did you kiss him?' Manda asked the minute they sat down and started tucking into their scrambled eggs.

'No,' Harlow said. 'Sorry to disappoint.'

'You're classy; I like it.'

'Anyway, it wasn't a date. I was buying him a drink to say thank you for rescuing me.' Yet the feel of his kisses on her cheeks was firmly imprinted on her mind...

'You know how dreamy that sounds – a gorgeous Greek guy saving you on a mountain road...' She gazed wistfully towards the sea.

'We talked, sat on the beach for a bit and then had these delicious Greek sweets at his aunt's.'

Manda raised an eyebrow. 'Is that a euphemism?'

Harlow laughed. 'No.'

Manda sighed. 'So you went home alone then.'

Harlow didn't say anything about a drunken Tyler ending up passed out in her bed. There was no need to go into that.

'Have you heard any other rumours about my mum?' she asked instead.

Manda finished chewing her mouthful of scrambled egg. 'Like what?'

'Oh, I don't know. Just wondered if there was any gossip.' Harlow watched as Manda carefully cut her toast. She could tell the question had made her uncomfortable, probably because there really was gossip and truth to what Tyler had blurted out last night.

'I, um...' Manda glanced up from her plate.

'It's okay, I shouldn't have asked. I know it's awkward me being related to Maeve.'

'It's not that.' Manda looked thoughtful as she gazed across the pool. 'It's just hard to know what's true and what's not. I don't want to tell you something that ends up being a crock of shit.'

'But there is something. Possibly about my mum and Jim?'

Manda's eyes snapped back to Harlow's face. Harlow knew there was truth in it without Manda needing to confirm or deny a thing. 'I've worked on projects Maeve's headed up before. There's always gossip. It doesn't necessarily mean anything, but maybe the reason I'm surprised that nothing happened between you and Adonis is because I assume you take after your mum more than you actually do.'

'What does that mean?'

'Let's put it this way.' She lowered her voice. 'If it was your mum in your shoes last night, she'd have had plenty of gossip for me this morning...'

Coupled with Tyler's drunken comment, Manda confirmed what Harlow was thinking. She actively avoided reading anything in the media about her mum, but that was why things like this took her by surprise. From the little she knew about him, Jim didn't seem to be the type of bloke her mum usually went for – he wasn't an actor or well-known. He came across as a nice guy and down-to-earth. But then again, her mum never talked to her about her personal life. Maybe that was something she needed to change, except that would have to work both ways. Was she ready for that amount of sharing or to know what her mum really got up to?

16

WEEK FOUR – THIRD WEEK OF FILMING

Harlow was glad to have the distraction of work to occupy her mind after a social weekend that left her with a growing number of questions. After sorting out a replacement tyre for the hire car before spending the rest of Saturday with Manda and her make-up colleagues, Harlow had returned the spare tyre to The Olive Grove on the Sunday only to be disappointed when Adonis wasn't there. He did message her though, about the walk the following weekend, which gave her something to look forward to.

Filming during the week was a mix of the Glossa villa location and Panormos beach. With Tyler busy making preparations for the following week, it meant Harlow was on her own at the location a lot of the time, although she had enough production assistants to help out. She quite liked not being bossed about by Tyler – in person at least; he still bombarded her with messages. But she was grateful they didn't revisit the events of Friday and his drunken episode.

Harlow did have plenty of chances to keep an eye on her mum. After everything that had been said, first by the American tourist at The Olive Grove, and then Tyler and Manda, Harlow paid particular interest when her mum was with Jim. But because the idea that something was going on had been seeded, Harlow wasn't sure if she was imagining things or not. Her mum was professional with everyone; she always was. She was also quite tactile, often talking to the director, the cameraman or the head of costume with a hand on their shoulder, but perhaps it lingered longer when she was chatting to Jim. Not that any of it should bother her. What her mum got up to in her personal life was private, exactly as Harlow's was. The difference was that Maeve Fennimore-Bell was in the public eye and at the centre of everything.

* * *

The weekend arrived and Adonis made good on his promise of taking Harlow on one of the walking trails that crisscrossed the island. Harlow didn't have walking boots, so she made do with her trainers, dressed appropriately for a hike and doused herself in citronella. She crept from her room, closing the door silently behind her, even though she knew that Tyler, after a long and stressful week plus another big night out, wouldn't surface until much later. She'd heard him return at gone two in the morning, so she figured he wouldn't miss the car. She hadn't wanted to have an awkward conversation about why she needed it. There was nothing going on between her and Adonis, yet she didn't want Tyler to know that she was spending time with him. Silly, she knew, yet she was aware how easily Tyler would turn their blossoming friendship into something sordid.

The solar lights lit the paths and the hotel grounds were quiet. She drove out of the car park and along the nearly empty road towards Glossa. The sun was beginning to rise on the other side of the island and the sky became gradually lighter the closer she got to The Olive Grove. A wash of mauve seeped on to the horizon as the Aegean shimmered in the half-light.

It was still magical to arrive at The Olive Grove and walk beneath the avenue of vines. She skirted the restaurant and took the path that ran alongside the orchard up to the villa where Adonis and his family lived.

Adonis was already outside, tucking a flask into the side pocket of a rucksack. With proper walking boots, olive-green combat-style shorts, a beige T-shirt and a hat, he looked like he was ready for a hike.

He caught sight of her and smiled. '*Kaliméra*.'

'Morning. Not sure I'm dressed right.' She gestured to her trainers.

'You're fine. You don't need hiking boots, but it can be slippery walking on the pine needles so just go carefully. You have your swim things though?'

'I do.'

'Let's go then.'

They headed up the hill behind the villa and over the wooden fence that separated the olive grove from the forest beyond. He'd warned her that the walk would be steep in places and he wasn't wrong. Harlow's calf muscles were protesting by the time they'd navigated their way through the dense trees and joined a dirt path edged with Spanish broom. She understood why he'd suggested leaving early in the day before the sun blazed high in the sky.

* * *

They stopped about forty-five minutes into their walk and perched on a rock to have breakfast. The view across olive trees to the pines sweeping down to meet the azure water that circled the island took Harlow's breath away.

She liked how Adonis didn't feel the need to fill the silence with mindless chatter. She was more than happy to quietly sit, munch on cheese pies and simply soak up the surroundings. Flakes of filo fell on to her knees. The salty feta was delicious mixed with the crunch of the pastry.

Although there was no one else about, the hillside was alive with wildlife. The longer they sat, the more they spotted. Butterflies fluttered in front of them, their black wings with orange and yellow edges dancing, before disappearing in the undergrowth to be replaced by another with large yellow wings that seemed to glow in the sunlight. Birdsong filled the tree canopy and birds swooped from the shade of the treetops down the hillside.

Harlow sighed inwardly with satisfaction and popped the last bit of pie into her mouth. 'Did you make these?' she asked, wiping crumbs from her lips.

'No, my yiayia – my grandmother. I can make them, but it takes patience. She makes the filo too.'

'What, from scratch?'

He nodded. 'That's why they're so good.'

Harlow remembered she'd briefly met his grandmother; she was the lady who'd spoken to her in Greek when she'd tried to find Adonis during the shoot in the olive grove. Dressed in black with a weather-worn but kind face, she was exactly as she'd imagined a Greek grandmother to be.

'She's your dad's mother?'

'Yes. All the family on Baba's side are on Skopelos.' He looked thoughtful as he gazed into the distance. 'Mama was from Athens. Very different to here, although she grew up in Italy and spent a couple of years in England before coming to Greece. She fell in love with the island – and Baba – and stayed. She was the opposite of Baba.' He glanced sideways at her. 'A lot younger and, uh, fun. She was the life in the house. How do you say it in English?'

'The life and soul of the party?'

'Exactly. Her dad was Greek and her mother half English, half Italian. She was the best of the three cultures, full of life and energy.'

Harlow was hesitant to ask the question, but it felt like the right time. 'What happened to her?'

'She was very ill,' he said quietly. 'She died when I was sixteen. Nearly half my life ago.'

'I'm so sorry.'

He looked away. 'I find being on the island hard, particularly now with your film being made. I associate the movie *Mamma Mia!* with her. Everyone was so excited when they filmed on the island. Friends would go down to the beach where they were filming and watch from the trees. Everyone, and I mean everyone, knew someone who was an extra in the film. Nothing ever happened here and then a movie like that. Everyone was talking about it.'

Harlow waited for him to continue, aware that he was fighting his emotions. His fingers were tense on the rock, the knuckles white as though he was trying to stop what he was feeling from overwhelming him.

'My cousins and friends went; I didn't. Mama was very ill that summer. It was her last. She was the one who was most excited about them filming. She adored ABBA and she loved Pierce Brosnan. She always teased Baba that he was the Greek version of him. He wasn't so grumpy back then. She had a good friend who was in the dancing scene on the dock – you know the one when they all jump in the water. She visited every day after filming and told Mama all about it. Every detail. She never got to see the finished film though. She died before it came out.'

All Harlow wanted to do was erase his pain, but she had no words that would help. She slipped her hand into his and held it in her lap, clasping it tight, hoping to convey how much her heart ached for him. 'She sounds like she was a beautiful person. Full of joy.'

A tear trickled down his face and caught in his beard. He wiped it away with his free hand. 'She was. And she would have loved the film.' He shook his head. 'I hated it though. I hated everything about it because it reminded me of what we lost that summer. And this film...'

She held his hand tighter. 'I get it; it must dredge up painful memories.'

'And it's crazy because nothing happens here and I should be pleased something different is going on. Normally it's work, day after day, and tourists in the summer season, then it goes quiet. The island feels dead over winter. *I* feel dead.'

'Because there's nothing to do?'

He shrugged. 'There's always work to do, we're busy with the olive harvest. But I feel like I'm not free.'

'Why didn't you go for *The Batchelor* when it was offered? It would have got you off the island.'

'Baba would have struggled; friends would have laughed. It is nothing that I want to do. I don't want to be famous... Have you seen the show?'

'I've seen bits of the UK and US version. But have you never thought about leaving, not to do anything like that, but something *you'd* want to do?'

'I'm trapped by family and responsibility.'

The anger that had laced his voice the first time they'd met had returned. His hand tensed in hers but he didn't pull away. She knew it wasn't her he was angry with, not now or previously, but the situation he was in. She understood that well enough. Anger, frustration, uncertainty, doubt – they'd all plagued her at one time or another.

Harlow wanted to take him in her arms and hold him, try and

unburden him of just a fraction of the hurt he was holding on to. 'And that's why you're conflicted about us filming at The Olive Grove...'

He nodded.

'I'm so sorry, if only I'd known the pain it would have caused you.'

'You have nothing to be sorry about. It's something I have to deal with. I'm sorry if I've taken it out on you.'

'How does your dad feel about it? He's obviously okay with us filming there.'

'I don't know if Baba feels the same way. Maybe he doesn't associate the filming with Mama like I do. Or maybe he just thinks the money's worth it.'

'You haven't asked him?'

'We don't talk about things like that. We never talk about Mama.'

'Oh Adonis, that's hard.'

He shrugged. 'I have Ereni for that; she's always kept Mama's spirit alive by talking about her lots. Baba keeps everything in here.' He pressed his fingers to the centre of his chest. 'Ereni is open and has looked after me in ways Baba can't. He's older and stubborn. He finds it difficult to talk.'

'About his emotions?'

'About everything.'

'You and your dad have been grieving in a different way to everyone else. You lost your mum, your dad lost his wife – I can't even imagine how that must feel, particularly when you were growing up. I found it hard enough to deal with my parents divorcing and I was already used to my mum being absent a lot of the time.'

Adonis let a ladybird crawl on to his finger and placed it on the ground. 'She wasn't around when you were growing up?'

'Not much, and when she was, she wasn't really involved. It was my dad who raised me.'

'Your mum is very well known?'

'Yeah, she's made quite a name for herself. She won an Oscar a few years ago and that catapulted her to even more fame. I've always been in her shadow – don't get me wrong, out of the limelight is where I prefer to be, and if I can help it, I don't advertise the fact that she's my mum. But people know, particularly in this business.'

'You follow her though, by working in movies?' He packed the coffee flask and empty tinfoil wrappings back into his rucksack.

'Not exactly. I mean, yes, I work in the industry, but I'm not following in her footsteps, however much she'd like me to be. I've massively disappointed her with my lack of ambition – she's said as much. Like you and your dad, we don't talk, at least about things that are actually important. I think we hide a lot from each other.'

'Can I tell you something?' He got to his feet and Harlow slid off the rock after him. 'My mama was always there for me; she loved being a mother and would have loved more children too if things had worked out, so I have no experience of what you've been through with a mother who wasn't there, but...' He breathed deeply and gripped the rucksack straps like he was trying to control his emotions again. He looked at her with such an intense and serious expression. 'I'd do anything to have more time with my mama. You have a mum; however difficult it is, you'll miss her when she's gone. Make the most of her now.'

17

Harlow and Adonis made their way along the track down the forested hillside. The sun was inching higher, heating up the day, making the sea sparkle and the trees a deep soothing green. They didn't see Agios Ioannis Kastris, the *Mamma Mia!* church, until they almost reached it. The sight of the steps cut into the rocky outcrop instantly reminded Harlow of Meryl Streep running up them to the tiny white church at the top. It was familiar from watching *Mamma Mia!* countless times as a teenager. Tufts of grasses and shrubs edged the uneven path. The sea on either side shimmered in the sunshine and looked inviting enough to dive right in, clear turquoise water turning a deep blue further out.

Harlow followed Adonis, whose calf muscles strained with each step, 'The Winner Takes It All' playing over in her head as they wound their way up. She concentrated on getting to the top and the reward of far-reaching views.

The church was dark inside, cooler and surprisingly small, although Harlow was aware that the interior of the church in *Mamma Mia!* had been filmed in a studio and not on location. Religious paintings adorned the white stone walls. Candlelight flickered from the handful of slender candles at the back of the church. Adonis took an unlit one, held it to a flame and added it to the group. He made the sign of the cross and bowed his head.

Tears pricked at Harlow's eyes. After their conversation on the hill, the gesture was simple yet meaningful knowing he'd lit it in memory of his mama. She'd been moved by his heartbreaking story and by the passion with which he'd voiced his belief that she should connect with her mum. He was right about how difficult that would be.

Harlow left him alone with his thoughts and went back outside. The trees that dotted the top of the rock provided much-needed shade. Every direction she turned was peaceful and beautiful, a soothing mix of earthy tones, vibrant greens, bright white and varying shades of blue.

The view stretched endlessly along the coast of Skopelos and across the water to Alonissos. Dense green shrubs dotted the steep hillside all the way down to the chalk-white rocks that disappeared into the sea. Clear aquamarine water revealed darker blue patches beneath the surface. A yacht was anchored off the coast, and another sailed further out, the only thing to disturb the deep blue sea. A gentle breeze buffeted Harlow as she soaked up every inch of the view.

'I told you it was worth it.' Adonis joined her, his bare arm brushing against hers as they gazed out together. It was magical, worth every second of the climb and getting up so early on a Saturday.

'I'm used to seeing how locations look on film compared to in real life, but this is something else.'

'Without the hundreds of people walking the steps every day, it is.'

It was the absolute peace that struck her the most. They were somewhere iconic, yet they were alone. She loved that they were experiencing it together and that Adonis had wanted to share it with her. They were slowly getting to know each other. He was opening up to her, just as she felt she could open up to him. It was good to talk to someone who wasn't associated with the film, who didn't care who her mum was or have any preconceived ideas about her. Someone who had nothing to do with her past.

'It will get busier the later it gets.' Adonis motioned towards a couple of people who were walking along the track that led to the bottom of the steps. 'It's quite a hike back – are you ready?'

'Of course, as long as we can stop for more of those cheese pies.'

They made their way back down the winding steps, Harlow flicking her attention between the view and her footing. They passed the couple making their way up and nodded hello. The narrow rock formation opened out at the bottom, with the island spreading in both directions. Pale grey rocks jutted into the turquoise water. Dense trees carpeted the hills, shady and inviting now the sun was pounding down.

Adonis paused at the bottom of the steps. 'There's the beach we could see from the church, but there's another one I'd like to show you a bit further round.'

They retraced their steps into the trees but instead of continuing the way they'd come, they went past another church and followed a dirt path that headed back towards the coast. The ground beneath the trees was speckled with sunlight sneaking through the branches.

The path opened out on to a desolate beach with patches of sand and fine pebbles. The water lapping the shore was so clear and shallow, Harlow could see the pale pebbles on the sea floor, shimmering turquoise and sea-green. The surrounding rocks, topped with bushes and trees, narrowed to form a sheltered bay with another wedge-shaped rock rising out of the Aegean in the gap between.

Adonis took a towel out of his rucksack and laid it over the pebbles. 'Pretty special, huh?'

'I'll say.' Harlow sat next to him, relieved to get the rucksack off her hot back.

'Fancy a swim before we walk back?'

Harlow could think of nothing better. She followed Adonis's lead, eagerly peeling off her top and shorts. She had her bikini on underneath, while Adonis was wearing swimming shorts. She couldn't help but admire his tanned and toned chest. It took her right back to the first time she'd met him in the olive grove.

They made their way down the beach together, splashing into the shallows and watching their footing on the smooth jumble of pebbles. The water was shallow and warm but refreshing after walking for a good chunk of the morning. They waded further out until it was a little deeper.

Harlow sank down, letting the water caress her hot skin. Adonis puzzled her. He'd hinted at his desire to leave the island and she'd witnessed his frustration, yet he looked so content now, swimming out to the edge of the bay where the rocky headland on each side ended, his arms slicing through the clear, calm water. She floated on her back, gently paddling her hands and gazing up at the sky. Perhaps it was the same for him as it was for her; there was much about her life that frustrated her, while there were moments she loved too. This job for one – at least this place. The island had completely stolen her heart.

They swam and messed about in the sea for nearly an hour. Adonis went back to the beach first, took a towel from his rucksack and started rubbing his hair dry. Harlow emerged a few minutes later, aware of his eyes following her from the shallows up the beach.

She sat down next to Adonis, sharing the small space on the towel with him, her damp shoulder touching his arm. Far away from villages, roads and people, it was beyond peaceful, the only sound the sea bubbling on to the beach. The sun wrapped around them, warming them up and drying them off. She'd thought about kissing him a week ago when they'd been sitting together on the moonlit beach. Now it was all she could think about. The way he was staring ahead, his arms tensed around his knees, made her wonder if perhaps he was too.

Harlow decided to let her emotions rule her head. What would be the worst that could happen? She leaned closer, her hand finding its way across his toned stomach.

'Thank you for today,' she said, letting her hand rest on his side.

He looked at her and smiled; their lips were inches away from each other. She brushed hers against his. He returned her kiss, but properly, not tentatively like she had been. He manoeuvred himself to slide his hands around her bare waist, holding her closer until she was enveloped in his warm embrace.

'I've wanted to do that since I first saw you,' he said.

'Really? You could have fooled me.' She laughed.

'I told you I was upset, but not with you. I'd had an argument with Baba, stormed off and taken my anger out on the ground. I'd needed to dig it for ages. Then you showed up, just gorgeous and happy and, I don't know, you took me by surprise, but there was something about you.'

She'd been holding back for too long, afraid to give in to her feelings, afraid of what they meant and how Adonis would react. She needn't have worried because he felt the same. 'You kinda took my breath away too.' Harlow slipped her hand into his and looked into his deep hazel eyes. 'I mean, it totally helped that you were topless and hot as hell. I wasn't expecting *you*. I was expecting your dad, a grumpy farmer.'

'I was grumpy.'

'Yeah, grumpy and hot.'

Adonis laughed, and squeezed her hand tighter.

'What had you argued about, with your dad?'

'The same thing we always do. If I suggest doing something differently or a new idea, he shuts me down. He's stuck in his ways and won't allow me any freedom when it comes to the farm.'

'I'm so sorry.'

'It just makes me angry; I can't help it.'

'Let's change the subject then.'

'Let's not talk at all.' He kissed her again and ran his hands up her bare sides, caressing across her bikini.

* * *

Harlow had no idea how long they stayed wrapped in each other's arms. She hadn't wanted to stop kissing, but eventually they dried off and got dressed. The hike back was harder than the way there. Not only was it a steep climb but the sun was high and edging towards the hottest part of the day. At least the trees provided shade and the swim had left Harlow refreshed. She also felt as though she was walking on air, wrapped in the deliciousness of their time on the beach. She really did have gossip for Manda now. Yet part of her wanted to keep Adonis all to herself. Manda would have noticed that she'd been out all day, and possibly Tyler too. She definitely didn't want him to know anything.

Hot and with aching legs, they made it back to The Olive Grove. They emerged from the pine forest bordering the olive farm and Harlow saw the full size of the land. The restaurant, villa and the whitewashed outbuildings formed an L-shape, with pockets of gardens, terraces and fruit trees. The orchard and olive grove spread out across the hillside, with the parched wildflower meadow and the field of goats furthest away, then nothing but sea and sky. From this high up, even Glossa was hidden. Apart from the murmur of chatter from diners in the restaurant, there was only nature, sunshine and beauty.

'You can shower here if you don't want to wait until you get back?' Adonis said.

'Oh that's okay, it'll be easier at the hotel.'

'Stay and have lunch then.' He took her hand and looked at her. She couldn't refuse. Not that she wanted to; she didn't want the day to end.

The terrace was full, so they sat in the courtyard beneath the shade of an olive tree. They shared a Greek salad, little dishes of creamy smoked aubergine and another of hot smooth feta along with tender chicken souvlaki. After their hike and swim, Harlow was ravenous and didn't think she'd ever eaten a better meal. It really had been a good day; one of the best. The tingling feeling she got whenever she looked at or thought about Adonis filled her with a mix of joy and trepidation.

As they ate, their conversation moved from food to their childhoods and growing up in different countries with such different parents. Yet Harlow sensed a connection. She wondered if Adonis did too. They didn't mention the kissing, but it remained imprinted on Harlow's mind. And when he walked her back to the car and said goodbye with another kiss, she left The Olive Grove with her heart soaring.

* * *

'Where have you been all day?'

Tyler was of course the first person Harlow bumped into after arriving back at the hotel. They met on the villa stairs – Tyler on his way out, Harlow on her way up to her room.

'For a walk.'

Tyler raised an eyebrow. 'What, all day?'

Harlow held his gaze. 'Did you know the network of old paths across this island and the trails through the pine forest are completely stunning?'

'Okay,' he said slowly. 'You really can be a nerd sometimes, Harlow.'

She narrowed her eyes. 'What, because I'm interested in nature and walking and stuff like that?'

'Exactly. I've been waiting for you to come back with the car all afternoon. You finished with it?'

'Yeah, sorry. I thought I'd be back sooner.'

'Someone kept you out, did they?' He smirked and took the car keys from her. 'You not going to ask where I'm going?'

'No, why should I?'

He shrugged. 'See you later.'

She watched him clatter down the stairs. He obviously wanted her to ask where he was going, or more likely who he was going with. He was still playing games.

* * *

After showering and changing into fresh clothes, Harlow messaged Manda about meeting up. She wandered down to Villa Sporades. Manda's room was on the ground floor and had a small terrace that opened right on to the pool. They sat outside with a drink and soaked up the late-afternoon sun.

'So, where did you go today?' Manda asked with a knowing grin.

'You sound just like Tyler.'

'Oh, sorry. He was asking earlier if I knew where you were. I said I didn't, but I had my suspicions.'

'I went on a hike to the *Mamma Mia!* church with Adonis.'

'I knew it!' she squealed.

Harlow glanced at the girls from the make-up team lounging around the pool.

'And...?' Manda said, lowering her voice.

'We had a lovely time.'

'You know exactly what I'm asking. Did he kiss you?'

'Actually, I kissed him.'

'Oh my goodness, you lucky, lucky thing. I presume he kissed you back?'

Harlow nodded. 'We didn't actually talk about it though. That kinda worries me.'

'Why? What are you going to say? That was a nice kiss? You're worrying for nothing.'

'I've just never been good at knowing where to go from here.'

Manda folded her arms on the table. 'You go out again. You kiss a lot more. Then when you're ready...' She raised her eyebrows.

'I've been in this position with Tyler and look where that's got me.'

'Tyler is a flirt. When he's not with you, he's chasing someone else. And Adonis isn't Tyler. You can't compare everything to your relationship with him. It's messed up – I know it is, you know it is, and I'm sure Tyler knows it is. And just because you have this weird, messed-up whatever-it-is with Tyler, doesn't mean any other relationship will be like that.'

'Maybe you're right.'

'I mean, you've had other relationships besides Tyler, right? Other boyfriends?'

'Tyler has never been my boyfriend. But yes, there have been a couple of other guys, nobody I've ever been really serious about. My longest relationship lasted a little over a year.'

'But Tyler?'

'We've been a thing for twelve years. Not together, but not really apart. Friends but more than friends, and we always end up together when we do see each other. When I've been with someone else, I've purposefully avoided seeing Tyler because I know what happens.'

'Have you slept with him here?'

'No.'

'Honestly?'

Harlow nodded. 'For the first time ever when we've both been single, nothing's happened.'

'Maybe this is your chance to break the cycle. It's toxic. I know how he makes you feel. And I know you're drawn to him and there's lots you like about him, but still... Time to let go, I think. When you've got someone like Adonis, there's no competition. Boy would I have liked to have been you earlier today.' She grinned. 'Honestly, I love my husband dearly, but Adonis, phew, he's something else.'

'I get it.' Harlow held up her hands. 'He's hot.'

'There's nothing to lose by getting to know Adonis better. See where it leads.'

18

WEEK FIVE – FOURTH WEEK OF FILMING

Monday soon came around and Harlow was plunged back into the busy routine of the shoot. It was intense working on location in another country. There were local politics to navigate, tourists to manage, cordons to police, local extras to organise, all while working to a tight timeline. And of course there was no escaping the film environment. Downtime was spent with colleagues and everyone was living and working together twenty-four-seven. Gossip was rife, mainly about how much time Crystal and Dominic were spending with each other outside of filming, but also about Tyler and production assistant Olivia. Rumours about Jim spending *a lot* of time at Maeve's villa had also reached Harlow.

It was a strange situation with Adonis. Their walk to Agios Ioannis Kastris had undoubtedly brought them closer together, yet she was still hesitant. They had each other's numbers, but neither of them had messaged or called. Harlow had thought about texting but didn't know what to say. As the week marched on, she found it harder to make contact and then worried because he hadn't contacted her either. Maybe he was just as confused. She was also aware that she was the one dealing with The Olive Grove as a location, yet she was messing around with one of its owners. Well, not messing around – they'd spent some time together, talked and had got to know each other. And kissed of course. He'd opened up to her, spilling his hurt.

So, of course, as she'd always done when a situation felt complicated, Harlow didn't deal with it, despite Manda banging on all week about how she should get in touch with Adonis. The longer she left it, the harder she knew it would be.

* * *

It was the end of the week and the Glossa villa was baking. The air conditioning wasn't working and filming had been paused. Cast and crew stood about in the shade fanning themselves. Harlow could see her mum talking on the phone, her hand on her hip, looking angry enough to fire someone. It was times like this Harlow was glad she had little responsibility. Keeping the shoot on time and to budget fell largely to her mum; it was no wonder she looked stressed.

Harlow's mobile buzzed in her back pocket. She pulled it out. Dad. She glanced around. Tyler was deep in conversation with the assistant directors and everyone else was just hanging about. She slipped away, on to the dusty earth of the makeshift car park.

'Hey, Dad.'

'Can you talk?'

'Yeah, there's an unexpected break in filming. Don't ask.'

'Can you see Skiathos from where you are?'

'Yes. Why?'

'Give us a wave then.' Her dad chuckled.

'You're not?' Harlow looked in disbelief towards the hazy outline of Skiathos across the deep blue Aegean.

'The girls are staying with Granny and Grandad for the week.

Gina and I thought, why not have a Greek island escape? We've never been to Skiathos. We got a last-minute deal, plus it's conveniently only a ferry ride away from you.'

Harlow beamed. 'I can't believe you're here, well there.' She gestured to the distant island. 'Not far away.'

'You're not working tomorrow, are you?'

'No.'

'Well then, we'll come over to Skopelos, unless you fancy a day out in Skiathos?'

'I would love to see you over there – you can show me the sights.'

'Gina suggested you invite your mum too.'

'You have got to be kidding.'

'I don't mean for the whole day! We're not masochists. See if she fancies having an early dinner with us.'

The truth was, Harlow wanted her dad all to herself, Gina too. She'd always got on with her step mum, not least because Gina was everything that Harlow had wanted in a mother: maternal, family-orientated, a good listener, selfless, loving, caring – the list went on. The fact that it was her suggestion to invite her mum proved that. Harlow knew that Gina had given up things to raise a family, while her own mum had put her career first. The two women were very different, not that there was anything wrong with that.

* * *

The next day couldn't come around quick enough. Because of the delay, the Friday shoot dragged on until late into the evening and Harlow didn't get a chance to talk to her mum until they'd wrapped.

'Your father's on Skiathos?' There was an edge to Maeve's voice and she looked pissed off.

'They're on holiday without the girls and want to see me. And you too.'

'Right.' She looked away and waved at someone over Harlow's shoulder. 'I don't have time tomorrow to swan off to Skiathos.'

Of course not, Harlow thought. *Too busy with Jim*.

She turned to go.

Maeve caught hold of her arm. 'If they can come over to Skopelos on Sunday, we can have lunch together then.'

That was certainly better than nothing and to be honest Harlow was pleased she'd get her dad and Gina to herself for the day. Harlow couldn't remember the last time all four of them had been together. She suspected that her mum wasn't thrilled with the idea, but she had agreed and that was something.

* * *

Harlow was up early and got a taxi to Glossa the next morning. It had been nearly five weeks before that she'd sailed to Skopelos, a bundle of nerves about what the shoot would hold. It felt good to be sailing away for a short time. She hadn't realised how much she wanted to see her dad. Spending time with her mum evoked memories she'd rather keep buried. It also made her question everything she was doing. Time spent with her dad usually had a grounding effect. She always thought more clearly around him and felt less stressed. Her good childhood memories were wrapped up in him, and as the ferry powered through the deep blue of the Aegean, she realised most of the happy ones as an adult were tied up with him, Gina, her sisters and her grandparents too.

It was another typically Greek island view that greeted Harlow as the ferry docked. Pockets of green studded the hillside between square, white buildings with red-tiled roofs. Sapphire water lapped the harbourside. She spotted her dad and Gina, holding hands, looking happy and relaxed outside a taverna with painted blue chairs and white and blue chequered tablecloths.

Her dad greeted her with a bear hug and Gina's smile was warm as she hugged her too.

'I can't believe you're here,' Harlow said once she was released from their embrace.

'We thought it was the perfect opportunity to combine a much-needed holiday with seeing you,' her dad said.

'Plus the kids adore spending time on the farm with your grand-parents.'

Her dad put on his sunglasses and hooked his arm in Harlow's. 'I see it's just you.'

'Mum made her excuses; said she's busy today.'

'Why doesn't that surprise me.'

'But, if you can come over to Skopelos tomorrow, we can all have lunch together. Mum's suggestion.'

'And we get to see Skopelos too,' Gina said. 'Bonus.'

Harlow knew it wasn't the most comfortable situation for her mum to spend time with her ex-husband and Gina, but she liked the way Gina and her dad were at least willing to, even if it stemmed from making the effort to all get together for Harlow's sake when she was growing up. She liked that about Gina, how easy-going and upbeat she was about things, so open to socialising with her husband's ex-wife. It couldn't be easy for her either, although she never made an issue of it. Perhaps that's what her mum had a problem with; Gina was too lovely to ever bitch about.

Gina hooked her arm in Harlow's. 'We thought we'd walk around this morning, have lunch, then relax on the beach before you get the ferry back.'

'Sounds perfect.'

The only time Harlow had felt like a tourist on Skopelos was during the day out with her mum. Even visiting the *Mamma Mia!*

church hadn't felt like a touristy thing to do because she was with Adonis, a local. But she was excited about today, getting to explore an island unknown to her, while spending the day with her dad and Gina.

* * *

Skiathos Town was reminiscent of Skopelos Town, but larger and less traditional. Its narrow streets bustled with tourists and it was a relief when they left the busy centre for the quieter and more picturesque Bourtzi – a tiny peninsula on the other side of the port. Shaded by tall pine trees and surrounded by the glimmering Aegean, the area was more chilled out than the heart of the town.

They had lunch at Marmita, a restaurant housed in the courtyard garden of a traditional building with green shutters and exposed stone.

'I guess we'll either love it or hate it,' Harlow's dad said as they were led through a gated entrance to a table. 'Get it? Marmita... Marmite...'

Gina caught Harlow's eye and shook her head at his 'Dad' joke.

Harlow basked in the warmth of the sun-drenched garden and the comfort of being with her dad and Gina. They tucked into delicious food: a green bean salad with pear and walnuts, plus spicy meatballs for her and slow-cooked lamb with fennel and greens for them. They talked about Abi, Ellie and Flo, what they'd be getting up to on the farm and how much they were looking forward to seeing Harlow when she was back in the UK.

Harlow loved every minute of sitting with them and sharing a bottle of wine, surrounded by luminous green leaves and hot-pink flowers. The simple white-painted wooden tables and chairs were offset by the saffron-yellow and salmon-pink stone walls. It was easily one of Harlow's favourite days since arriving in Greece. The only one that topped it was the day she'd spent with Adonis, hiking to the church and swimming in the sea. She'd loved everything about that day.

Stuffed full of good food and wine, they strolled back to the harbourside and got a taxi along the coast to the beach in front of the hotel where her dad and Gina were staying.

Unlike the beaches on Skopelos, this one was sandy. The large hotel loomed behind, with a beach bar with rows of umbrellas and sun loungers. They found three empty loungers on the row closest to the sea. Harlow was relieved to peel off her dress and lie down in just her bikini. There was barely a whisper of wind and she was immensely glad of the cooling frappé that was brought down to them from the bar. This was the life. Working on a movie on a Greek island was hardly a chore, but there had been little chance to relax during the week and she hadn't been able to enjoy the beautiful locations like a tourist.

'I might go see if I can hire a jet ski,' Harlow's dad announced after they'd been sunning themselves for an hour. 'Either of you two fancy joining me?'

Gina laughed and Harlow shot him an 'are you kidding me' look. She was perfectly happy lounging beneath an umbrella with nothing but sand and sea in front of her. She adored her dad's enthusiasm though. Although he was edging close to sixty, Harlow still thought of him at the age he was when she was in her teens and they'd go hiking together, play tennis and badminton, swim, run and spend weekends exploring places. Maybe he hadn't aged because of a younger wife and three more children – although with the girls heading into their teens, perhaps that would change. They were a sporty family though. She always got a stab of jealousy when she heard about her dad taking the girls wild camping or that they'd gone on a ten-mile hike or cycled through the woods. They lived in the Norfolk countryside with places they could escape to on the doorstep, the opposite of where Harlow lived in London.

Harlow and Gina ordered another frappé each and settled back on their sun loungers. Harlow had lost sight of her dad, who had disappeared further down the beach.

Gina sipped her frappé. 'How are you, Harlow? I mean really. Your dad said you sounded strained when you last spoke.'

'He caught me at a bad time. Things are fine.'

Gina looked at her over the top of her sunglasses. She raised her eyebrows.

'Honestly, I'm fine. It's just not been the easiest situation being around Mum, and her getting me this job last minute pissed Tyler off, and it's been weird with him, cos, you know, we've not seen each other for ages and things had begun to get weird with us before. I've sort of been put in a position I didn't want to get myself into.' Harlow chuckled. 'That all came spilling out.'

'It's good to talk,' Gina said. 'I'm glad you're spilling. We haven't seen you anywhere near as much as we should do. As much as we'd like to see you. The girls miss you like crazy.'

'I miss them too.'

'I know things have been difficult over the last few years and your career has taken you away lots of the time. You've been busy; we certainly have with the girls and work. We've seen less of you and I want you to know you're welcome any time. Really, Harlow, any time. I mean that.'

'I know.' A lump caught in Harlow's throat at Gina's sincerity and openness. 'It's just I feel like my loyalties are always being challenged. Not by you and Dad; I know you're happy to see me whenever, but Mum, I don't know... She has this way of sending me on a massive guilt trip if I spend time with you guys over her. Yet when I'm around her it's obvious how much of a disappointment I am to her.'

'You are absolutely not a disappointment, Harlow.' Gina reached out and squeezed her hand.

'Maybe not to you but you really don't know her the way I do, or Dad does. I think she believes the more influence she has over me and the more time we spend together, the more likely it is I'll miraculously turn into a version of her.'

'It's true, I don't know her the way you do, but I do know you're nothing like her, however much influence she has. You're smart to not be reeled in by that. I've seen and heard enough to make my own mind up.'

'She's clever at manipulating me and making me feel guilty. She's always telling me I should spend time out in LA with her, then because she travels loads and is in London for work, it's hard to spend time with you all if Mum's going to be alone in London.'

'But she's not really alone, is she? She has loads of friends and usually a bloke she likes to spend time with.'

'Still, doesn't stop her sending me on a guilt trip.'

'For someone who's always been so independent and wasn't around when you were growing up, you really shouldn't feel you owe her anything.'

'Easier said than done. She has a way... You've seen what she's like, even from afar.'

'I know the hold she had over your dad. I admire him for eventually standing up to her. He could have ended up having a miserable life staying with her. Don't let her controlling nature impact your life, is all I'm saying.'

'I'm well aware of what she's like,' Harlow said with a resigned tone.

'I know you are, but... it was just something your dad said about your mum not really giving you a choice about working on this movie.'

'It's a brilliant opportunity.'

'Yes, but that doesn't answer the question of whether you actually wanted to do it, to be here with her?'

'You and Dad both know the answer to that.'

'Then why did you say yes?'

Harlow looked at her step mum. 'You said it yourself about her controlling nature and how proud you were that Dad got out when he did. Maybe I'm not as strong as he is.'

'Oh Harlow, you are.'

'Growing up, the time I spent with you and Dad was healthy. Time I spent with Mum wasn't.'

'What do you mean?'

Harlow faltered; her hands were sweaty and her heart raced. 'All sorts went on at those parties she held. Stuff that would turn Dad's hair white.'

'Oh goodness, Harlow. I had no idea. We had no idea. Your Dad—'

'Doesn't know and doesn't need to know. I've said too much.' However much she trusted Gina, there were some things she wasn't comfortable opening up about, even though being here with Tyler and her mum had stirred it all up.

'Did anything happen to you?' Gina's voice wavered.

'I shouldn't have said anything. It's in the past and doesn't need to be dragged up again.' The conversation had turned serious. Harlow didn't want to be feeling this wound up when it was the weekend, she was with her family and they were relaxing on a beach. She shifted on her sun lounger to face Gina. 'I appreciate you asking how I am though.'

'Of course. And really, if you need to talk, I'm always here. I mean, if there's something you don't want to say to your dad.'

'We've always been open with each other about most things. Dad was who I talked to about boys, periods, friends, worries, the whole works. But there are a few things I don't want to say for fear of driving him and Mum further apart. They tolerate each other and that makes my life easier. I don't want to mess that up.'

Gina nodded, sipped her frappé and gazed out at the sea. 'I get that, I really do.'

Harlow sighed and rested back, stretching her legs out and enjoying the gentle heat beneath the shade of the umbrella.

'Oh lordy. Is that Derek? I think that's your dad.'

Harlow lowered her sunglasses and looked in the direction Gina was pointing. Wearing a bright yellow lifejacket and looking as though he was holding on for dear life as he whizzed through the water behind a boat speeding across the bay, it was unmistakably her dad.

'There we go. Your dad, at the age of fifty-eight is still following his heart. You should follow yours too, Harlow. Life's too short to not pursue your dreams and try to make yourself happy, whether romantically or professionally. Your dad changed his life for the better, however hard it seemed at the time. I sense you're unhappy and if that's true, then follow your gut about what you want to do. That's helped me in the past. If I hadn't listened to my gut and taken courage from knowing I'd be better off on my own, I might have remained with an abusive boyfriend instead of meeting your wonderful dad. Follow your heart, you deserve to be happy.'

19

Harlow parked on the edge of Skopelos Town and made her way to the harbourside. She was early, so found an empty table at one of the cafes overlooking the water. She ordered a vanilla milkshake and waited for the ferry to arrive. Yesterday had been so good, but it had also made her realise how much she missed her dad and Gina. She was aware her job would take her away a lot of the time, but wasn't that partly why she'd switched from a directing role to one that would allow her to travel and eventually scout locations? What she loved was being outdoors. Was working in film and TV really the best way to achieve that?

The ferry arrived and a flood of people disembarked, her dad and Gina among them. She couldn't help but smile at her dad in his sunhat, sunglasses, FatFace camper-van T-shirt chosen by the girls, and knee-length shorts that showcased his pale legs in flip-flops. He was holding hands with Gina, who was looking effortlessly summery.

Harlow slurped the remainder of her milkshake and tucked five euros in the shot glass with the bill. She waved at them and weaved her way through the flood of people heading in the opposite direction.

'Well, isn't this a treat.' Her dad gave her a big hug. 'Getting to see you two days in a row.'

He let go and she hugged Gina.

'Mum's offered to do lunch.'

'She has?' her dad said in disbelief.

'I'm not sure if she's cooking or getting takeaway or what, but she seems keen to have us over.'

Her dad raised an eyebrow but refrained from saying anything.

'She seems to want to make the effort.'

'Well then, I'm sure it will be good.'

Harlow loved her dad's positivity. He could even see the best in things when it came to his ex-wife, and Gina was just as positive. They were the perfect couple. She also got the sense that it annoyed her mum no end, seeing them so happy together. Not that her mum would ever want to get back with Harlow's dad, but she did wonder whether she'd actually like a relationship as stable and happy.

Harlow took them the longer but picturesque way through the town, up patterned steps between gleaming villas, past wooden tables and chairs clustered outside cafes. There was no rush to get to her mum's villa, not when there was the opportunity to see the island sights. In the back of Harlow's mind, the longer they avoided seeing her, the better.

* * *

'This is quite a place,' Gina said as they got out of the car in the driveway behind the villa. Off a lane on a quiet road, the peace was only broken by the ever-present cicadas and the distant bleat of a goat.

'Bit out of the way for your mum, isn't it?' her dad said under his breath. He clutched a bottle of wine that he'd bought on their way through Skopelos Town. 'She always used to like being at the centre of everything.'

'She still does, Dad. You'll see when we go round the back – it's the perfect place for parties.' *And for having a fling*, Harlow thought.

She led them along the side of the villa and through the gate to the terraced garden.

Her dad lowered his sunglasses as they walked onto the top terrace with its sweeping view down to Panormos. 'Ah, I see what you mean.'

'Wow,' Gina said. 'Puts where we're staying in Skiathos to shame.'

'Apart from we have a proper sea view, love, even if the room's a little on the simple side.'

'I thought I heard you.' Maeve swept out of the villa wearing a long but semi-sheer dress over a low-cut swimming costume. Her blonde hair was perfectly tousled, large sunglasses shaded her eyes, while her red lips matched her toenails. She was dressed for a pool party and not a relaxed lunch. 'Derek,' she said, kissing him on both cheeks.

She did the same with Harlow and Gina. Harlow could see Gina looking Maeve up and down. In Harlow's eyes, Gina looked just as gorgeous as her mum but was dressed in a more relaxed and appropriate way in sandals, a white maxi skirt and floaty top, her make-up subtle, if she was wearing any at all. Harlow knew her mum had always had an issue with Gina because she was younger – only by seven years, but it seemed to make all the difference.

'What can I get you to drink? You still partial to a beer, Derek? There are bottles chilling in the fridge.'

Her dad wandered over to the outdoor bar beneath the large oak.

'Do you like prosecco?' Maeve asked, handing Gina a glass. 'Do you want one, Harlow, or are you driving?'

'I'm driving. I'll get myself a soft drink.'

'It's quite a place, Maeve,' Gina said as Harlow joined her dad. 'I was saying so as soon as we saw that view.'

Derek popped the lid off a beer. 'I was wrong,' he said under his breath. 'She can still be centre of attention here. It is quite a place. Hard-pressed to see why you refused to stay here now.'

'You know exactly why, Dad. Working with her is enough. Anyway, you know as well as I do that she was probably relieved I did say no. The idea of me living here would be appealing for a day or two, after that not so much.'

'Is she staying here on her own?'

She knew where her dad was going with that question. 'I think so,' she answered truthfully. She knew as much as her dad did, besides the inevitable rumours that were doing the rounds, but he didn't need to know about those.

They re-joined Gina and Maeve. Gina had nearly finished her prosecco and Harlow could tell she was nervous. Her mum thrived on entertaining people, whereas Gina was far more comfortable spending time with her family.

'Is there anything I can do to help?' Gina asked.

'Goodness, no. You relax. Harlow can help.'

Gina caught Harlow's eye and gave her a sympathetic smile. Harlow followed her mum into the villa without argument. It was open plan and surprisingly airy, with sunlight flooding through the shuttered windows. There were splashes of colour from the cushions on the mink-grey sofa, leafy green indoor plants and wooden beams cutting across the ceiling.

Maeve started taking dishes from the fridge and placing them on the work surface. 'I had the hotel restaurant make up some food.'

That didn't surprise Harlow one bit. She wasn't sure her mum had ever cooked, and certainly not when she had guests to entertain. The parties she held in London when Harlow was in her teens were usually catered affairs so her mum could spend all her time socialising. This seemed to be no different, minus the waiters.

'Can you take these outside.' Maeve handed her bowls of olives and nuts. 'By the way, Jim and Tyler will be here in a bit.'

'Excuse me?' Harlow backtracked into the kitchen. 'I thought this was supposed to be a family lunch?'

'It is, with a couple of extra guests, that's all. They're bringing the salads, so they'd better turn up.'

'Oh for goodness' sake, Mum.'

'Don't be pissed with me, Harlow. I'm making an effort. We're all together, aren't we? Just on my terms.'

Harlow gripped the bowls tighter and left the kitchen. This had always been the problem, her mum wanting to do things her way. Harlow had thought it too good to be true that she'd willingly agreed to spend time with them. There were always conditions; Jim and Tyler were it.

She emerged back into the bright sunshine, her mum on her heels.

'Derek, you always were king of the barbecue,' she said, handing him tongs and a bag of charcoal. 'You want to get it started.'

It was an order rather than a suggestion, but Harlow knew her dad would be glad to have something to do.

'Gina, let's sun ourselves by the pool.' She hooked her arm in Gina's and led her down the steps to the pool terrace. Harlow caught Gina's backward glance of longing at her husband.

'By the way,' Harlow said under her breath, 'Mum's invited a couple of other people.'

'Oh has she now,' Derek said with the resigned tone of someone who knew his ex-wife well.

'The first assistant director, Jim. There are rumours—'

'Say no more.'

'She's also invited Tyler too... So, you know, a fun, family afternoon.'

Derek tipped charcoal into the base of the barbecue. 'Things okay between you and Tyler?'

'Let's just say I'd rather not be spending today with him.'

'It'll be all right, Harlow, we're here.'

'I know you are, Dad.'

He put his arm around her shoulders and hugged her.

'I'd better make sure Gina's okay.'

She took the bowls of nibbles down to the pool and placed them on the table between Gina and her mum's sun loungers. Harlow settled herself on the other side of her mum and rested back, enjoying the manageable heat in the mottled shade of the overhanging olive tree.

Her mum was saying something about how peaceful the place was at night and that you could see the lights down on the coast at Panormos.

A car crunched into the driveway.

'They're here,' Maeve said, standing up.

'Who's here?' Gina looked at Harlow in confusion.

'Friends,' Maeve said by way of explanation.

'Not just us then?' Gina mouthed to Harlow.

Harlow shook her head, her heart skipping a beat as Tyler walked round the corner of the villa clutching a cool box to his chest.

Maeve kissed Tyler on both cheeks and kissed Jim on the lips. Harlow's eyes widened at the confirmation that the rumours really were true. Harlow and Gina wandered up to join them and Maeve made the introductions.

'This is Jim, and of course Derek, Gina, you both know Tyler.'

20

Harlow hadn't paid much attention to Jim before; she didn't have that much to do with him during the shoot and she'd so far avoided going out with Tyler and the others. He was older than she'd first thought, but it was difficult to pinpoint how old – he could be anywhere from his late thirties to mid-forties; younger than her mum by at least a decade though. Not that his age bothered her if he made her mum happy, but she'd seen it many times before, her mum bouncing from one meaningless fling to another – or so it seemed. Was Jim being invited purely to rub her dad's nose in it? Not that he'd care. After trying his hardest to make his marriage to Maeve work, her dad had been happy with Gina for more than fifteen years.

'How's the shoot going?' Gina asked, looking between Maeve and Jim. 'This island must be an incredible place to film.'

Harlow liked how attentive her step mum was, always eager to ask about other people and keep the conversation flowing.

'It is, but it's also a complete headache,' Maeve replied. 'It will be worth it for how it'll all look post-production, but the locations aren't exactly the easiest.'

'Don't blame me,' Tyler said, holding up his hands.

'It's my own doing,' Maeve acknowledged. 'We wanted the authenticity of a Greek island rather than filming on location in Croatia or on a sound stage at Pinewood, which would have been technically easier.'

'You've always loved a challenge,' Derek said without a hint of irony in his voice.

'Yes, I have. And the locations are paying off, despite their awkwardness. The island has some beautiful beaches and we have an incredible villa just outside Glossa. And there's this stunning olive grove that Tyler and Harlow managed to secure.'

Harlow stopped listening and wondered what Adonis was doing. He didn't get the whole weekend off like she usually did. Working on the land and with animals meant there was always something to do. It had been more than a week since they'd spent the day together, but she'd thought about him every day since, worrying that neither of them had got in touch. She would message him later, as soon as she got back to the hotel.

'Don't you, Harlow?'

'Don't I what?' She looked across the terrace at Tyler.

He grinned at her. 'Love the island and its nature. The locals too.'

Harlow held his gaze but didn't give him the satisfaction of a reply. This was exactly why Tyler being here – and Jim to a lesser extent – was going to ruin their day. Her mum just couldn't, not even for a few hours, be herself and relax around her ex-husband and his wife without bringing in support.

They stayed on the top terrace for a little longer chatting about the shoot, while Derek got the barbecue going. Once the coals were white hot, he placed skewers of chicken souvlaki over the heat, while Maeve, Harlow and the others wandered down to the pool terrace with their drinks.

Maeve, as usual, was centre of attention and chose the sun lounger in the middle. Harlow was happy on the periphery listening to her mum dominate the conversation, which was mostly centred around work and her life, sprinkled with the names of the famous people she'd worked with. Tyler and Jim chipped in every so often, and Harlow sensed her dad listening in from above as he turned the corn on the cob and the souvlaki skewers.

Harlow allowed herself to relax. Jim was next to her, focused on Maeve's every word. Tyler was on the other side of Gina, far enough away to not annoy her. The water in the pool looked cool, tempting her to dive in, but despite having a bikini in her bag, the sun bed was too comfortable to consider moving. The heat quite often felt an inconvenience while working, but lying down now with every inch of her being warmed by the sun was just blissful. With the chatter and birdsong lulling her, she could quite easily nod off.

'Food's ready!' Derek calling from the top terrace disturbed Harlow's peace, although the mouth-watering smell of the grilled chicken was worth it.

Harlow helped her mum set the table on the top terrace. Jim and Tyler laid out the extra salads they'd brought from the hotel, and Derek piled the grilled chicken, onions and corn on the cob on a plate and plonked it in the middle of the table.

Maeve waited until everyone had settled down before raising her glass. 'Well, cheers, everyone.'

'Cheers!' they all chorused, knocking their glasses together.

Spoons and forks darted from bowl to bowl and the souvlaki was passed around.

'The girls are with your parents, are they?' Maeve asked, looking at Derek.

He had his mouth full but nodded.

'Yes, they love it there,' Gina said for him. 'Like Harlow does.'

Maeve wrinkled her nose. 'My overriding memory is of freezing there one Christmas. Snow outside and blowing a gale. Derek and his father out in all weathers. Me left with a teething baby and Derek's mother too busy to help because she was always cooking or cleaning out fires. Not my idea of fun.'

Gina caught Harlow's eye. 'Well, they have central heating now. Malcolm has help on the farm and Eileen likes looking after us, but the girls and I help her as much as we can.'

'Easier when they're older.' Harlow knew her mum didn't like the suggestion that she was moaning.

Harlow had fond memories of Christmas on her grandparents' farm, but she only vaguely remembered her mum being there. They'd spent most summer holidays there too, but it was usually just Harlow and her dad, and when her mum did come, she never embraced the way of life: early mornings, working outside in all seasons, and hard, physical work. She worked long days and faced plenty of challenges as a film producer but that was because she wanted to. She'd always made it abundantly clear that she wasn't interested in the farm or Harlow's grandparents' way of life one bit, even while married to Derek.

The food was polished off and drinks were topped up. Harlow couldn't fail to notice that despite the lunch being hosted by her mum, she hadn't actually prepared or cooked a thing. She'd had the souvlaki skewers made at the hotel, the salads had been brought by Tyler and Jim, and her dad had cooked everything. Her mum liked to socialise and she wasn't a good cook. Harlow could hardly expect her to change now, particularly on her one day off.

Gina insisted on clearing away and Maeve didn't argue. Harlow helped, while Maeve went down to the lower terrace with Jim, Derek and Tyler. Harlow was quite glad to escape that conversation.

It didn't take long to put the leftover food in the fridge, stack the dishwasher and wash up the larger bowls, while Harlow chatted to

Gina about what plans she and her dad had for the rest of their holiday.

Gina wiped over the work surface, hung the cloth on the tap and turned to Harlow.

'Are you really doing okay here?' She put a warm hand on Harlow's shoulder. 'I don't know all the ins and outs with you and Tyler, but from what your dad's said and your reaction to him being here, I can see the tension.'

'I'm okay, honest, but thank you for asking. This time here feels like my chance to sort out my feelings about him, or at the very least get my head straight. It's not healthy feeling the way I do around him.'

'No, it's not. I care about you, the same way I do Abi, Ellie and Flo. I wouldn't want them to be messed around by someone; Tyler shouldn't be doing that with you.'

'I know, but it's not always been like this. There was a time when it at least felt like we cared for each other.'

'What happened?'

'I'm not really sure.' Except she did, a series of events that had put a strain on them both and made Harlow feel as if she owed him; nothing she could easily put into words.

'You'll figure it out. Like you said, this time here is the perfect chance.' She smiled at Harlow. 'Come on, we'd better join the others and save your dad.' She headed for the door.

'Can I tell you something, Gina?'

She turned back. 'Of course, always.'

'I've sort of met someone here – a local, not anyone associated with the film…' Harlow trailed off, not really knowing where she was going with this, but feeling a need to confide in Gina.

'And you like him, this local?'

'Yeah, a lot.'

'Well then, don't let Tyler mess that up.'

* * *

Harlow stood on the threshold of the villa and gazed across the terraces shimmering in the afternoon sun. The barbecue coals had burnt down to little more than ash and the pool still looked inviting. After her chat with Gina in the kitchen they'd joined the others and spent another hour on the sun-baked lower terrace with its unspoilt view of the sweeping valley until Harlow had needed a wee and come inside. She hovered in the shade by the villa. Jim had his arm along the back of her mum's chair, while her dad and Gina were sitting opposite holding hands. They were still very much in love fifteen years and three kids down the line. What did her mum think about that? She also wondered what they were all talking about – she had no desire to join them yet.

Tyler sidled over from the outside bar and handed her a bottle of Diet Coke.

'Just for the record, I'm as surprised as you that I got invited.'

'Really.'

'Oh come on, Harlow. I think your mum wanted to even up the numbers. Her and Jim are an item; think she figured you could do with some company too.' He sipped his beer and watched her.

'Trust me, I would have been perfectly comfortable without your company. Mum doesn't have a clue about us.'

'Is that so.' He smirked.

'I just feel sad that she still feels the need to rub Dad's face in it. That because he's moved on she needs to prove that she has too. But her and Jim, it's just another mindless fling.'

'How do you know that? Have you talked to her? Have you talked to Jim?' He folded his arms and looked at her. 'No, you haven't. You're making assumptions.'

'I know what she's like, Tyler.'

'I've spent quite a bit of time with Jim and we've talked a lot. They sound pretty serious to me.'

Harlow turned to him. 'That's not how you described things between him and my mum when you were drunk the other weekend.'

Tyler's eyes narrowed. 'You said I didn't say anything.'

'I said you were talking gibberish.'

'So I did say something?'

'You told me that Jim was banging my mum. Doesn't sound like a serious relationship to me.'

'I was drunk, Harlow.'

'Yes you were.' She wasn't going to tell him that he'd also told her he loved her. Twice.

'What's going on with you and this Adonis?'

'Oh God, don't you start. There's nothing going on.'

'Is that why you went bright red and off with the fairies earlier when your mum talked about The Olive Grove?'

'I didn't.'

'If you say so.' Tyler swirled the beer in his bottle and stared out over the valley. 'You slept with him?'

Harlow clenched her hands. 'That has nothing to do with you.' He had no right to ask such a personal question and she felt no need to tell him that she hadn't. Let him wonder.

* * *

The intensity of the afternoon sun made them move back up to the top terrace, where the trees cast long shadows across the patterned paving. Harlow was the only one not drinking. Yet after a big lunch and too much sun and relaxation, she was struggling to stay awake. The day was naturally drawing to a close, with her dad and Gina looking as though they were ready to go. Tyler was over by the bar pouring himself another drink and Jim had disappeared inside.

Maeve had wandered off and was gazing out at the view, but as Harlow walked past to collect her mobile from the table on the lower terrace, she noticed her holding a glass of bubbly in one hand, while the other clutched her chest. Harlow backtracked and walked over to her.

'You okay, Mum?'

Maeve turned in surprise. 'God, Harlow, you made me jump.' She dropped her hand from her chest. 'I'm fine.'

Harlow nodded, unconvinced. Sweat trickled down the sides of her mum's face. During the shoot, even in the intense heat, she always remained cool and calm – at least she looked that way, even if her insides were a jumbled mess. But right now she looked sweaty, pale and flustered.

'I think we're about to leave,' Harlow said. 'I need to get Dad and Gina to the ferry.'

'Well, let's go and say goodbye then.' Maeve dabbed the sides of her face with a tissue. 'Just a hot flush; you'll understand all too well one day.'

Harlow sighed as her mum paced back up the steps to where her dad and Gina were gathering their things.

'It was lovely to see you after so long,' Maeve was saying to Gina.

Tyler wandered over, downing the last of his drink. 'Can I get a lift back with you? Jim is staying.' He raised his eyebrows.

'Sure,' Harlow said, realising she had no choice unless she made him call a taxi, which she knew she wouldn't do. The last bit of time she had with her dad and Gina would be spent with Tyler as well.

They all said goodbye. Maeve kissed everyone's cheeks and linked her arm in Jim's. They followed them out to the car.

Harlow was about to slide into the driver's side when her mobile pinged. Her heart skipped when she realised the message was from Adonis.

If you're free tonight, come to The Olive Grove. It's Ereni's birthday and she's invited you. Would love to see you. 8pm.

She thumbed a quick reply before getting into the car.

I'd love to, thank you. Will see you later x

21

Maeve and Jim looked quite the couple, standing in front of the villa with their arms around each other's waists, waving them off. More than two decades after divorcing, her mum was still trying to prove she'd moved on, making a show of being with Jim, particularly when she'd kept their relationship hidden – at least from Harlow – until now.

'Well, that was…' her dad said with a hint of laughter on his lips.

'Lovely,' Gina finished for him. 'It's been a really lovely day.'

Harlow caught her step mum's eye in the rear-view mirror and smiled. She was sat in the back with her dad, while Tyler was next to her in the front.

'Actually, in all seriousness, it really was,' her dad agreed. 'No arguments, no unpleasantness, just a lovely few hours. I'm not sure we've ever had a day like that all together.'

'That's because we weren't on our own, Dad.'

'See, I can be a positive influence,' Tyler chipped in.

'You're practically part of the family, anyway,' Derek said with a laugh.

Harlow caught Gina's eye again. It was true, in her late teens and early twenties, Tyler had spent a lot of time with her family, both at her dad and Gina's in Norfolk, and at her mum's house in London. Whether that could class him as 'like family' was debatable, but he knew her family well and they knew him, that couldn't be argued with.

* * *

Harlow was sadder than she'd thought possible as she hugged her dad and Gina goodbye. She got back into the car and watched them walk towards the harbourside and the ferry that would take them back to Skiathos.

'You okay?' Tyler put his hand on her thigh.

She tensed. 'I'm fine. I miss them, that's all.'

He removed his hand from her leg. 'Gina doesn't like me much, does she?'

'Whatever gave you that idea?' she said in all seriousness.

'She avoided talking to me.'

'You're being paranoid.'

'I'm really not, Harlow. You talk to her a lot?'

'I talk to them both, but Gina has a tendency to ask pertinent questions that perhaps my dad doesn't want to hear the answer to.'

'You've talked about me, huh?'

'Don't flatter yourself.' Harlow reversed into a side road and carefully pulled out and headed back up the hill. 'I talk to my family – Dad, Gina and the girls at least.'

They drove back to the hotel with the radio on and the windows open. Warm air buffeted Harlow's face as she navigated the winding roads. Seeing her dad had left her feeling even more homesick. Not that it was home or being back in the UK that she was missing; it was the people she loved. Her choice of career had taken her away from them. While they'd moved away from London, she'd ended up staying because it was more convenient for work. And because she worked in the film industry, she was always pulled back to her mum. That and she had a habit of making her feel guilty about not spending time with her, not concentrating on her career... guilty about everything.

It was strange to think of Jim alone with her mum at the villa. They seemed pretty comfortable in each other's company. It only surprised Harlow because she tried not to pay any attention to her mum's love life. It was highly unlikely she was going to gain a step-father. Her mum had had numerous relationships since she'd divorced, but no one who ever seemed serious or permanent, and those were just the ones Harlow was aware of. There was lots Harlow didn't know about, like this affair with a Hollywood actor her mum was supposed to be having. Yet here she was hooking up with Jim, a first assistant director. Harlow didn't know what was true. Her mum liked her own company and didn't want to be tied down, yet she didn't seem to want to be on her own either.

They turned into the hotel car park and Harlow parked in the shade of a cypress tree. It had been a non-stop weekend filled with good things, but emotional too, and she still had the prospect of an evening with Adonis and his family.

She switched off the engine and turned to Tyler to ask him about borrowing the car again that evening, then thought better of it; he'd drunk far too much to be driving anywhere. He didn't need to know where she was going.

'You want to go to the bar and get a drink?' Tyler asked as they got out of the car.

Harlow wrinkled her nose. 'No, thanks. I'm going to have a siesta.'

'Suit yourself. Might see if Olivia's around.'

They split off in different directions; Tyler towards the beach bar and Harlow back to Villa Aegean. She'd had enough of his company; she was looking forward to an evening with Adonis.

* * *

After a long, hot day, Harlow felt refreshed following a siesta and a shower. Nerves attacked her stomach, a combination of seeing Adonis again and the prospect of spending the evening with his family. It was a birthday party for Ereni, so she popped on a summer dress and stopped in Neo Klima on the way to buy a box of Greek sweets from the bakery.

The Olive Grove was only open for lunch on a Sunday, so apart from a couple of cars, the car park was nearly empty when she arrived. From high on the hill and surrounded by the green of the forest, the retreating sun cast a shimmer of gold across the horizon.

Clutching the box of sweets and her bag, she walked beneath the tunnel of vines, past the deserted restaurant towards the sound of music and laughter.

The garden behind the villa didn't have the sweeping view that the terrace at the front did, but it was an oasis of green backed by the pine forest. A paved area was edged by fruit trees and a large table was filled with food. Harlow was immediately greeted by Ereni, and hugged and kissed on both cheeks.

Harlow handed her the box of Greek sweets.

'Thank you, that's so kind,' Ereni said. 'You know us Greeks and our sweet teeth well. Come, meet everyone, and eat. Adoni!' She waved across the garden to where he was standing by the barbecue. 'Harlow's here!'

Before Adonis had a chance to join her, Ereni pulled up a chair for Harlow and someone else handed her a plate filled with grilled meats and a rainbow of colourful salads.

Toe-tappingly catchy Greek music filled the garden, along with the smell of chicken grilling. Stephanos might be a grumpy farmer and Adonis troubled over his past and worried about his future, but Ereni made up for their quiet reserve with her energy and a large and happy family. Even Adonis's grandma, who Harlow had briefly met when they'd filmed in the olive grove, seemed friendlier somehow, with a twinkle in her eye as she sat at the table clasping a glass of ouzo and a plate of strawberry and cream-topped cake.

Adonis came and sat next to Harlow and smiled shyly. 'It can be full on when we're all together.'

Harlow watched his aunt, uncle and dad talking in Greek at what felt like a hundred miles an hour.

'It sounds like they're arguing, but they're really not. We speak with passion.' He reached for a bottle and took the cap off. He offered it to her. 'Do you want a beer?'

'I'd love one, but shouldn't. I need to drive back later.'

'You don't have to,' he said. 'You can stay here.'

Harlow met his eyes, unsure of his meaning and aware of the fluttering in her chest. 'I have work first thing in the morning.'

'Yes, but you're filming here,' he said with a smile. 'And we have a guest room.'

Harlow had been organised too, preparing all the paperwork on Friday ready for Monday morning. There really was no reason why she couldn't enjoy herself tonight. She took the bottle from him. After sitting in the sun all day longing for a cold beer, she couldn't think of anything better than sharing one now with Adonis.

'The call time isn't until nine for the actors, but I still need to be up early.'

He knocked his bottle against hers. 'We're always up early. We live and work on a farm – it's normal.'

In the sultry heat of the evening, the cold beer was refreshing and washed down the food nicely. It was like watching a scene from *My Big Fat Greek Wedding* or even *Mamma Mia!*, with tanned Greeks laughing and shouting together, surrounded by enough food to feed a hundred people. Three of Ereni's young grandchildren were running around with cheeky grins. Sam padded across the paved terrace, sniffing about for food before settling down at the foot of an almond tree. Adonis seemed happy to sit with her and listen to his family, their voices and laughter loud in the still night. There were no neighbours close by to disturb, only the insects in the undergrowth, the goats further down the hillside and the owl in the trees, its boop boop call fighting to be heard over the music, voices and cicadas.

The evening was full of laughter and Harlow was made to feel welcome and part of the celebrations, not an outsider, something that was often in the back of her mind even with her family, as she hadn't grown up with Gina and the girls. Being that much older she often felt like an aunt rather than a sister. She saw a similarity with Adonis; his immediate family was tiny, just him, his dad and his grandma hidden away up in the hills, while his aunt, uncle and cousins were loud and all-encompassing.

The food was as good as the meal she'd had in their restaurant the weekend before, tender herbed chicken and a variety of salads, all washed down with copious amounts of beer. As soon as her bottle was empty, she was handed another. There was no reason to say no.

As the food was finished off and the drinks flowed, the volume of the voices and laughter increased. The music was turned up and Adonis's uncle Kostas, who'd been snoring on the sofa when she'd eaten those loukoumades at Ereni's, started dancing on the edge of the courtyard. With flushed cheeks, a deep tan and a beer belly, he was mesmerising to watch. He danced effortlessly and with passion, slowly to begin with but matching the pace of the music as the beat increased. Some of the others began to join him, making a circle. A cheer went up when one of the grandchildren, who couldn't have been much older than seven or eight, took hold of his grandfather's hand.

Adonis was tapping his foot and Harlow couldn't resist either. The beat and atmosphere enveloped her. Ereni broke the circle and came towards them with a grin. Harlow shook her head, laughing with Adonis as Ereni took their hands and drew them into the dance. With her arms linked with Ereni on one side and Adonis on the other, Harlow was clueless about what she was doing, but attempted to copy Ereni as the family circle moved around the courtyard. Adonis's movement was sure and fluid, as if he'd been doing it all his life, which he probably had. Trying not to trip over her own feet, she glanced at him and caught the happiness on his face as he grinned and mouthed the words to the Greek song.

* * *

By the time Ereni and her family bundled themselves into their cars to head to the coast, Harlow's legs were tired from dancing and her mouth ached from laughing. Ereni offered to give Harlow a lift, but it was pointless as the car she shared with Tyler was in the car park. Ereni gave her a knowing smile and kissed her on both cheeks before she left.

The food had already been cleared away. Adonis's yiayia had disappeared inside and Stephanos called for Sam to follow him, nodding and saying '*kalinychta*' to Adonis and Harlow as they passed him on their way to the villa.

Harlow had loved everything about the evening, spending time with Adonis and his family. She didn't mind that they hadn't been alone, and now that they were as they climbed the stairs, she began to feel nervous.

They reached the landing and Adonis pushed open the first door.

'The guest room,' he said, switching on the light.

It had a tiled floor, white walls and was plainly furnished with a double bed facing the window.

'The bathroom's opposite.' There was no expectation from Adonis, or pressure. She liked that about him even if a small part of her was disappointed.

Harlow turned to him. 'Thank you for inviting me and for a lovely evening.'

'You enjoyed yourself?' He took her hands.

'I really did.'

They stared at each other for a moment, neither of them dropping their gaze. Harlow was pretty certain they were thinking the same thing. Adonis made the move this time, leaning in for a kiss, his hands leaving hers and finding her waist, gently caressing her sides as she kissed him back.

Stephanos's footsteps on the stairs forced them apart. Adonis blew her a kiss and she retreated into the guest room, closing the door just as Stephanos reached the landing. The feel of Adonis's hands and his lips on hers remained as she heard their hushed voices talking in Greek. It was a good thing to be left wanting more. But with not long left on the shoot, wanting more could be a problem.

22

WEEK SIX – FIFTH WEEK OF FILMING

Harlow woke to a cockerel crowing. She yawned, then smiled as she stretched out on the comfortable bed. The sound reminded her of waking up in her grandparents' farmhouse. The difference here was she was warm and the room was flooded with sunshine streaming through the curtainless window. In winter at her grandparents', she'd wake with frozen breath puffing into the room, and even in summer the thick stone walls of the farmhouse kept the inside cool, particularly the north-facing back bedroom. She didn't mind being woken early here; not to that sound and in a place like this.

She got out of bed and padded across the cool-tiled floor. The window was wedged open, and the early-morning sun cast warmth over her bare arms and shoulders. The olive grove was bathed in sunlight and the distant sea glittered. She could just see Skiathos too and imagined her dad and Gina would soon be waking up to spend the day exploring the island.

An engine started. Harlow caught sight of the pickup truck driving out of the car park onto the dusty lane. She wondered who was leaving so early in the morning; hopefully Stephanos and not

Adonis. She went back to bed and lay on top of the sheets, enjoying the warmth of the sunlight falling across her. Her eyes shot open. It was Monday – how could she have forgotten. After such a wonderful evening which she hadn't wanted to end, she'd pushed everything else to the back of her mind.

Shit, Tyler, Harlow thought. She really hadn't thought things through. They should be driving here together, and while she was already here, lying in Adonis's spare room, Tyler would be back at the hotel knowing she hadn't come back last night. She could go and pick him up, but that would be a waste of time when there'd be plenty of crew he could get a lift with. Her staying here was innocent – nothing had happened – but that's not how it would look to anyone else.

She took a deep breath. The production assistants shared a car. She messaged Olivia.

Hi Olivia. Any chance you can give Tyler a lift to the LOC this morning, please. And pass out the call sheets – they're already printed and in the production office. Thanks, Harlow.

There, done.

A minute later, her phone pinged with a message from Olivia.

Harlow Sands you dirty stop-out (this is Tyler btw). No prob O giving me a lift. Hope you had a good night ;-)

Harlow grimaced and glanced at her watch. To be with Olivia this early in the morning, the chances were he'd spent the night with her. She decided to refrain from sending a reply. Anyway, she'd see him later. There was no getting away from that.

She dragged herself out of bed. She only had the dress she'd worn yesterday to put on, but at least she had a bikini in her bag that she could swap for the underwear she'd slept in.

Footsteps creaked along the landing and stopped outside her room.

'Harlow, are you awake?'

Adonis. Harlow breathed easy.

'Yes, morning,' she said, going over to the door and opening it a crack. Adonis was standing outside with wet hair and just a towel wrapped around his middle.

'If you want a shower, the bathroom's free.' He handed her a clean folded towel.

'Thank you,' she said, trying her hardest to keep her eyes fixed on his face, while the memory of last night's brief kiss on the landing flooded back.

'Come find me outside after.'

The bathroom was simple but functional and the blast of luke-warm water woke Harlow up. She hurried back to the guest room, slicked on deodorant, chewed a toothpaste tab she had in her bag and got dressed. She dabbed on lip balm and mascara, left her hair to dry naturally and went downstairs. She could hear Adonis's yiayia in the kitchen, humming a tune as she pottered about.

Harlow poked her head round the door. '*Kaliméra.*'

The old lady beamed at her. '*Kaliméra. O Adonis eínai éxo. Exo ekeí.*' She jabbed her finger towards the open door.

Harlow escaped outside. The early-morning sun filtered across the terrace that ran the length of the villa and in front of the outbuildings. A small ginger cat was curled on a paving slab, licking its paw and basking in the sun. She caught sight of Adonis outside the workshop. As he walked over, a vehicle pulled into the car park.

'What time should everyone be arriving?' Adonis asked as he reached her.

Harlow glanced at her watch, a knot of worry tightening in her stomach. 'In about half an hour.'

Then the morning's peace would be shattered and she'd be plunged back into filming. There were worse things to be doing on a Monday morning, but she had an overwhelming desire to keep this place and Adonis to herself.

Stephanos appeared from around the side of the restaurant with Sam trotting behind him. 'I bring bougatsa.' He handed Adonis a small, white plastic bag.

'Ah, thank you, Baba.'

He nodded and walked off, talking in Greek to Adonis's yiayia who'd come outside to feed the chickens.

Harlow and Sam followed Adonis down to the wrought-iron table outside the workshop. Harlow scratched Sam's ears as Adonis unwrapped the bougatsa, put it between them and handed Harlow a wooden fork and an apricot juice.

'This is a treat.'

'Every time Baba has errands in Glossa early morning, he gets bougatsa. Will set you up for your busy day filming.'

Sam settled himself at Harlow's feet, and they tucked into the cream-filled filo sprinkled with icing sugar. There was so much Harlow wanted to say to Adonis, but she couldn't find the words. She loved spending time with him and adored how they could comfortably sit in silence and just be in the moment. She caught him gazing off into the distance, watching the birds swoop between the fruit trees.

The minutes ticked away too fast. Harlow was desperate to stay with Adonis, looking out over the orchard. All too soon, they'd finished eating. Adonis gathered together the leftover paper and the empty cartons of juice.

Harlow stood up and stretched. It was going to be a blistering day and they needed to get the scene shot and wrapped by the end of the afternoon.

'I hope today goes well.' Adonis moved closer and kissed her cheek.

'Thank you.'

'Have dinner with me later – if you have time.'

Harlow nodded. Of course she'd stay and have dinner with him; she was thrilled he'd asked.

* * *

Harlow's peace was shattered less than twenty minutes later with Tyler and Olivia's arrival. Even with sunglasses shading their eyes, they looked tired and hungover as they walked across the car park towards her.

'The others aren't far behind.' Tyler waited until Olivia had gone on ahead. 'You had a good night with the "Greek God"?' Tyler said with a smirk. 'I've heard what Manda and the make-up girls are calling him.'

Harlow kept calm. 'It's not what you think.'

'Yeah right.' He leaned closer. 'You forget how well I know you.'

Harlow folded her arms. 'And you had a good night with Olivia then?'

'Yeah, I fucking did. And I'm not afraid to admit it.'

Harlow told herself it didn't matter what Tyler assumed; she knew the truth and he could think what he liked.

Olivia looked sheepish as they followed her into the restaurant courtyard. Harlow wondered how much she knew about her and Tyler, or if she was just feeling awkward having spent the night with her boss. Her discomfort was not Harlow's problem, and neither should what Tyler thought be an issue. But she had no doubt that they were all relieved when the rest of the crew began to arrive and the restaurant was taken over by cameramen, sparks and sound. While all of that was being set up, Harlow escaped to the car park to check on everything.

A small marquee had been erected on the grass edging the car park, and hair, make-up and costume had already set themselves up ready for the extras to arrive.

Manda waved her over. 'Tyler said—'

'Don't listen to him, Manda.'

'So you didn't stay here last night?'

'I did...'

Manda squealed.

'But it's not what you think.'

'Okay, I believe you, crazy lady. You're taking things slow.'

'Exactly.'

'I will point out that we have less than two weeks left. Don't take it too slow.'

* * *

It was a short scene shot from two angles, one facing the actors on to the terrace with people dining behind them, and then the other way looking at them and beyond into the olive grove. There'd been a casting call for locals before shooting had started and so a dozen were brought in to act as other diners, with a couple more as the waiters. Adonis had made himself scarce, although Harlow knew that he was happily tucked away in his workshop while he had the chance. He could have been one of the extras – the restaurant staff had been asked and most had jumped at the chance of being involved in the film. She knew him enough by now to know he wasn't interested, not to mention his good looks would likely have distracted from Crystal and Dominic.

Harlow had persuaded Stephanos to open the restaurant

kitchen to make fresh dishes for the cast and extras to eat, to ensure the scene looked authentic. With the filming needing to take place before it got too hot on the terrace, it was a busy morning with everyone working hard to get the shots in the can and wrapped on time. It also meant that Harlow and Tyler spent little time together, and her mum wasn't on location either. The last couple of days had been a whirlwind of events and emotions, finished off by a successful shoot at the location she had organised. The feeling of contentment as they wrapped was something she hadn't felt for quite a while.

23

The last of the crew left in a trail of dust as they drove off down the lane. Everything had been packed away and taken back to the base. Harlow removed the last of the signs and put them in the boot of the car. The restaurant would be opening soon for real diners and Harlow was hoping to be one of them.

The clang of pans, voices talking in Greek and the delicious smell of something roasting drifted from the kitchen as she walked past the restaurant towards the villa and the outbuildings. The workshop doors were open but Adonis wasn't inside. She shaded her eyes and gazed across the orchard. She spied movement through the trees, so set off that way, relishing the peace now that everyone had left.

Adonis was fixing a section of fence at the end of the orchard. He waved when he caught sight of her.

'Are you finished for the day?' He tightened the wire on a wooden post.

'Yeah, all done.'

'It went well?'

Harlow reached out and touched his arm. 'We don't have to talk about the filming, but yes, it's all good. In the can, as we say.'

'I'm done too.' He tucked the tools into his belt.

Harlow waved her hand around them, at the endless space, the beauty of the orchard leading to the olive grove and the view over Glossa. 'I would love to live somewhere like this.'

'You would?' He looked at her as if she'd gone mad. 'But you live in London.'

'So?'

'It must be an amazing place to live, no?'

'I only live there because it's where most of the work is.'

'You don't like the city?'

'No, never have done. Okay, that's a lie, I did enjoy it when I was a student. I made the most of city life and going out, but the appeal wore off.'

'If you like this' – Adonis motioned to the fig and plum trees – 'then come with me.' He offered his hand and she took it.

They left the patchy shade of the trees for the large meadow and the blazing sun. The grass was yellow and straw-like and scratched their bare legs as they walked together.

'This area is covered in wild flowers in spring.'

Harlow gazed around. 'I can only imagine how beautiful it is then – even more than now.' She turned back to him. 'And you'd seriously want to live in London?'

'Maybe. Any city really. I want to experience life away from Skopelos.'

'You've never been anywhere else?'

'If you count a couple of other Greek islands, a few holidays visiting family in Athens and a cousin's wedding in Italy, then yes.' He laughed. 'I'm a country boy; you're a city girl.'

'A match made in heaven if you ask me.' The words were out before she'd thought them through.

Adonis looked at her intently with smiling eyes. Harlow suddenly felt self-conscious. Why was she feeling shy around him? Maybe because they were alone again and there was an expectation of what might happen.

'I'm not actually a city girl at heart,' she said, trying to change the subject.

'No?'

'The times I've been happiest have been when I've stayed with my grandparents on their farm in Yorkshire.'

'Yorkshire, like the pudding?' Adonis asked in all seriousness.

Harlow laughed. 'It's up north – way further north than London. There's the Yorkshire Dales and the Moors. My grandparents live in the Dales. Think beautiful green open spaces, fields with pockets of woods, lots of sheep, farms, few people. An old TV series was set there. I used to watch it as a kid. One of my grandparents' favourite programmes. Waking up here this morning reminded me of staying there.'

They reached the end of the meadow where a wooden fence separated it from another field with grazing goats and short, cropped grass shaded by the trees edging it. They rose steeply, coating the hill in a sea of green.

Adonis gestured to a bench, which was carved from a piece of wood set on top of two squat tree trunk legs. They sat down with their backs to the trees and looked out over the meadow and the grazing goats to the sea and sky beyond.

'It's my favourite spot,' Adonis said quietly.

Harlow nudged him, her bare arm briefly connecting with his. 'See, there is something you like here.'

'It was Mama's favourite place – she used to bring me here when I was little and read me stories.'

'Oh, Adonis, I'm so sorry...'

'Don't be.' He shook his head and put his hand on her arm.

'Honestly, don't be. There is much I like about Skopelos, but much I'm frustrated with too.' He ran his fingers along the wood. 'I made this so we had a permanent place to sit and remember.'

'You made it? It's beautiful.' It really was. The grain and natural beauty of the wood shone through.

'Your grandparents' farm is your favourite place?'

'Yes, always has been. Not sure anywhere could top it, certainly not for its remoteness, but its beauty – well, this place is hard to beat. I've always been happier when I've been there, usually only a week or two in the summer holidays when I was a kid and at Christmas. Maybe that's the thing; I've always left wanting more. Trudging across the fields at dawn, helping to feed the sheep. I loved it.'

'You *loved* it. You don't go any longer?'

'I haven't done any of that for a long time; I've not visited much, apart from a fleeting one- or two-night stay.'

'You've not seen your grandparents?'

'I have, when they've been at my dad's. I've just not made the effort to go up and see them.' Guilt stabbed at her insides.

'Why not?'

Harlow stared out at the heat haze shimmering in the distance. Adonis's question was a good one. Why had she put off visiting? And the times she had been there, why hadn't she thrown herself into the way of life like she had when she was younger?

'The more I'm there, the more I realise how unhappy I am when I'm not there. Nothing about my life, my job, my relationships fulfils me. Nothing about my life actually makes me happy,' she found herself admitting for the first time.

'You don't like being here filming?'

'Oh, I do. I love being *here*. I adore the island, its beauty, its nature, its greenness, the people...' She cast a quick glance in his direction, wondering if he'd pick up on her meaning him in particular. 'But the job... I don't know, if I'm honest I don't know if working in film and TV is actually what I want to do or if it's really my mum's dream for me.'

'You said she's the producer on the film, yes?'

'Yes, she calls the shots – on set and off in my case.'

'She wanted you to be a location manager?'

'An assistant location manager, God no. If she'd had her way, I think her desire was for me to act – and not just theatre or bit parts in TV, I mean be a famous movie star, and when she realised that I was more comfortable behind the scenes, then she wanted me to be a director or a producer like her.'

'So you did want to work in film?'

'Only because I didn't know anything else. I've been around the industry my whole life. It's all I know. My mum lives and breathes movies, particularly after she divorced my dad. I got pretty used to dinner and garden parties at our house with film stars and well-known directors popping over.'

'And your dad?'

'He's the head teacher of a private secondary school, as down-to-earth and as different to my mum as you could get.'

'You didn't want to teach?'

'I don't know. I spent more time with Dad, yet somehow Mum had a greater influence.'

A patch of sunlight had crept across Harlow's leg and she could feel the intensity of the heat on her bare skin. She shifted until she was completely in the shade. She couldn't get over the stillness, unlike back home where there was the constant noise of people and traffic.

Harlow wafted away a mosquito. There was only an occasional bleat from a goat, the buzz of a bee, and of course the ever-present chirruping cicadas.

'I know I shouldn't be frustrated.' Adonis's voice cut through the stillness, deep and lilting. 'But I can't help it – my life has been dictated – is that right?'

Harlow nodded.

'It's been dictated by Baba.'

Harlow immediately felt the connection with him; it was how she felt about her mum. Dictated was the right word.

'I feel guilt.' He shook his head. 'So much guilt, if I even think about leaving the island because I'd be leaving him and the family business. I had dreamed of going to university in England to experience life away from here, but that was before Mama died. Everything changed after that. Everything.'

Adonis abruptly stood. He smoothed down the front of his shorts. Silhouetted against the early-evening sun, Harlow only got the sense of his outline, his broad shoulders and toned torso in a fitted T-shirt, and the way he seemed to be fighting his emotions with clenched fists and jaw.

She stood and wrapped her arms around him. He tensed, for only a moment, then relaxed against her, his arms encircling her waist. They stood in an embrace, Harlow's head against his chest, his chin resting on the top of her head, for what felt like an eternity. Harlow didn't want to break free. She breathed in his scent, a delicious mix of fresh deodorant and hot skin, while they held each other tight.

Adonis took her hand and they walked together back through the orchard. It was obvious that he didn't want to continue their conversation and dredge up a painful past, and Harlow didn't push it. They'd said enough, their embrace saying more than words could.

Away from the shade of the trees, the evening sun sizzled on Harlow's skin. She loved the endless summer days, the guaranteed sunshine and knowing that bare arms and legs wouldn't result in goosebumps as soon as a cloud shaded the sun. It had been another perfect filming day, the deep blue sky untainted by even a smudge of cloud.

She followed Adonis along the well-worn grassy track in front of the restaurant. She glanced back at the orchard and wildflower meadow beyond. It was a spot that begged to be discovered, not that it should be overrun with people, but it seemed such a shame to not share it.

The busyness of the restaurant terrace was a stark contrast to the peace of the meadow. Having spent the day filming the restaurant scene, it was good to see real couples and families enjoying dinner while soaking up the olive grove view.

'I promised you dinner earlier.' Adonis turned and took her hand. 'You don't have to go back yet, do you?'

With him looking at her in the way he was, she had no intention of going anywhere. 'I've been longing to have another meal here.'

They went up the steps to the sun-flooded terrace. He nodded to a family, said '*yasas*' to an older Greek couple and pulled out a chair for Harlow at a table tucked between a lemon tree and the stone wall.

'What would you like?' he asked.

'Anything. You choose; whatever you think is best.'

Adonis caught the attention of a waiter. Harlow watched them chatting together, the Greek flying between them. A few words jumped out at her as Adonis placed the order – *horiatiki*, *tirokafteri* and *tzatziki* – words that had become familiar after a few weeks in Greece.

After working all day, it was a joy to sit and bask in the evening sunshine with Adonis. His company was as relaxed and as easy-going as it had been on their walk to the *Mamma Mia!* church. Whatever he thought of living on the island and working at The Olive Grove with all the memories it held, right now he seemed at ease.

The waiter brought over a selection of dishes and laid them on the table. Harlow noticed him wink at Adonis before leaving.

Adonis picked up the jug of wine and Harlow covered her glass.

'I really do need to drive back this evening,' she said, despite part of her hoping he'd suggest she stayed again.

He poured her a glass of water instead and pointed at the bowls of food between them. 'The olive oil is made from our olives – the tomatoes are grown here. We even make a small batch of our own wine.'

'You sound as proud as your dad does talking about this place.' Harlow stuck her fork into a large chunk of tomato, the juice and olive oil dripping on to her plate before it reached her mouth.

Adonis's eyes shifted away from hers and he shrugged.

'It's not a bad thing to be proud of something, even if it's not what you want to be doing,' Harlow said, thinking that it was probably good advice for her too.

He waved his hand around the restaurant. 'This place is family, that's why it's so hard to leave. It is memories; it is home. It is everything I know. Maybe I'm too scared to change things.'

'I understand that.'

'You do?'

'Yes, because it's how I feel about upsetting my mum or taking a chance on something new.' She pressed her fingers to her chest. 'Something *I* want to do.'

They continued eating in silence, their forks dipping in and out of the bowl of Greek salad.

Adonis tore off a chunk of bread and dipped it into the juice at the bottom of the bowl. He popped it into his mouth and chewed thoughtfully, his eyes lingering on hers. 'Maybe we should make a promise to each other.' He wiped the juice from his beard and lips. 'Before you leave, we make a decision to do something that scares us. Maybe we should decide for each other.'

He took her hand and stroked his thumb along hers. 'What do you think?'

'I think it depends on what it is.'

'But that's the point, it will be whatever I choose for you, and what you decide for me.'

Harlow laughed. 'That seems like such a bad idea.'

'That's why it's perfect. Do you want to make a promise?'

24

It seemed like a mad idea, but Adonis was serious. They agreed to think on it and let each other know what they'd decided the following weekend. With only the one day slated for filming at The Olive Grove, the shoot was moving to a different location and Harlow's chance to spend more time with him was fizzling away.

The rest of the week was dedicated to preparing for and shooting the challenging out-of-the way beach scenes at Perivoliou. Even though it had been Tyler's decision and ultimately her mum had signed off on it, Harlow still felt the pressure at being involved. They had two days to make it happen and get the shots. Two days of the beach being closed to the public.

The cliff that overlooked the pebble beach provided pockets of shade for the cast and crew. Harlow watched the scene from there, perched on a rocky outcrop. The bay was sheltered and a suntrap. The air was still and smouldered with heat. With no public nearby, it was strangely quiet once the director called 'action'. A handful of extras were sunbathing in the back of the shot and Crystal and Dominic were sitting on a towel having a heart-to-heart. The sea swooshed rhythmically onto the pebbles, but apart from that, nothing, only the actors' voices carrying into the air. Even the birds seemed to have gone quiet. As soon as the director called cut, one of the production assistants would go straight over to the actors with bottles of water and an umbrella to shade them. The monitor where the director and Maeve sat was shaded by a small marquee. Harlow could see how red-faced they both were.

For such an incredible setting, underlying tension simmered as much as the heat did. Tyler, usually relaxed and eager to joke, looked serious and was more focused on getting the job done than she'd ever seen him before. And although Maeve managed to come across as relaxed and in control while looking effortlessly chic on a beach in 35C heat, Harlow noticed the worry etched across her forehead and the perspiration sliding down the side of her face. Jim seemed flustered too, pacing about checking his watch numerous times while shots were reset. Olivia had a face on her like she'd been slapped. The pressure was on to get wrapped on time, but Harlow sensed there was more to it than just being hot, uncomfortable and tired. Tyler avoided Olivia as much as he could and when he did need to speak to her, it was purely about work, or he did it via Harlow.

'Next break, get Olivia to clear away those empty bottles, could you, Harlow.' He pointed to the bit of beach behind the monitor.

'Of course,' Harlow replied.

It was a melting pot of tension, everyone stuck all day on a beach with little respite from the sun or each other.

Just before they stopped for lunch, Maeve ordered everyone to cool off in the sea, and so the shallows were filled with cast and crew splashing about. It was the respite everyone needed.

They wrapped late and Harlow was the last to leave to ensure nothing was left behind. Tyler had already left with Maeve, who wanted to discuss the next day's shoot with him. After being surrounded by people and frayed tempers all day, Harlow was relieved to have a moment to herself.

She picked up the last empty bottle she could find and stood looking out at the sea which glistened golden with the retreating sun. After shouts of 'cut', 'first positions', 'background action' and the general chatter of people in between shots, Harlow relished the utter peace. No voices, no traffic noise, only the rhythmic wash of the Aegean lapping the pebbly shore. Birdsong from the surrounding cliffs mixed with the harsher call of a seabird flying overhead. Her legs and back were stiff from standing about all day and her skin was hot and sticky with sunscreen and sweat. She sighed and left behind the perfect view for a run at the hotel, a much-needed shower and an early night before they were back at the beach first thing to continue the scene.

* * *

'And that's a wrap!'

Four little words Harlow had been dying to hear since six that morning. They finished just before they began to lose the light, the last shot proving to be the most difficult and time-consuming. They'd had to move everyone and all the equipment from the beach before the shot from a boat out in the bay was attempted. Anyone who was no longer needed was released, so as the day wore on there were fewer and fewer people.

For Harlow it had been the same as the previous day, with the last couple hours spent sitting around waiting, the only difference being that Tyler stayed until the end too. Maeve looked relieved and shattered, thanking everyone as they left the beach to make their way up the steep, uneven path.

'Great job, Tyler.' Maeve clamped a hand on his shoulder. 'You too, Harlow.'

As Maeve started up the hill, Harlow did one last sweep of the beach to check that nothing had been left behind before joining Tyler.

'Thank God that's over,' he said.

'You pulled it off.'

'We made the right decision sticking with this place.'

'*You* made the right decision; I had nothing to do with it.'

'I thought you had a word with your mum?'

Harlow shook her head but remembered the argument they'd had over dinner in Skopelos Town when her mum had asked her about this location.

They left the empty beach and drove back to the hotel. Harlow got a stab of longing as they passed Glossa and the road that led to The Olive Grove and Adonis.

'Have a beer with me,' Tyler said as they parked. 'We so deserve it after the last couple of days.'

Deep down, she knew it probably wasn't a good idea, but he looked so relieved after all the worry, she didn't want to say no.

'Sure,' she said, following him past the hotel reception and into the grounds.

'Not down at the bar.' He turned off the main path and walked towards Villa Aegean.

Harlow sighed but followed him. She figured he was still trying to avoid Olivia and there'd been talk earlier about everyone heading to the bar once they got back.

Tyler's room was baking. He turned on the air conditioning, grabbed a couple of beers from the fridge and opened the balcony doors.

It was good to finally sit somewhere comfortable and actually relax after two long and hot days. The relief they felt at the beach shoot being over and successful was immense. They drank and talked about it and about what was slated for the final week.

'What's happening with you and Olivia?' Harlow asked as Tyler returned to the balcony with another two bottles of beer.

'Nothing.'

'It was just a one-night thing?'

'Yeah, but literally the next day she was like let's go out again, let's do this, let's do that. So full on.'

'You slept with her. What did you expect?'

'Not a bloody relationship. I figured she understood that.'

'Did you explain that at any point?'

'Of course not, Harlow. Kinda assumed it was a given.' He shrugged and knocked his beer against hers. 'Getting pissed with you is much more fun.'

'She's young, Tyler.'

'We're young too; thirty-one is hardly old.'

'Well, she's younger, and you're her boss.'

'Don't go giving me all that professional shit. Practically everyone on this shoot is doing it with someone.'

'You're exaggerating. For one, Manda's not messing about with anyone and neither are the rest of the make-up team.'

He raised an eyebrow. 'You're so naïve sometimes. It's endearing. But, yeah, you're right about Manda and her group of friends. Can't say the same about you though – fraternising with a local.'

'I don't think there's any rule to say I can't make friends while I'm here.'

'Is that what you're calling it?'

She ignored him and gazed out at the blue pool, the glowing room lights and the silver of the moon catching on the glittering black sea.

'Do you remember that shoot in Scotland?'

Harlow turned back to him. He'd obviously decided to change the subject instead of continuing the conversation and pissing her off even more. She sighed. She might as well let her annoyance go and try and have an enjoyable drink with him.

'How can I forget? Most difficult shoot ever. Your fault mind, finding that castle.'

Tyler swigged his beer and shook his head. 'Wasn't down to me. I was only an assistant back then. I did all the grunt work, like you do now, except then I was freezing my bollocks off and you get to hang about in the sun here.'

'You forget I was a third AD. I remember trying to keep the spirits up of about twenty extras who were playing the soldiers about to go to battle. Do you remember that holding room? It looked like a dungeon – massive, freezing cold and damp too and these tough guys all chosen cos they were fit and big and bearded were just like, is this ever going to end.'

'Everywhere was like that, even in the rooms where we were filming you could see your breath.'

'Pretty authentic for a medieval costume drama, mind.'

'That's why it was chosen. Just a shame the shoot wasn't in spring or summer rather than February.'

'Made it memorable though.'

'Your mum produced that one too.'

'Yeah, she picked up a Golden Globe for it. Funny how she wasn't on set very often though.'

'A supposedly haunted castle in the depths of Scotland in winter doesn't have quite the same appeal as a Greek island in July. Although, to be fair, she was the money, rather than the hands-on person.'

They reminisced more and swapped beer for vodka. After weeks of tension and being annoyed at him, it was refreshing to talk about the good times. Harlow had worked hard in her twenties, swiftly working her way from third to second assistant director and ending the decade as a first assistant director. Looking back, she could see how the assumption could have been made that she'd got where she was because of her connections. Doors opened the moment anyone realised who her mum was. It worked both ways too; not only had Harlow benefitted from more work, but directors loved who she was related to.

'I miss this.' Tyler nudged his shoulder against hers.

Harlow sighed. 'I do too. But just this, right this moment, when it's pleasant and us chatting normally, like we used to. Not any of the bullshit you've been pulling up till now – propositioning me, accusing me of nepotism. None of that was cool, Tyler.'

'I know, I'm sorry. I just miss you, that's all.'

'You've got a funny way of showing it.'

'I miss us, like we used to be, you know, way back.'

Before things got messy, Harlow thought.

Tyler reached for her hand and held it between them on the rattan sofa. It was a gentle and affectionate gesture and she didn't pull away.

'I think I've struggled since, you know…' He trailed off. 'You've seen me at my most vulnerable. You're the only person who's seen me like that. I find that hard to deal with.'

'It shouldn't have changed anything. With or without your demons, you're still my friend. You've been trying your hardest to push me away, yet there are times when we seem to slot back to being twenty-one again and happy and, I don't know, good for each other. Most of the time, we're not.'

'I know I've not helped in the slightest. I'm not sure I know what I want. I suspect you kinda feel the same.'

Harlow gave a hollow laugh. 'You're right about that.'

'Why have we never talked about this before?'

'You said it yourself – the times we've been together in the past, we've done little talking. And we've not seen each other for a long time. I've changed; I'm pretty sure you have too. I'm unfulfilled and struggling with where my life's going in every way. I hate feeling like that. Being here is beginning to make things a little clearer.'

'It's good to talk.'

'Free therapy.'

'Don't we both need it.'

'Speak for yourself.' But she knew he was right, not that she thought a therapist in the traditional sense would help. She needed to figure things out for herself about what would make her happy.

'Maybe we should give it a proper go,' Tyler said, pulling her back to the moment.

'What do you mean?'

'Us.'

Before she could react, he kissed her. His hands found her waist, dipping beneath her silky top, hot on her skin. Everything about him was familiar, the way he was kissing and touching her, taking her back to a time when she'd reciprocate and want a whole lot more. She let her guard down and kissed him back, lost in the comforting sensation of being in his arms. But was that how she really felt? As his fingertips brushed her thigh and crept upwards, she knew where it was leading. This was not what she wanted. Tyler was not who she wanted.

'Stop.' She moved away from him. 'Tyler, please stop.' She held her hands against his chest, her heart thudding, confusion washing over her. Her immediate reaction had betrayed rational thought. Just because he was familiar and they'd kissed hundreds of times before, didn't make it right to do so now. She didn't want to go down that road again, particularly after the way he'd treated her these past few weeks. All she could think about was Adonis and how it felt as though she was betraying him, despite nothing more than a kiss happening between them. But something *was* happening, from the way he made her feel to just the thought of spending time with him filling her with joy.

Tyler's eyes drifted across her face as if he was studying her. One hand still touched her bare thigh, teasing and tempting her.

'You want to stop because you slept with this Greek guy. I knew it.' There was an edge to his voice.

'Actually you don't, because I haven't. We've kissed, that's all. I didn't want to be doing this with you even before I met Adonis.'

'Well, that's charming.'

'We're wrong for each other. I know that sounds harsh after we've just spent an enjoyable couple of hours together... But if you can't see it by now—'

'Maybe you can't see how right we are. We always make each other feel better...'

'You're just talking about sex.'

'So? What's wrong with that?'

Everything, Harlow wanted to scream. His assumption that they should do it just because they had many times before was exactly the problem.

'We have a connection, Harlow.' His eyes didn't waver from hers. 'You can't deny that. Plus, we've always looked out for each other. Always.'

Harlow tore her eyes away as a rush of emotion flooded through her. She knew exactly what he was talking about. But they couldn't keep doing this; they couldn't keep dredging up the past as if it was the reason why they should be together now, not when it felt so wrong. What upset her the most was the tiny voice inside telling her it was so right too.

'I do care, Tyler, I really do. That's why we have to break this cycle.' She stood, the movement forcing him to drop his hand. 'We're done; we both need to move on.' She leaned down and kissed his cheek, not wanting to storm out, because deep down she cared for him. She'd always cared for him, but it didn't make how he'd treated her right.

25

Are you free this evening?

Harlow's heart pounded as she stared at the message from Adonis. She should have messaged him before now; she felt guilty for not having done so, as if she was trying to hide what had happened with Tyler. Her fingers hovered over her phone.

It's my mum's birthday and she's having a last-minute party, wanted to invite you if you fancy it? It's going to be at the hotel beach bar this evening.

He replied almost immediately.

Sounds great. Will be there.

She sat on the end of her bed and put her head in her hands. Nothing had happened the night before with Tyler beyond him kissing her, and yet, despite her putting an end to it, she felt as though she'd done something wrong. How emotional she felt was made worse by her dad ringing to say goodbye after his and Gina's holiday on Skiathos.

'We've missed your company this week,' he'd said, making Harlow feel even sadder. 'We're looking forward to seeing you when you get back to the UK. Wish your mum a happy birthday from us.'

Harlow saw Tyler at breakfast and they did their usual thing of saying hello, then completely ignoring what had happened the evening before as they headed to the Glossa set for the day. Back at the hotel, she had a swim in the villa pool before getting ready for the party.

With the sunset, Harlow began to feel flustered about everyone being at the beach bar together. Was it a mistake to have invited Adonis? Not only would Tyler be there but her mum would be too. She was making a rare appearance at the hotel rather than inviting only a select few to her villa in the hills.

However, it was too late to change her mind now. And anyway, Harlow wanted to see him.

* * *

The night air thumped with the beat of the music carried from the beach bar. Laughter and chatter reached Harlow as she waited on the shadowed path for Adonis. He'd messaged to say he'd parked and she decided to wait for him so he didn't have to walk into a bar full of strangers. She was surprised he'd even wanted to come; she was pretty certain he wouldn't relish the idea of being surrounded by actors and a film crew all evening. She wondered if he'd said yes just to see her. A rush of joy was immediately replaced by guilt over the stupid kiss with Tyler.

From the path, she could see the bar was packed. Her mum was at the centre, wearing a low-cut maxi dress and bright red lipstick with a glass of champagne clasped in her hand. Dominic and

Crystal were next to her, their arms around each other's waists, their laughter loud and attention-seeking. Tyler was standing with Jim and another of the assistant directors, while Olivia was sitting at a table with the production assistants looking miserable. Manda was with the make-up team. Harlow hoped it wasn't going to be this cliquey all evening.

Her hands were sweating. She really shouldn't have invited Adonis; it was asking for trouble. She wasn't sure how she should introduce him to her mum. The evening she'd spent with him and his family had been so easy and happy. They were a family who were relaxed around each other, sharing food, drink and laughter. She'd been welcomed with open arms, while here she was dreading what her mum would do or say.

'You look gorgeous.'

Lost in her thoughts, she hadn't noticed Adonis walking towards her.

He kissed her on both cheeks.

'Hey,' she said quietly. She longed to lead him through the dark wood to Panormos and away from anyone she knew. 'Are you sure you're okay doing this?'

'It's good to make myself do things and here is familiar. It'll be fine.'

He took her hand and she took a deep breath. She led the way to the beach bar.

They were met by a barrage of hellos from the crew and immediately swept up into the party atmosphere. A gin and tonic was placed in her hand and a beer was passed to Adonis. Manda welcomed them to her table and Harlow relaxed because Adonis seemed to be enjoying the attentive company of the make-up ladies.

It took nearly an hour for Maeve to make a beeline for Harlow. The drinks had been flowing, 'Happy Birthday' had been sung and the cake cut. Adonis had gone to the bar and Harlow had just finished talking to Crystal.

'Happy birthday, Mum.'

Maeve clinked her glass of champagne against Harlow's G&T. 'Thank you, and thank you for this.' She jangled the silver bracelet on her wrist. 'Is that the farmer?' She nodded towards the bar.

'He runs The Olive Grove with his father, yes.'

'He doesn't look like a farmer.'

Here we go, Harlow thought. 'What do you know about farmers?'

'My ex-parents-in-law are farmers.'

'I know they are.' Harlow shrugged. 'But it's not like you spent any real time with them.'

'You've been keeping quiet about him.' Maeve raised a perfectly manicured eyebrow and ignored Harlow's dig.

'There's nothing to say, except we've spent a bit of time together.'

'I bet you have.'

And there it was, just one of the many things that was wrong with their relationship, her *mum* insinuating that the time Harlow and Adonis had been spending together was far from innocent. No wonder Harlow had always tried to keep things from her. She remembered what Manda had said, that if her mum had spent the evening with Adonis, there'd have been plenty of gossip.

'Well, enjoy him while you have the chance,' Maeve said smoothly before sidling off to join Jim and the director.

Harlow clenched her fist and downed the rest of her gin.

'You look like you're in a world of your own.' Manda hooked her arm in Harlow's.

'Sorry, just been talking to Mum.'

'Say no more.'

'I don't understand how she manages to make me feel like shit so easily.'

'She's had plenty of practice from what you've said.' She squeezed her arm tighter. 'Ignore her and try to let it wash over you. Now, where's that Greek God of yours?'

Harlow laughed. 'You're incessant.'

'He was a hit with the girls, and I don't mean just 'cause of the way he looks. He comes across as a really nice guy.'

'That's because he is.'

When she looked over, Harlow realised Adonis wasn't at the bar any longer. She scanned the tanned and flushed faces of her work colleagues packing the outside bar. Her heart dropped when she finally laid eyes on him. He had his back to her, his broad shoulders, deep tan and dark hair now familiar. He was standing next to Tyler. Olivia was with them too. It seemed as though Tyler was doing all the talking, which made her palms sweat again.

'You look worried,' Manda said.

'Adonis is talking to Tyler.'

'Oh. *Oh*,' Manda repeated with an understanding of Harlow's concern.

Harlow was about to go and join Adonis when her mum strode back over, with Jim close behind.

'Harlow, I cannot for the life of me remember what I did for my fiftieth. Jim was asking. Do you remember?'

'Seriously, you don't?'

Maeve shook her head and her long earrings jangled against her neck.

'You had a pool party at your old house in LA during the day and went out somewhere with friends in the evening.'

'You were there?'

'Yeah, I was there.' Harlow shook her head in disbelief.

Jim looked at Maeve and laughed. 'You've just come over to ask Harlow what you did for your birthday – how could you not remember her being there?'

'There was a lot going on back then.' She waved her hand dismissively.

Harlow was beginning to like Jim. 'It was the summer I stayed with you in LA when you set up auditions for me despite knowing I was working as an assistant director,' Harlow continued.

'Huh, I'd forgotten about that. I figured you might just change your mind when you saw the opportunities Hollywood could offer.'

'I saw plenty of what it offered, but I wasn't interested in leading that life. But, yeah, that's what you did for your fiftieth, although you were pretty drunk by mid-morning, so I'm not really surprised you don't remember.'

'Well, I'll remember this one and it's not even a big birthday.'

'We could have had a pool party at your villa,' Jim said.

'We still can; the night is yet young.'

Harlow resisted rolling her eyes. She caught Manda's sympathetic look before she clocked Adonis weaving his way across the bar towards the path.

'Hold on a minute.' She left them and cut across the terrace, jogging to catch up with him. 'Hey, you're leaving already?'

'I'm staying at my aunt's.' He carried on walking. His tone was similar to the way he'd talked to her when she'd confronted him in the bar all those weeks ago.

'Adonis, what's wrong?'

He carried on walking beyond the first villa, stopped and looked at her with a clenched jaw. The moody, brooding look was back and it briefly crossed her mind that he'd never looked hotter, but the way he was glaring worried her.

'Do you think I'm a fool because I've been so sheltered, always living on this island?'

'What are you talking about?'

'My first impression of you was right.'

'What?'

'You work in movies and do what you like, mess people around.'

'I literally have no idea what you're talking about.'

'You and Tyler.'

A coldness flooded through her, the image of Adonis and Tyler talking together fresh in her mind. 'What about me and Tyler?'

'That you're together.'

'We're not. It's really not—'

'Please don't try to deny it. It's probably just as well I found out now before anything else happened between us.' He continued walking up the path.

Harlow wanted to run after him, to take him in her arms and tell him that whatever he'd heard wasn't true, except it wasn't that straightforward. She had been involved with Tyler and she had kissed him yesterday – even if it was him instigating it, she hadn't said no straight away. What a mess.

Adonis disappeared beyond the whitewashed villa and she was left standing alone on the path. She'd been looking forward to seeing him and now Tyler had ruined everything. And for what? To get back at her? After such a lovely couple of hours, Harlow was left with regret and intense anger tearing at her insides.

26

Harlow's eyes blurred with tears as she walked back through the grounds towards the beach bar. By staying at his aunt's, had Adonis's intention been to spend the night with her? She knew she'd wanted to – if she'd had the courage to suggest it – but of course Tyler mouthing off to Adonis had put an end to that. She clenched her fists. She'd put up with so much crap from Tyler over the last few weeks. He'd gone a step too far this time.

He was still in the bar. Olivia was nowhere in sight and neither was her mum.

Tyler must have sensed her rage because he left the table and his drinking buddies and met Harlow before she'd made it halfway across the terrace.

'What the hell did you say to him?'

Tyler held up his hands. 'Woah, calm down, Harlow.'

'Don't you dare tell me to calm down, not when you've messed up the one good thing that's happened to me in a long time.'

'It wasn't so much what I said. Olivia kinda put her foot in it. She seems to be as pissed at you as she is at me.'

'And why's that then?'

He shrugged.

'Are you actually enjoying this?'

'Of course not.'

'Then why don't you wipe that smug look off your face.'

Tyler took her arm and leaned closer. 'Let's take this somewhere quieter, shall we.'

He led her from the bar on to the beach, away from prying eyes, which was probably a good thing as there was already too much gossip. It was quieter and darker, the voices from the bar muffled by the surf hitting the pebbles, but Harlow couldn't shrug off the feeling of being watched. A couple were snogging on one of the sun loungers, so they retreated back up the beach to the hotel grounds.

Tyler paced ahead. Harlow caught up with him. 'What did you say to Olivia?'

'I might have suggested that me and you still had a thing for each other.'

'Oh for God's sake, Tyler.'

'It seemed the easiest way to let her down lightly, make her see that it was just a one-night thing, that me and you were messing around too.'

'We're not though.'

Tyler abruptly stopped next to a rose bush. 'We used to a lot though.'

'*Used to*, Tyler. You've just said it yourself.' Harlow shook her head and swept on past the blue-lit pool towards Villa Aegean.

Tyler matched her pace. 'I didn't think she was going to get all psycho about it or mouth off to your holiday fling.'

'He's not a fling. And you had absolutely no right to say anything to her, not even about our past, let alone make up a load of rubbish because things got awkward.'

She flung the main door to the villa open and took the stairs two at a time. She heard Tyler following behind. She didn't want to be anywhere near him, but they needed to talk this through. *She* needed to get what was bugging her off her chest. She reached the second floor and unlocked her room. She held the door open and waited for Tyler.

'We're not done talking,' she said as he appeared at the top of the stairs.

He brushed past her without a word. Harlow closed the door and stood in the centre of the room while Tyler made himself comfortable on the sofa.

'So he's more than a fling?' he asked.

'I don't know what he is, but I like him a lot. And you, sleeping with Olivia and not being able to keep your mouth shut about stuff you had no right to talk to anyone about has messed things up completely.'

'What the hell does it matter if he knows we've slept together?'

'Because if Olivia insinuated it was *still* happening that makes it seem like I've been messing him around.'

'Huh, you're actually serious about him.'

Harlow folded her arms.

'You kissed me the other night and you've slept with him… I can see how this is ending up a bit of a nightmare for you.'

'That kiss the other night, you know exactly what that was.'

'Yeah yeah, for old times' sake and all that…'

'Exactly like you keep suggesting. It was a mistake and you took me by surprise. Me and you, we do this, fall into the trap of it being familiar when all it does is mess with our heads. You can't do this, Tyler. You can't treat people like dirt. And I'm not just talking about me, Olivia too.'

Tyler stared at the floor and shook his head. When he looked up, her heart softened a little at how emotional he seemed. 'Look, I'm sorry. I shouldn't have used you to push her away.'

'It's what you do though, isn't it? You always do this; we get close, then you shut down. It's the same since we've been here, you playing games, all this teasing, blaming me because of who my mum is, yet in the next breath you're trying to sleep with me. When I think about it, you've been pushing me away for years. This, us' – she motioned between them – 'is messed up. And the crazy thing is, you don't want to be with me, yet it seems you don't want me to be with anyone else either. Ask yourself why we've never been a real couple.'

'I've never said I don't want to be with you, Harlow.'

'Yes, you have!' She wanted to scream at him for how he couldn't see how he'd behaved. 'I told you this the day we had the puncture.' She took a deep breath and tried to keep calm. 'The last time we slept together you suggested our relationship was very much one of convenience and sex. We've both known this for a long time, except it had been built on a foundation of friendship and trust, but the way you've behaved and the things you've said since being here, has destroyed all of that. So honestly, Tyler, I really don't believe you when you say you want to be with me in a serious way.'

'But I do, Harlow.' He stood up and came over to her. 'All this pushing you away is because I've been confused about my feelings. I have been for a long time. The stronger the feelings I have for you, the stronger my gut reaction is to run away. Maybe I'm scared of rejection, fearful of commitment... I don't know.'

'Or do you just want to be with me to further your career? Well, do you?'

'You know that's not the reason.'

Harlow shrugged. 'Maybe that's true because I'm nothing. I'm no one. An assistant location manager who happens to have a famous mum.'

'I hate how you see yourself. You're so much more. You're more to me than that.'

'But I also remind you of your problems. You've said as much.

What we are is messy and complicated and...' She ran her hand across her furrowed brow, uncertain how to explain.

'You saved me.' He took her hand. 'Making me go to rehab, being there for me when I was a total mess. Making hard decisions, even when you risked me hating you for it.'

'So you're punishing me now?'

'That was never my intention. I've been angry and not known how to deal with my emotions. You remind me of what *I've* done wrong. I find it difficult to separate how I really feel about you with the way I feel when I'm around you. And I've probably taken things out on you because you're the closest person to me... because I love you.'

His words were like a slap in the face. Deep down weren't they the exact three words she'd wanted to hear from him for more than a decade? Weren't they the words that had been on the tip of her tongue many times over the years? He'd drunkenly said them the night she'd found him stumbling about outside, but a drunken 'I love you' meant nothing. Now he'd said them when relatively sober... And they left her feeling... nothing. She felt numb. Yet she did love him, she always had done, but she wasn't *in love* with him. She suspected it was the same for him.

She removed her hand from his. 'I'm not sure you really mean that.'

'We have too much history to walk away from each other, Harlow.'

'That shouldn't mean we carry on the way we are just because we have in the past.'

'I'm not suggesting we carry on the way we have been. I mean, you know, a proper—'

'A proper relationship?' Harlow scoffed. 'I'm not sure you know the meaning of the word.'

'That's unfair. How's your track record when it comes to your love life?'

'It's always been okay until I'm around you.'

'Ouch.'

'I'm only telling the truth. I've met someone here who I really like and who makes me feel good about myself... He makes me feel a lot of things. But being here with you, and you gossiping to your... I don't know what she is, has ensured a perfectly healthy relationship has blown up in my face.'

'Well, sorry about that, but you didn't have to kiss me back last night.'

'I stopped it from going any further though.' *For the first time ever*, she thought. She needed to break the toxic cycle of their on/off relationship. It wasn't doing either of them any good. And yet, she didn't want to destroy their friendship. 'I've always loved you, Tyler. I love you like you're family, unconditionally, however you behave. Whatever you say to me doesn't change that. But I'm not in love with you.'

'Have you ever been?'

'I don't know; there was a time when it felt like we had something special. Things have changed over the years for both of us.' A lump formed in her throat as she looked at him. 'You saved me too, remember. I feel I owe you.'

'That was a long time ago. You owe me nothing; what I did was what any decent bloke would have done. What a friend would do. Anyway, you paid me back ten times over by helping me get clean.' He wrapped his arms around her and kissed her gently on the top of her head. 'If it wasn't for you intervening, paying for me to get help, persuading me to go to rehab, I don't think I'd be here now.'

'But it was my fault you ended up like that in the first place...' A sob caught in her throat.

'What *he* tried to do to *you* is not your fault, Harlow. You can't ever think about it like that.' He held her close, emotion shuddering through him as much as it was her.

'If we're to stay friends, you really need to think hard about how you treat me,' she said quietly, her voice muffled against his shoulder. 'I think you need to go now.'

He released her. Tears glistened on his cheeks. He ran his hand across his stubbled jaw, looked as if he was about to say something else, then walked to the door and left.

Harlow felt wrung out, emotionally and physically. She hated how upset Adonis had been earlier and now she'd hurt Tyler too. So much for her and Adonis making a promise to challenge each other; so much for them spending what little time they had left together. Manda and Gina were both right about how toxic she and Tyler were together, yet their history was like an umbilical cord connecting them. That connection had just screwed up a potential relationship with Adonis. Somehow she had to make it right.

* * *

Harlow lay in bed and stared up at the ceiling. With the balcony doors open, she could hear the sea and the sounds of the hotel drifting in. Tyler hadn't gone back to his room. After he'd left, she'd heard him clatter down the stairs. Perhaps he was going back to the bar to carry on drinking. What she'd said was true – she loved him like family, so she couldn't just stop worrying about him. But what she was most concerned about now was Adonis and what he was thinking. Worry tumbled through her head that he'd believed Tyler over her. She gave up trying to sleep. She got out of bed, slipped on shorts, a vest top and flip-flops and left her room determined to sort the situation out.

It was gone midnight and the music and voices that had been drifting across from the beach bar had eased. She didn't meet anyone leaving the villa and she hadn't heard Tyler come back either.

The path that led to the hotel reception was quiet, but an occasional voice or peal of laughter filtered into the night and a few room lights still glowed. Harlow reached the reception building and walked further along until she could see the balcony that ran the length of Ereni's apartment. It was empty. There was a light on inside, but it was faint. She stood with her hands on her hips and shook her head. What was she expecting? That it would be like a scene from *Mamma Mia!* or *Romeo and Juliet* and Adonis would be standing there gazing at her adoringly? However angry she was at herself, at Tyler, at poor Olivia, the idea of trying to put things right with Adonis in the middle of the night was foolish. She started to walk back.

'Harlow?'

Panicked, she turned. Ereni was in a dressing gown standing in the open doorway of the hotel reception.

'Are you okay?' she asked. 'I saw you out here. It is late.'

'Yes, I know. I'm sorry. I came to see if I could speak to Adonis, then thought better of it.'

Ereni nodded slowly. She wrapped her dressing gown tighter and wandered out into the night. 'He seemed... upset when he got here. He not say much. That's not unusual, but I think something is wrong. You had an argument?'

'Yeah.'

'He went to bed, but you can come up and see if he's awake...'

'Oh goodness no, it's probably best if I leave it tonight. I'll talk to him when he's had a chance to calm down.'

'Do you want to talk to me?' She reached a hand out and touched Harlow's arm. 'Adonis say you don't talk to your mama much. If you need someone, I'm a good listener.'

'He talks to you a lot?'

'Ah, you know, as much as any grown man talks. He is better than my brother at least. But, yes, sometimes he talk to me.'

Harlow glanced up at the dark balcony and wondered if he was asleep yet. Had he been playing out their argument over and over in his head like she had?

'We had a misunderstanding. It's difficult to explain and I feel awful because perhaps if I'd been open with him sooner about what my relationship with someone was, we wouldn't have been in this mess.'

Ereni's eyebrows furrowed. Harlow knew she wasn't making much sense, but she wasn't prepared to go through all the sordid details with Adonis's aunt.

Ereni lowered her voice. 'He is afraid. Afraid of losing someone he cares for again, the same as he lost his mama. You understand?'

Harlow nodded as she fought back tears. 'The last thing I wanted to do was hurt him.'

'He likes you. I see the change in him since he spend time with you. He's been happy – it is good to see. If what happened to upset him is only a misunderstanding, then tell him. Make it right. If there is truth in what happened, then don't hurt him more. I cannot stand to see that. Understand?' she said softly.

'I understand.'

'Now, it is late and we both need to sleep. *Kalinychta*.' She kissed Harlow on both cheeks and walked back towards the building.

'Ereni,' Harlow said before she disappeared inside. 'I really like him too.'

Ereni smiled and waved goodnight.

27

Despite going to bed late and sleeping fitfully, Harlow woke early. Apart from at last night's party, she'd barely seen Manda all week. They'd arranged to have breakfast together, but that wasn't for another couple of hours. She was hot and still annoyed with herself, but mostly annoyed with Tyler for allowing the situation to arise in the first place.

Instead of fighting to get back to sleep and getting more annoyed, she got up and went for a run. She loved the peace of the early morning. The break of dawn sent a wash of silver-pink across the sea. The backdrop of trees had a calming effect, so by the time she'd run along the forest path to Panormos and back, she felt less wound up and more able to face the day.

She'd only just got out of the shower when there was a knock on her room door. She sighed and tightened her towel. If it was Tyler wanting to continue last night's conversation, then she would send him packing.

She opened the door ready to give him an earful, only to be confronted with Adonis.

'Hey,' she said, taken aback.

'Sorry.' He briefly glanced down. 'I should have messaged... I can come back.'

'It's okay.' She stood back and let him in. He looked fresh-faced, as if he'd had a decent sleep, and as gorgeous as ever in jeans and a tight T-shirt. 'Do you mind if I quickly get dressed?'

'Of course not.'

No way was she going to have a conversation in just a towel.

Flustered, she grabbed knickers and the first clothes she came to in the wardrobe and shut herself in the en suite. Her heart raced. He wasn't doing the sultry, glowering thing that he had been doing last night; he seemed calm and wanted to talk. She threw the skirt and top on, unwound the towel from her head and ran her fingers through her damp hair.

She left the steamy en suite. 'I'm really sorry about everything that happened last night.'

Adonis was standing by the open balcony doors looking out. He turned and held up his hands. 'Ereni told me you came by last night and wanted to talk. She suggested I talk to you and maybe that I, how do you say it in English? Jumped to con...'

'Conclusions.'

'Exactly. So, do you want to tell me what's going on?'

Harlow perched on the end of the bed and Adonis sat on the sofa. He rested his arms on his knees and watched her expectantly. She breathed deeply; this was her chance to put things right, but she also knew she needed to tell the truth about her relationship with Tyler. If Adonis didn't like it, there would be no way forward for them anyway, although with the days ticking by, she wasn't sure what kind of future they could have. But if she wanted to find out, she needed to do this.

'Tyler and I have a long and complicated history. We met on the first day of film school when we were eighteen. We were in the same student accommodation and became friends quickly – I mean, like really good friends. He was someone I could talk to and tell anything to.' She stumbled, feeling her cheeks flush, not really wanting to divulge more to Adonis. 'Let's just say our friendship soon turned to something more than just friends.'

'You were boyfriend and girlfriend.'

'Not exactly.'

Adonis frowned.

'We were friends with benefits...'

'I thought, why would you want to be with me when he's from your world and I'm just the son of a farmer?'

'And I'm the granddaughter of a farmer and the daughter of a teacher.'

'And a movie producer.'

'Trust me, I have more in common with my dad's side of the family. And you should be proud of your heritage and what you and your dad do for a living.' Harlow clenched her hands in her lap. Tension whitened her knuckles. She wondered how she could make him understand the truth of how she felt about him. 'Have you ever felt that connection with someone – I don't know how to describe it. An understanding or a feeling of wanting to spend all your time with that person.'

'I have friends, good, close friends, and there have been girls over the years, but no one I feel like that with.' He held her gaze. 'Until you.'

Harlow's heart fluttered. 'And I feel the same about you. I want to spend time with you. I was so happy you were there last night. The last thing I wanted to do was upset you. And honestly, it's not what you think with Tyler.'

'But that girl—'

'Olivia?'

Adonis nodded. 'She was very clear what you are to each other.'

'What we *were*.'

'So you didn't kiss him the other night?'

'Well, I, um... We'd had a bit to drink and he kissed me. He took me by surprise, but I put a stop to it. I promise you.'

'But why were you with him?'

'I wasn't "with him" in the sense you mean. We had a drink together after a long and difficult couple of days and one drink turned to a few. He's been my friend for a long time.'

'But you've already said you were more than friends.'

'Our relationship was... how can I put it.' It was ridiculous how hard she was finding it to explain the intimacy of her relationship with Tyler. Just the thought of saying the words out loud made her feel like she was cheating on him.

'You slept together.'

And now he'd said it for her. 'Yes. Many times over the years.'

'I get it.' He held up his hands, a glimmer of a smile beginning to creep on to his face.

'The last time was two years ago. Apart from the other night when he made a move, nothing has happened. And I don't want anything to. Not any longer. That's not to say that I don't value his friendship, because I do, but how we behave with each other has to change. He had a one-night stand with Olivia. She wanted more, he didn't, so he used me and our past as an excuse not to see her any more. She was understandably hurt and has taken it out on me. I'm sorry you ended up in the middle of all of this. I would have told you if I thought it was something you ne—'

A knock at the door stopped her mid-sentence.

Please, please, please let that not be Tyler, Harlow thought.

'Harlow? You still asleep?'

Manda. Panic over. She mouthed 'sorry' to Adonis.

Harlow opened the door a crack.

'Hey, sleepyhead,' Manda said. 'You coming for breakfast?'

'Yeah, I will. Can I meet you there? Give me ten minutes.'

Manda looked at her thoughtfully, then broke into a grin. 'Do you have company?' she said under her breath.

'It's not what you think.'

'O-M-G,' she mouthed, and then whispered, 'Take your time.'

Harlow closed the door and turned back. 'That was Manda. I'm supposed to be having breakfast with her.'

Adonis came over and slipped his arms around her waist. His fingers caressed the bare skin beneath her top. 'I'll go so you can join her.'

Pressed against his firm body with his lips inches from hers, the last thing she wanted was for him to leave.

'You don't have to.' She let her arms rest on his shoulders and gazed into his eyes. 'Trust me, she'll more than understand if she has to wait a while.'

'I got angry too quick last night.' He leaned closer and rested his forehead against hers. 'I find it hard to let people in. I fear getting hurt again, of losing someone.'

'Your aunt said something along those lines.' She closed her eyes. His fingers caressed slowly upwards, tickling and teasing. 'I didn't mean to upset you. I really like you.'

Harlow tugged him closer and they kissed. Their tongues explored as his hands smoothed across her bare back. The more they kissed, the more Harlow wanted. Breakfast was the last thing on her mind. Manda wouldn't care one bit if Harlow rocked up late with some serious gossip, or didn't rock up at all...

Adonis pulled away and gazed at her. 'I'm so sorry. I really have to go.' His breathing was fast. His hands remained hot against her bare skin. Still held tight against him, it was apparent just how much he didn't want to go. 'I'm late already and Baba needs me back. Come over this evening though and have dinner. Maybe we can carry on with this...'

Harlow grinned and they kissed again. She could think of nothing better.

* * *

Over breakfast, Harlow filled Manda in on the events of the past couple of days. If she was disappointed that Harlow didn't have more gossip about what had happened with Adonis in her room, she hid it well. Harlow was relieved to not see Tyler or Olivia.

At Manda's insistence, she packed a bag and joined her and some of the costume and make-up girls on Panormos Beach for a day of sunbathing, swimming and reading.

Despite the beauty of the location and the bliss of being able to relax on a beach instead of working in the heat, Harlow found herself wishing the day away. All she could think about was Adonis and continuing what they'd started that morning.

After another shower and changing into a short daisy-print dress and white trainers, she packed clean underwear and her wash things into her bag. She drove all the way to The Olive Grove with a smile on her face, eager to spend the evening with him away from the hotel and everyone there.

Harlow parked and walked beneath the archway of vines towards the restaurant glowing in the darkness.

'I thought I heard you arrive.' Adonis was waiting outside, a big smile on his face.

'Hey,' Harlow said as she reached him.

He kissed her, took her hand and led her along the path.

'We're not eating in the restaurant then?'

'No, we're not.'

Instead of leading her towards the villa, he took the path that ran in front of his workshop and into the orchard. The nearly full moon did a good job of lighting their way along the path beneath the trees. The chatter from the restaurant terrace ebbed away the further they walked.

A picnic blanket was laid out on the edge of the meadow and a handful of lanterns hung in the branches of a fig tree, pooling light through the leaves on to the grass.

'We had them left over from a birthday party Ereni organised at the hotel,' Adonis said, pointing at the colourfully lit tree.

'It's beautiful.'

Harlow sat down on the blanket. The night was sultry, but the faintest of breezes reached them high on the hill. Glossa glowed below, while out in the blackness of the Aegean, the towns on Skiathos twinkled. Apart from the call of an owl and the cicadas, it was utterly peaceful, the light breeze barely rustling the leaves.

'I thought we'd do something different.'

'It's magical. Even though I know there's a restaurant full of people back there, it feels like we're the only ones for miles.' Nobody had ever done anything like this for her before.

'Baba and Yiayia are up at the house too,' Adonis said smiling.

'What do they think of this?'

'Baba is not impressed.' He shrugged. 'But Yiayia said it's romantic.'

'Your yiayia is right.'

'I know.' He opened up a wicker basket and started taking out bowls of food and packages wrapped in greaseproof paper. 'I hope you're hungry.' He handed her a fork and motioned to all the food spread out.

Harlow had purposefully not had much lunch. She hadn't been hungry anyway; the heat of midday hadn't helped, nor the fluttering in her stomach at the thought of seeing Adonis later. She was starving now and happy to tuck in. There were squares of spanakopita, as well as a sweet cinnamon and sugar pastry, along with a variety of meze dishes, like creamy spiced feta, rice-stuffed vine leaves and chunks of sweet watermelon. Adonis fed her olives and wiped away the watermelon juice dribbling down her chin. Their hands brushed against each other, teasing and tempting, reminding Harlow of the desire she'd felt that morning.

Harlow rested back on one hand with her legs outstretched. Adonis's shoulder touched hers. He was sexy and handsome, but he also came across as dependable, thoughtful and sensitive, not just emotionally but how he thought about others. He'd been a hit with Manda and the girls the night before, yet he was definitely more comfortable in an environment far removed from the glamour of the hotel and the movie.

Adonis poured the wine into two glasses, handed her one and tapped his glass against hers.

'You should do this for guests,' Harlow said. 'A picnic in the orchard or the olive grove. People would pay good money for it. The solitude, the romance, the peace.'

'I have thought about it before, but...' He sighed.

'But what?'

'Baba.'

'Doesn't like the idea?'

'I don't know.'

'You've not suggested it?'

'He's not very open to change.'

'But there are things you'd like to do?'

'Of course.'

They sipped the wine in thoughtful silence, kept company by the owl and an occasional rustle in the undergrowth.

Adonis packed away the picnic and they lay back, resting on a couple of cushions, gazing up at the star-sprinkled sky. Adonis's hand found hers. She was acutely aware of her heart beating, of her hand in his resting against his firm stomach. She didn't want the moment to end as much as she didn't want her time on Skopelos to be over either.

'There are lots of things I want to do.' Adonis moved a little to face her. 'The olive harvest with tourists, cookery and woodworking workshops...'

Harlow shifted until she was gazing into his eyes. A moth fluttered around one of the lamps in the branches above. Adonis stroked his hand across her cheek to her collarbone, skimming her arm and coming to rest on her hip.

He kissed her. Whatever else he wanted to do with The Olive Grove would have to wait for another time. Kissing Adonis beneath the lantern-lit tree was perfect. Harlow tried not to worry about what would happen when the shoot came to an end and she headed home.

They moved closer, their hands dipping beneath clothes, caressing warm skin. A goat bleated and they pulled away, laughing. Harlow felt flushed and heady from the wine, from his touch, from being this close to him.

'Remember what we promised the other week.' Adonis rested on his elbow and gazed at her. 'I know what you should do, before you leave.'

'Oh yeah, what?'

'Talk to your mum. Tell her exactly how you feel about... about everything.'

Harlow shook her head. 'You're mad. It's such a bad idea.'

'It's a promise, remember.' He tickled her sides and kissed her again.

'Okay, fine. If we're doing this and you're going to hold me to that, I have a challenge for you too.'

'Okay.'

'I think you should leave the island.'

Adonis shook his head. 'I can't, you know I—'

Harlow held a finger to his lips. 'You said for us to do something that scares us. This is what scares you. Do you think I want to talk to my mum and open up old wounds, create new ones?'

'It's just talking, Harlow.'

'You might think that's what it is, but I know it will be anything but talking – arguing, yes, probably shouting, hating each other.'

'I can't leave though.'

'Yes you can, for a short time, I'm sure you can.'

'What good will that do?'

'It's a break, a new experience. But maybe the first step is to talk to your dad about the way you feel. Maybe tell him your ideas about this place.'

'I can't...'

'It's just talking,' she said with a sly grin.

Adonis laughed and they left the conversation there. They folded up the blanket and walked back through the orchard, Adonis holding the picnic basket and her hand. They got to the paved area by his workshop and slowed as they reached the villa. Warm light pooled from its windows, inviting in the darkness.

'Stay the night.' Adonis's hand tensed in hers, but he held her gaze.

Harlow nodded. It was a no-brainer.

They went inside and Adonis left the basket and blanket in the kitchen. The sound of a TV filtered from one of the rooms off the hallway.

'Adoni, *esý eísai*?' Stephanos called from the back room.

'*Naí*, Baba.'

Adonis motioned to Harlow to follow and they clattered up the stairs together, past the guest room she'd stayed in last time and into Adonis's room at the end of the landing. He closed the door behind them.

'Baba will start talking; Yiayia will ask questions...' He drew her to him.

She kissed him, wanting nothing more than to be alone with him, wanting to forget all about his family downstairs.

'I tell you what really scares me,' she said. 'Leaving this island and saying goodbye to you.'

He took her face in his hands. 'That scares me too, but—'

With a kiss, she stopped either of them saying more. She slipped her hands beneath his T-shirt and prised it off, dropping it on the floor and sliding her hands up the firm chest she'd admired the first time she'd laid eyes on him.

He made light work of her dress, tugging it off over her head, kicking off his shorts and leading her to his bed. They lay down together, their bare skin hot and sticking to each other as they explored, kissed and removed what was left of their clothes.

Adonis's beard tickled as his lips travelled toe-curlingly slowly from her neck downwards, lingering on her breasts, trailing across her stomach, teasing more and more the lower he got. Harlow closed her eyes and gripped the edges of the pillow, her breath shallow, perspiration erupting on her skin as Adonis's lips explored.

Footsteps thudded on the stairs.

'Adoni!'

Stephanos.

Adonis looked up from between Harlow's thighs, grinned and held a finger to his lips.

'Adoni!' Stephanos again, an edge of panic to his voice.

'*Óchi tóra*, Baba!'

Harlow bit her lip to stop herself from laughing out loud.

'*I yiayiá sou. Voítheia*!'

Adonis's smile disappeared.

'What's wrong?' Harlow asked.

'I don't know. My yiayia.'

He slid off the bed, put on his shorts and left the room.

Harlow sat up. She suddenly felt incredibly naked and vulnerable, alone in Adonis's room, everywhere still tingling from his touch. She looked around and scooped up her knickers from the floor. She found her dress, turned it the right way and put it on too.

Now what?

Adonis had left the door open and voices filtered up. Urgent, strained voices. It was no good, she couldn't hide away upstairs while there was some kind of family emergency going on. She slipped on her trainers and crept downstairs.

Adonis was pacing the hallway with his mobile clamped to his ear, the strain in his voice evident even though she didn't understand a word he was saying. Stephanos was kneeling next to Adonis's yiayia who was lying awkwardly in the doorway, blood pooling on to the stone floor from a gash in her head.

28

Everything seemed to be conspiring against her. First Tyler and his big mouth and now Adonis's yiayia. Except Harlow felt horribly guilty as soon as the thought popped into her head. Adonis had lost his beloved mama when he was only a teen and now she was upset that her night with him hadn't gone to plan because his poor grandmother had collapsed. She berated herself, but was still conscious that the time she had on Skopelos was slipping away. She wanted to hold on to it, slow it down, perhaps stop time entirely. And she wanted to erase Adonis's pain. She desperately wanted his grandmother to be okay, not for her benefit, but for his. The glimpses of sorrow she'd seen in the short time she'd known him were heartbreaking.

On top of that, she'd suggested he leave the island, the one thing he couldn't do, particularly now. Would she have felt the same if she'd grown up in a different way? If her parents hadn't split, if her mum hadn't spent her life travelling the world and socialising with famous people, and if she'd grown up in a place like her grandparents' farm – peaceful, secluded, with a slower pace of life.

Perhaps then she'd find it just as hard to leave behind family and the memories associated with the place.

And wasn't what Adonis had everything she'd ever wanted? A permanent place to call home? Her childhood home had been sold when her parents divorced. It was where she'd felt safe and grounded. Even if her mum had been absent, her dad had always been there, dependable and loving, but once the divorce happened, she had to split her time between parents. It was agreed Harlow would stay with her mum two days a week unless she was working away, which happened frequently. Having been used to a mother who rarely spent time with her, it was a shock to be alone with her without her dad. And then he met Gina and was happy again, while Harlow struggled.

Her dad had at least waited until she was eighteen and at MetFilm School to move to Norwich for a new teaching job and to buy a forever home with Gina in the north Norfolk countryside.

Becoming an adult changed things further. Harlow was tied to her mum, first as a film student in London, supported by her when she, Tyler and a couple of other friends moved into a house her mum owned. After that, she'd never been able to shrug off her mum's influence. Her dad, Gina and the girls felt like a distant dream, the same as her grandparents in Yorkshire, somewhere that felt homely, safe and welcoming. She'd never managed to find another place that gave her that kind of feeling. Not until she'd come to Skopelos. Was it selfish of her to tell Adonis to leave?

Adonis's yiayia had been taken by ambulance to the island hospital after her collapse. Adonis and Stephanos had gone with her. With tears in his eyes, Adonis had kissed Harlow goodbye and apologised profusely, which made her long for him even more. She'd cried her eyes out on the lonely drive back to the hotel. She'd cried for Adonis and the hurt he was feeling; she cried for his yiayia and hoped that she'd pull through. She even cried for grumpy

Stephanos, clearly upset by witnessing his mum hurt herself so badly.

* * *

She woke the next morning with anger churning her stomach at how unfair life was – not because her night with Adonis was interrupted, but because bad things happened to good people. She didn't want Adonis to suffer any more or lose anyone else he loved. Despite the drama of the night before, by late morning he was thoughtful enough to message her and she relaxed a little knowing the worst hadn't happened.

Yiayia's going to be okay. She had a small stroke and a head injury from the fall. I went with her last night to the hospital in Volos on the mainland. Baba had to go back to the farm. I am so sorry how last night ended.

Tears pricked her eyes as she replied.

Oh Adonis, don't be. You concentrate on your yiayia. Sending love and kisses x

She held the phone in her lap. Now what? Her thoughts were with Adonis and the last thing she wanted to do was spend the day surrounded by people. Not even lovely Manda, not today, not when the first thing she'd ask is what happened the night before. Harlow drummed her fingers on the bed. With a fire still raging in her chest, perhaps this was the perfect opportunity to make good on her promise to Adonis.

She messaged her mum.

Do you mind if I come over and see you?

By the time, she'd had a shower her mum had replied.

What's the occasion, Harlow? Of course you can come over.

* * *

'You look pissed off. What have I done?' Maeve emerged from the pool, slicked her hand through her hair and left wet footprints on the pale stone as she padded over to the sun lounger.

'You've done nothing. Today at least,' Harlow muttered under her breath as she walked down the steps and joined her on the middle terrace.

'I didn't get to say goodbye to you on Friday night. I see you went off with that Adonis. Is that his name?' She threw on a floaty kaftan over her wet swimming costume. 'I presume you had a good night?'

Harlow shook her head. 'Things are not quite how you imagine them to be.'

'Oh?' Maeve sat down on the sun lounger and patted the one next to her.

'Life seems to be conspiring against me.'

'You're being cryptic, Harlow. Just tell me straight.'

'Okay, I will, but not about Adonis as that's private. I want to talk about us.'

Maeve opened her mouth to say something and closed it again.

'What about us?' she eventually said as Harlow sat down. 'Do I need a stiff drink for this?'

Probably, Harlow thought, wondering how on earth she was going to start. She took a deep breath. 'I'm not like you, and I don't want to be like you.'

Maeve's nostrils flared. She reached for the bottle of prosecco cooling in an ice bucket, poured herself a glassful and downed it.

'Feeling better?' Harlow asked.

Maeve refilled her glass. 'Where the fuck did that come from?'

'I can't keep doing this, pretending everything's okay and I'm happy with my life, because I'm not. You're constantly interfering, trying to steer my career in the direction *you* want it to go in, making choices for me. You weren't around for most of my childhood, yet in adulthood you've been meddling in everything. Maybe I could understand it if you'd been interested in me when I was growing up, but you chose your career over your child.'

'Oh wow, we're going there, are we?'

'This talk is long overdue.'

'And so you choose now, towards the end of a pressurised shoot to give me an earful about my parenting.' She downed the second glass of prosecco and folded her arms.

'Yeah, I choose now, because being here has given me the time to think about things. Like why you preferred to work rather than spend time with me when I was younger.'

'Don't be ridiculous, Harlow. It's not that I preferred work over you. It's just...' She breathed deeply and steadied herself. 'I much prefer you as an adult.'

'Well, that's charming.'

'I didn't know how to deal with a child. I'm not maternal. Never have been. I've never been someone who gets all mushy over babies, and don't get me started on the hell of toddlers. I much preferred teenage you than toddler you.'

'You liked me being older so you could have parties and live the life you wanted. It was all about you.'

It was difficult to make out her expression behind her oversized sunglasses, but Harlow noticed her knuckles whitening as she gripped the edge of the sun lounger. 'The truth is I didn't want to fail at everything. I made a choice, to concentrate on one aspect of my life I could actually be good at.'

'And you chose work.'

'Yes. Yes, I did. I'd never have been the kind of parent your dad was and still is, and so I chose to be the best I could at my career. If I'd compromised, I wouldn't have got where I am now and I still wouldn't have been a great parent. I'd have failed at both, rather than winning at one and failing at the other.'

'You don't know that, Mum.'

'Oh, but I do, Harlow. I was not cut out for motherhood, not because I didn't love you, because I do, but I didn't know how to mother you. I certainly wasn't a natural like your father.'

'But surely that's the same for every new mother? You've got to learn as you go along.'

'Oh please, that's a load of bull and you know it. Of course it's not the same. I had friends who found the whole experience a breeze while I...' She looked away, her cheeks clenching as though she was trying to steady herself. 'I had postnatal depression. I felt like a failure because I couldn't bond with you. Everything was so hard. You cried constantly; *I* cried constantly. And your dad unintentionally made things worse by bonding with you on an epic scale.'

Harlow leaned back on the sun lounger in shock as she tried to process what her mum had said. 'Why did I not know about this?'

'About PND? It wasn't something that was discussed back then. I didn't feel able to talk about it with anyone – not even your father. You were only three or four when you kept asking about having a brother or sister. Too young to understand why you weren't going to have a sibling – from me at least. I felt like I'd lost my identity and my drive to make a name for myself. Work was the only thing I was good at, so I threw myself into it. You might think that's selfish, but it's the truth and how I felt, so I did something about it. If or when you have children you can make different choices.' She shifted on the lounger, looking flushed and flustered. If it wasn't for all the Botox, Harlow was pretty certain she'd be frowning. 'This is a pointless conversation and unhelpful.'

'No, it's not,' Harlow said, her tone softening with a new understanding. 'This is the first time you've properly talked to me about stuff – I had no idea you suffered with postnatal depression.'

'If you really want to know the truth, I was driven by a desire to succeed to prove myself to my father.'

Harlow looked at her mum sharply; she couldn't remember the last time she'd mentioned him. She rarely talked about her parents and had been estranged from them since she was twenty. Unlike her grandparents on her dad's side, her mum's parents had never been a part of Harlow's life.

'He'd wanted a son but got me. He spent the whole of my childhood drunk and bitter. He never showed me affection, only his belt when I displeased him. My mother was weak and never stood up to him. The last thing I wanted was to be like her. So I made myself strong and determined, left home as soon as I could and worked my arse off to escape my father's disappointment. I foolishly thought by becoming successful I could make up for not being the son he wanted. And of course the stupid bugger died before I really made a name for myself. I doubt he'd have cared anyway.'

'He might have been proud.'

'Oh, I don't think so. I've made mistakes, I'll be the first to admit that, but I did my best. It's not like I had the experience of a loving family to shape having a family of my own. That's not an excuse, just a fact.' She sniffed hard and swiped the back of her hand across her face, wiping away a lone tear. 'What's this all about anyway? What good is it to go back over the past and things we can't change? To make yourself feel better? To simply have a good go at me?'

It was Harlow's turn to shift uncomfortably. Her mum was glaring at her, her body language hostile. She'd opened up to her more in the last few minutes than she ever had before. Harlow was baking in the full glare of the sun. Sweat trickled down the side of her face. She'd told Adonis that being honest with her mum would be a bad idea, but something about him willing her on, and years of pent-up emotions had brought her here. There would never be a good time to have this conversation, so why not now?

'You've been frustrated with me for years because I've done nothing along the lines of what you've wanted me to do.' She held her mum's gaze and tried to keep her voice from wavering. 'Nothing that *you* can shout about or show off to your friends. It's you who wanted me to be an actor, then a director, or a producer like you, certainly not an assistant location manager, but, hey, if I was going to do that you had to go and get me a bloody cushy job. Notice how everything is about you, not about me and what I want. I'm sure, given a choice, we'd both want different things from each other. I can only imagine how hard having PND must have been and I'm so sorry you went through that. But I wanted a mum who was present – on the occasions you did spend time with me, I wanted you to be fully there, not still working, on phone calls, wishing you were anywhere but with me. Have you ever once thought to ask what *I* want?'

'What do you want, Harlow? Do you even know?'

'I know I don't want to continue as I have been, jumping from one thing to another because I'm not happy.'

'Oh, you do surprise me, not being happy as an assistant location manager after working as a first AD. Shock.' Harlow imagined her rolling her eyes behind her sunglasses.

'Actually, I'm happier now than I was as an assistant director, and it's not because, as you mistakenly insinuated, I couldn't deal with the pressure. It's because there's more opportunity to work outdoors and travel – things that do make me happy.'

'Well yes, Harlow, who wouldn't love to spend the summer on a

Greek island? You're hardly shocking me with that revelation. You have me to thank for that too.'

'And yet, you know so little about me, you had no idea how difficult it would be to have Tyler as my boss.'

'If you're meaning I don't know about you and Tyler, of course I do. I know you've been on and off with each other for years.'

Harlow looked at her sharply. 'Did Dad tell you?'

Maeve looked at her over her sunglasses and scoffed.

'Did Tyler tell you?'

'Of course not. You and Tyler are the worst-kept secret. Everyone knows. Come on, when you two were at film school and came and stayed with me, did you really think I believed you were upstairs revising?'

'There is no me and Tyler any longer. There never has been anything, no proper relationship.'

'You just have sex, do you?'

'Mum!'

'Oh please, don't go all sweet and innocent on me. I know the score.'

'We're not emotionally involved, let's put it that way.' Saying that out loud sounded like the lie it was.

'Pull the other one, Harlow. Emotion always gets in the way. That's why there's still something between you two. You can't let each other go.'

'I've moved on. There isn't anything. We're not together in that way, not any longer.'

'Because you like this Greek guy?'

'Yes, I do like him.'

'Then have a fling while you've got the chance. Get him out of your system. Tyler will be there when you go back to the UK.'

Harlow looked away. She didn't want to just have a fling with

Adonis. Emotions were already involved, yet she knew he couldn't be more than a summer romance.

She turned back. 'Is that how you think of relationships? Have a fling and move on to the next one?'

'Sometimes, yes.'

'Like with Dad?'

'Your father was not a fling. I loved him and we married for the right reasons, despite our differences. It's laughable really that we believed it could work – a school teacher from Yorkshire who'd moved to London for a better job, while I had my sights set on Hollywood. We just weren't right for each other. He held me back and I made him miserable. You know as well as I do that we're better apart. He's happy, isn't he?'

'Yes he is, very.'

'Well, good for him.'

'Are you jealous?'

'I don't want to be with your father any longer. Gina's perfect for him and I'm not jealous of her either.'

'I believe that, but are you jealous of the solid, loving, happy marriage they have? Don't you want that with someone?'

Maeve's cheeks clenched. She'd hit a nerve there.

Harlow decided to push her further. 'What about Jim?'

'What about him?'

'Are you two serious?'

'We are what we are.'

'Now who's being cryptic.'

'I don't want to talk about my relationship.'

'And yet you're quite happy to have your love life splashed across the internet.'

'You read that crap?'

'No, but I hear things. I just want you to find someone who treats you right and loves you for all the right reasons. The same as

I want a relationship like Dad and Gina have – they love each other, support each other, communicate. Put family first.'

'Gina made a choice, the same as I did. She chose to give up her career and concentrate on her children.'

'She didn't give it up; she put it on hold.'

'Either way, Harlow,' Maeve continued with a hardness to her voice, 'if I'd done the same, I wouldn't be where I am today.'

'But at what cost?'

Maeve ignored the comment and poured herself another drink. Harlow noticed how she hadn't offered her anything, not that she would drink as she was driving, but her throat was parched and the blistering sun pounded down relentlessly.

'Do you know, it's sad you've never asked if I'm happy.'

Maeve clenched her jaw. 'What would make you happy, Harlow?'

'Falling in love, being with someone I want to spend the rest of my life with, doing something I'm passionate about. I'd love to work outside, feel exhausted by the end of the day and go home to somewhere as warm and welcoming as Granny and Grandad's farmhouse. It's everything I've always wanted and I've never been able to admit that to you. I've never been able to admit it to Dad either.' As the words spilled from her, she realised everything she really wanted was here on Skopelos. 'Are you happy, Mum?'

Maeve downed her third glass of prosecco and lay back on the sun lounger. 'If you've said your piece, I think it's time you left.'

29

WEEK SEVEN – FINAL WEEK OF FILMING

Harlow woke early on Monday morning with a feeling of dread, like there were stones in the pit of her stomach. In seven days, she'd be on a plane heading back to the UK.

After the confrontation with her mum, she'd come straight back to the hotel and hidden in her room, in no mood to see or speak to anyone else. She'd managed to avoid Tyler since her mum's birthday party and she wanted to keep it that way. She ordered room service and even ignored texts and a phone call from Manda. There was nothing from Adonis, not that she expected him to update her or be thinking about her while his grandma was in hospital.

Before starting work, she went for a run, hoping that pounding the path beneath the trees would alleviate some of the stress. It didn't, but it did at least energise her. She showered, dressed, packed a bag and went to the hotel restaurant for breakfast.

'What's going on, Harlow?' Manda slid on to the empty seat opposite. 'I've been worried about you. What's happened?'

Harlow looked up from her bowl of fruit and yogurt. 'Sorry, I was having a bad day yesterday. I didn't mean to ignore you, just didn't want to speak to anyone.'

'Hey, it's fine. I understand. Are you okay now? Do you want to talk about it?'

Harlow sighed. 'Where to start.'

'Bit like that is it?' Manda wrinkled her nose. 'Give me the potted version.'

'I confronted Mum yesterday. Kinda told her how I felt about everything.'

Manda's eyes widened.

'Of course that didn't go down too well,' Harlow continued. 'And she pretty much told me where to go.'

'Okay, but what happened on Saturday night with Adonis?'

Harlow sighed again. 'We had *the* most amazing and romantic evening with a picnic in the orchard.'

'And...' Manda raised her eyebrows.

'I ended up staying and we were in his room, kinda doing stuff... I mean he was doing stuff...'

'Oh my goodness, Harlow, this is the stuff of dreams.'

'Yeah it is, up until the part his grandma had a stroke.'

'What?'

'She collapsed and hit her head. Stephanos called Adonis down to help, and that was it...'

'Is she okay?'

'She's going to be.'

'Well that's good. You've still got time to see Adonis and continue where you left off...'

'Except he's on the mainland with her at the hospital. And, I don't know, even if he was here, I'm not sure it's a good idea. The more I get to know him, the more I want to know and I... Oh. We're leaving in a few days. If more happens, I'm just worried how it's going to make me feel.'

'Because you really like him.'

Harlow nodded and glanced at her watch. 'I need to get going.'

Manda hugged her. 'Don't worry about it. Things have a habit of working themselves out. With your mum too. It's a good thing you finally talked to her.'

* * *

Harlow could no longer avoid Tyler. They met as usual in the hotel car park and managed to drive halfway to the Glossa set before saying more than 'hello' to each other.

'I apologised to Olivia,' Tyler suddenly said.

'You did?'

'After you told me to get out on Friday night, I went and found her.'

He was gripping the steering wheel and his eyes were fixed on the winding road.

So that's where he'd gone.

'You were right about the way I treated her and I put her right about us too.'

'Good, I'm glad.' She felt the pressure inside her ease, knowing he had listened.

They were the first ones there and they got things ready while the rest of the cast and crew began to arrive and the set became busy with activity. The cast had gone through costume, hair and make-up back at the base. With just final touches to be done at the location, they were ready for the first take by nine.

While the first shot was being set up, Jim came over looking worried.

'Hey, Harlow. I don't suppose you know where your mum is?'

'Erm no, sorry.'

Jim frowned.

'Why? What's going on?'

'She should have been here nearly an hour ago and I haven't seen or spoken to her since yesterday afternoon.'

'You've tried ringing her?'

'Multiple times. Just goes to voicemail. I'd go up to her villa and check, but I'm needed here, so would you mind?'

'No, of course not. I think Tyler's about to head back to the base – we'll swing by on the way.'

'Thank you,' Jim said. She met his eyes and he nodded. Whatever his relationship with her mum was, there was no doubt he looked worried. 'First positions, please!' he called, striding away.

* * *

Harlow was back in the car with Tyler, but now their attention had turned from each other to her mum.

'Maybe she decided to have a lie-in and switched off her phone,' Tyler suggested as they followed the road they'd come along just a couple of hours earlier.

'My mum doesn't lie in, not even on a weekend.'

'You think something's wrong?'

'I don't know.' Harlow gazed out of the window at the forested hillside zipping by. Worry gnawed away at her. Not turning up for work, not having her phone on and not communicating with anyone was not her mum's style.

Maeve's car was still in the driveway when they parked outside her villa. Harlow and Tyler glanced at each other as they got out and walked round to the back. Everywhere was still and quiet in the early-morning sun, the view lush and green all the way to the sparkling sea.

The patio doors were wide open. Harlow poked her head inside. 'Mum?'

Her bag and car keys were on the side, as though she was ready to leave, and a pot of coffee was on. Harlow walked over and switched it off.

'Harlow!'

The worry in Tyler's voice made her go back outside.

'Down here,' he called from the middle terrace.

Maeve was lying on the pale stone that surrounded the pool.

Harlow jogged down the steps and knelt beside her. 'Mum, are you okay?'

Maeve's eyes fluttered open. 'I feel... so dizzy...'

Tyler grabbed a cushion from the nearest sun lounger, gently raised her head and put it underneath.

'What happened?'

'I don't... know. I was fine, then sudden pain... dizziness, nausea, difficulty breathing. Felt like. I was. Going to die.'

'Why didn't you call someone?' Harlow looked round. 'Where's your phone?'

'Pool. I collapsed by the pool. It must have fallen in.'

'Oh my goodness, Mum. We need to get you seen.'

'No. I need to. Get to... set.'

'Mum, you can barely keep your eyes open. We're taking you to hospital.'

Tyler was thumbing something into his phone. 'There's a medical centre in Skopelos Town.'

'Okay, let's try sitting you up.'

With Harlow on one side and Tyler on the other, they gripped Maeve's shoulders and helped her up until she was sitting against the wall with her head resting on a cushion.

'Maybe we should call an ambulance,' Tyler said.

'No. No ambulance. Give me a minute. Get some water.'

Tyler ran up to the villa, while Harlow dipped the end of a beach towel in the pool and dabbed her mum's forehead and cheeks. Her usually tanned face was pale and sweat beaded her forehead.

Tyler returned with a bottle of cold water and held it to Maeve's lips. She gulped some down and rested her head back against the cushion.

'Thank you.'

While Maeve sat and sipped water, Harlow phoned Jim to let him know what had happened.

'But she's okay?' he asked.

'She's conscious and talking to us, just feeling dizzy still. We're going to take her to the medical centre in Skopelos Town.'

'If you need me there...'

'I'll let you know. I'll message you when we know what's going on.'

'Thanks, Harlow.'

She put the phone down and bit her lip. Maybe she was wrong assuming their relationship was a fling. He certainly seemed concerned. Perhaps he was more invested than her mum was?

* * *

They managed to get Maeve to the car and found the medical centre in Skopelos Town. They seemed to be used to dealing with foreign tourists and everyone spoke English.

'Tyler you'll be needed,' Maeve said after she'd been taken to a room to be seen by a doctor. Even lying on a hospital bed she was still giving orders.

Tyler glanced at Harlow and she nodded.

'Okay. I hope you feel better soon, Maeve.' He touched Harlow's arm. 'If you need anything...'

Harlow nodded. 'Thanks.'

She watched him until he disappeared down the corridor, then turned back to her mum. 'Do you want me to wait with you?'

'No, it's fine. Wait outside. We'll see what the doctor says, then you'll need to get back to work.'

'Mum, this is more important.'

Maeve huffed and closed her eyes.

Harlow looked at her for a moment. She had a little more colour in her cheeks now and certainly looked better than when they'd found her. But her usually perfect hair was tangled and she was without her trademark red lips. She looked small and vulnerable lying on a hospital bed in a tired-looking room, a long way from her normal glamorous self and surroundings.

Harlow did as she'd been asked and waited outside. With time on her hands, her head raced with a million thoughts from what could have happened if her mum had collapsed in the pool, to how Adonis was doing. She hadn't heard from him since his text the morning before. Maybe he was thinking the same thing she'd been saying to Manda over breakfast – what was the point of trying to start something that was going to fizzle out in a week's time? She considered messaging him but didn't know what to say, particularly when she was sitting in a hospital waiting for news about her mum.

It was another two hours until a doctor with a bald head and a greying beard came over to her.

'Harlow?'

She nodded and stood up.

'Your mother has asked me to come and speak to you about what has happened. What she's suffering with is severe anxiety,' he said in fluent English. 'We call it generalised anxiety disorder and it can manifest in physical symptoms as well as mental ones, like the symptoms your mother suffered today. The dizziness, an irregular heartbeat, feeling sick, shortness of breath and the pain.' He indicated to the middle of his chest.

'So, it was a sort of panic attack?'

'A severe one, yes.'

A memory flashed into Harlow's mind of the lunch at the villa with her dad and Gina when she'd walked past her mum standing on her own looking out of sorts – sweaty and holding her chest. Had she been having an attack then? Harlow wondered how long it had been going on for.

'She's getting some rest and we'll keep her in for a few more hours. Can you come back later?'

'Of course.'

Harlow left the stuffy medical centre, relieved to get out into the sunshine and breathe the fresh sea air. She felt wrung out. It seemed unimaginable that her strong powerful mum would suffer from anxiety. It just proved that everyone had an Achilles' heel.

30

It was Jim who Maeve contacted to collect her from the medical centre. Harlow didn't know if she was upset or relieved that her mum had chosen him over her.

Back in her room, she did something she'd never done before. She googled Maeve Fennimore-Bell and scrolled through page after page of gossip blogs and articles about her mum's supposed love life mixed in with serious interviews and photo shoots. There were grainy photos of her in a clinch with an actor half her age, the one the American woman at The Olive Grove restaurant had commented about when they'd been filming, while an article with *Vanity Fair* focused on her career and her achievements, and the front cover of *Empire Magazine* featured her clutching her Oscar. But it was the gossip that reduced Harlow to tears, the comments on everything from her mum's weight, the way she looked, whether she'd had help from a surgeon, to why this guy was with her and whether she was messing around with that bloke. Hurtful, cruel words were splashed everywhere. Everyone had an opinion; everyone found fault and talked about her in such a personal way that Maeve's male contemporaries would never be spoken about.

When Harlow got a message from Jim that evening saying 'your mum wants to see you', she jumped in the car and drove along the dark winding road into the hills, leaving behind the remnant of the sun bleeding into the horizon.

'How is she?' Harlow asked as Jim let her in.

'Being stubborn,' he said under his breath. 'I persuaded her to go to bed, but she's still working. She wanted to see you, but I also thought you might have a better chance of talking some sense into her.'

Harlow laughed. 'If she's not listening to you, she's hardly going to listen to me.'

'Just talk to her, please.'

Harlow hadn't made much time for Jim. Her assumption was he was in it to further his career, because Maeve was a good person to be involved with. Yet here he was when things had got tough.

She put her hand on his arm. 'Thank you for being here for her.'

'I know we've not talked much and I know it must be awkward for you... she's your mum and...' His cheeks flushed and it was obvious that he was struggling to find the words. 'Maeve and I have known each other a while – we've worked together a few times. We get on well and I like her. I just want you to know that.' He motioned to the stairs. 'Anyway, she's waiting for you.'

The villa's master bedroom was all white apart from the wooden ceiling beams and splashes of magenta and Aegean blue from the paintings of typically Greek views. Her mum was propped up in bed against a pile of pillows with her laptop open in front of her. She looked up at Harlow.

'Everyone's treating me like an invalid.'

Harlow walked over and perched on the edge of the bed. 'Jim's concerned and rightly so.'

'Oh, not you as well. I thought you'd have little sympathy and tell me to get on with it and back to work.'

'Mum, you had an anxiety attack so bad you passed out. It could have been so much worse; you could have had a head injury or fallen in the pool. Who knows what would have happened then? I don't even want to think about it.'

'You're being dramatic, Harlow.'

'No, I'm not.' Harlow closed the laptop lid.

'What are you doing?'

'Making you listen.' She put the laptop on the bedside table and turned back. 'How long have you been feeling like this?'

'I've been feeling fine.' She looked at her defiantly, her nostrils flaring.

'Really? So this just came out of the blue did it? You've not been stressed or anxious?'

'Of course, but it's nothing new. My job is stressful, but I thrive on it.'

'What about everything else?'

'What about it?'

'The way you live your life is toxic, Mum. I don't look at the trash that's written about you online, but I have done today, and my goodness. How can you stand it?'

'I've got used to it over the years.'

'You shouldn't have to get used to it.'

'What do you propose I do, huh?'

'I don't know... change things. Don't stand for it. Don't make it easy for them to target you. Slow down a little. Don't invite controversy.'

'All easy for you to say.'

'Actually, no it's not. I've told you this already that I loathe you interfering in my life, constantly telling me what I should be doing. The last thing I want to do is the same to you, but then you've ended up in hospital after chest pain and collapsing, so it's a different situation.'

'It's stress-induced that's all, not a bloody heart attack.'

'It's put you in hospital though and you've just admitted it's to do with stress. The amount of pressure you're under with work, I totally get – it's part of your job and you've been doing it long enough to know how to handle it, but all this other stuff, there is something you can do about that. Surround yourself with good people, like Jim. He's just told me you've known each other a while. If you like him, give it a proper go; don't go messing about with a famous, married film star.'

'That was blown out of all proportion.' She folded her arms. 'And I do have good people around me.'

'Really?'

'Yes. You're just not aware of who my friends are because we don't spend as much time together as we used to.'

'No, we don't, but then forgive me for assuming that you're still surrounded by a load of wankers.'

'What the hell's that supposed to mean?'

Harlow took a deep breath. 'I can't even remember how many times I was propositioned by "friends" of yours. Back in the Notting Hill house when you used to have a party every weekend.'

Maeve's eyes narrowed, but Harlow held her gaze. She'd bottled up the truth for too long; it had eaten away at her for years. If she wanted to start building a proper relationship with her mum, then honesty was the only way forward.

'I was like eighteen, nineteen. I think they were surprised when I wasn't interested; I had zero desire to act or be famous. So many times I was told they'd make me a star...' Harlow's voice wobbled. 'It just came with conditions...'

'What conditions?' Maeve's voice was steely, but the colour had drained from her face.

'The kind of conditions that the #MeToo movement has been trying to eradicate.'

'Oh my God, Harlow.' Emotion now wrapped itself around her words. Tears brimmed in her eyes. 'Why didn't you tell me?'

'Would you have believed me?'

'Of course I would have.' Her voice was unsteady. 'I'm well aware of what it used to be like for young actresses in particular.'

'I wasn't even an actress.'

'No, but you're my daughter.'

'Mum, you were so wrapped up in that glamorous world and lifestyle you'd created for yourself; I'm not sure you'd have seen past any of it back then. And calling out any of your producer and director friends on their behaviour would have destroyed your career. I guess from your reaction you weren't even aware. But I had my head screwed on enough to know what was really going on.'

'Thanks to your dad,' she said quietly.

'Yeah, thanks to Dad.'

'Does he know?' Panic coated her words.

'About what happened to me at the parties? No. It's the only thing I've ever hidden from him. Tyler does though.'

Maeve looked at her sharply.

'You probably don't remember, but he came to a few parties towards the end of our second year. I tried to keep film school and being your daughter separate. I knew how it looked with a film producer mum and I wanted friends to be my friends because they liked me, not because of who you were. But Tyler was different somehow; I trusted that he wasn't trying to use me for his own gain.'

Harlow paused as a wave of nausea hit. This was the first time she'd talked to anyone other than Tyler about this.

'One particular party someone spiked my drink with God knows what. Tyler caught him with me in one of the guest bedrooms and dragged him off me. Gave him a black eye too.'

Maeve gasped. Realisation crossed her face as tears trickled down her cheeks. 'I was completely out of it for the next few hours; wouldn't have known a thing if Tyler hadn't been looking out for me.' Harlow gave a shuddery breath. 'I'm assuming the intention was rape. Tyler saved me.'

Maeve reached for Harlow's hand and gripped it. '*He* did that to you?' Her voice was full of horror, her eyes puffy with tears, her face contorted in anger.

'You know who I'm talking about?' Harlow asked quietly.

Maeve swiped her free hand across her eyes. 'He was outed about sexual harassment during #MeToo. Why didn't you speak up?'

'I would have. I wanted to, but I feared your association with him would bring you down too.'

'Oh Harlow!' She clutched her and sobbed. 'You should have told me. About everything. I wish you had.'

'They were your friends and colleagues. It wasn't that straightforward. You were even in a relationship with his best friend for a time.'

Maeve put her head in her hands. 'But you suffered in silence. You really didn't tell your dad?'

Harlow shook her head.

'And you didn't tell me...'

'I had Tyler.' Harlow plucked a tissue from the box on the bedside table and handed it to her.

Maeve dabbed her eyes, steadied her breathing and looked at Harlow. 'Is that why you struggle with long-term relationships?'

'Talk for yourself.'

'That's different. I don't have trust issues – I just don't have the desire to settle down. But Tyler.' She sighed and wiped her eyes again. 'I can't thank him enough for being there and saving you. Do you feel you owe him? Is that why you can't let him go?'

Tears caught in Harlow's throat. She was reliving the pain and upset that she'd repressed for years. 'I feel responsible for his career stalling the second we graduated. He couldn't get work on anything that was associated with that producer. He had a drink problem that turned into a drug problem and spiralled out of control. I helped him get clean, but I've felt a mixture of guilt and owing him ever since. And he's my friend.'

'Maybe it's not just me who needs to change and let go of things. Yes, Tyler's your friend – he did exactly what a true friend should do, looked out for you and protected you when you needed him to. But you don't owe him anything except your friendship. If anything, it's me who owes him for protecting you when I didn't. *That man* is a monster.' Anger threaded through her words; she couldn't even say his name, but her determined look said it all. 'I was blind to it back in the day when I foolishly called him my friend. I didn't stand by him when the truth came out. Those poor women. They were who I stood with. And you... That's before I even knew about you... You're my daughter.' Her voice cracked and she pulled Harlow into a hug.

Harlow froze for a moment, the gesture from her mum unfamiliar, but at that moment very much wanted. She hugged her back.

'Don't let guilt or the past stop you from moving on.' Maeve gently took hold of Harlow's chin and made her look at her. 'Yeah?'

Harlow nodded. For once, she agreed with her mum.

'And I can say the same for you, except the other way round.' She grabbed a tissue and wiped away her own tears. 'Think about what you really want too and don't lose a good thing in Jim, if he makes you happy.'

31

The summer season was in full swing, with the island enjoying an extra influx of holidaymakers, just as the film crew and its stars were wrapping up, about to head back to the UK to finish the rest of the shoot at Pinewood Studios. Harlow would be back on familiar territory, yet she could think of nothing she wanted less.

Maeve was back working from the villa the day after she'd collapsed and was on set for the final two days of the island shoot. Harlow spent the whole week on autopilot: early start, busy day on set, late finish, back to the hotel for dinner. And repeat. She spent her spare time with Manda and her group of friends within the hair, make-up and costume departments. They'd all have another three weeks working together back in London, but Harlow knew she'd miss her company once filming ended. After that, who knew. And that's exactly what Harlow didn't know: what she'd do next. The things that made her happy had become clear over the past few weeks, it's just she had no idea if she could hold on to that happiness.

Apart from Monday when Harlow had found her mum

collapsed, Adonis had messaged her every day, yet he remained with his yiayia in Volos. Time was slipping away.

On Friday, the last day of the Skopelos shoot, Harlow showered and got dressed with a heaviness that made her stomach ache, the reality of leaving just the other side of the weekend finally sinking in.

She was about to head to the base when she was surprised by a knock on the door. Ereni was standing on the landing, tiredness and worry etched on her usually smiley face.

'Is everything okay?' Harlow asked.

'Yes, sorry. I wasn't sure if I see you in time. I go to Volos to be with Mama until she can come home. As you leave Monday, I want to say goodbye. I will be sad to see you go.' She clasped Harlow's shoulders and kissed her on both cheeks.

'Oh Ereni, that's so thoughtful of you. I'm going to miss you all too and being here.' A lump caught in her throat. She'd been trying so hard to keep on top of her emotions.

'Adonis will be back tomorrow; you should see him, before you go. I know he will like that. You have been good for him.' She gave a nod and walked away.

'Ereni!' Harlow grabbed her key card and followed her on to the landing. 'What do you think about him leaving the island? Is it something you think he should do? I know he's afraid of upsetting Stephanos.'

Ereni stopped at the top of the stairs. 'It is very difficult, for everyone. For my mama, for my brother, if Adonis leaves.' She walked back over to Harlow. 'But I worry if he don't he will end up resenting them, my brother in particular, and one day they might lose him forever. The Olive Grove already belong to Adonis – a third at least – and eventually Stephanos will leave it all to him. It is his inheritance, his future, if he stay on Skopelos. But it is memories, hard ones but happy ones too. I hope he can have many more happy times here, but he is grown and his own person.' She shrugged. '*Then xéro*. I don't know.'

'Is it because Stephanos can't cope on his own?'

'Tsch. It hard for him to cope with Adonis. There is tension between them. Adonis has ideas, new ideas I think – it is difficult, he don't say much to me because he is fearful Stephanos will find out then, ah, it is difficult. They have help at busy times, the olive harvest and in the summer at the restaurant, temporary staff for a short time only, but of course that is difficult to manage too. I cannot see how Adonis can leave without someone to replace him. Someone good and reliable is hard to find. Stephanos can be... what is the word, very hard? I worry they will one day fall out and that would be a disaster. I wish to help but I have the hotel, a husband, a family of my own to look after.'

'I'm so sorry that it's a difficult situation.'

'It is life. Never easy.' She shook her head. 'I hope one day we see you again.'

* * *

Harlow spent the rest of the day mulling over her conversation with Ereni, and as she worked, a nugget of an idea began to form. Maeve was back at work and in control, looking and acting as if nothing had happened, but Harlow knew. She'd witnessed a vulnerability within her mum that she'd never seen before. For once they'd properly talked and Harlow had said stuff that she'd bottled up for years. She'd been brutally truthful too. Her mum had reacted with disbelief and anger that had morphed into compassion. It was a relief to get the truth out in the open. She'd also been truthful when she'd told her that she was leading a toxic life – at least some aspects of it.

There were only two more full days on Skopelos and Harlow knew she wanted to see Adonis again, so when a message from him pinged on to her phone that evening she didn't have to think twice about her reply.

I'll be back on Skopelos by 8 p.m. tomorrow. Can I come and see you?

Of course. Can't wait. x

And from that point onwards, rather than willing time to slow down, she willed it to speed up.

There was a wrap party at the hotel bar that evening, a fitting end to this part of the project before they took the shoot to the interior set at Pinewood.

Maeve briefly showed her face at the beach bar and disappeared early; Harlow noticed Jim's absence too. Was that a good thing? She wasn't sure, but she knew she liked the idea of her mum having company up in her beautiful but lonely villa in the hills.

Harlow spent the evening in Manda's company with the rest of the hair, make-up and costume teams. She was immensely pleased to have rekindled their friendship.

'I'm dying to go home now and see Emma and Rob. It's the longest I've ever been away from either of them,' Manda admitted. 'How are you feeling about leaving?'

'Dreading it.'

'Oh, hun. You going to see Adonis before you go?'

Harlow showed her the message from him.

Manda squealed and hugged her. 'This is goodbye then as I'm flying back Sunday and tomorrow you'll be spending the night in Adonis's arms.'

'This is hardly goodbye, you silly mare. We'll be working together next week.'

'Indeed we will and you can give me *all* the gossip then.'

* * *

Early the next evening, Harlow walked through the trees clustering the edge of the bay and along the beach at Panormos. A few families and couples were still camped out, making the most of the retreating sun. The tiny stones crunched together as she walked. She stood for a moment, wanting to commit not just the view of the pine-clad hills and glistening sea to memory, but the warmth of the sun on her shoulders and the feeling of contentment that had been missing for so long. She didn't want to leave; she didn't want to return to her life in the UK and the uncertainty of what she was going to do next. Most of all, she didn't want to say goodbye to Adonis.

Harlow headed back to the hotel just before eight and her stomach flipped when Adonis messaged her to say he'd parked. She spotted him first, striding towards her along the path between the villas, a gorgeously familiar figure, the way he looked at her leaving her flushed and feeling all kinds of delicious things.

He wrapped her in his arms and they kissed.

'Hey,' Harlow said once he released her. 'I've missed you.'

'I've missed you too.'

Adonis took her hand and she led him to her villa and upstairs to her room. She handed him a beer from the fridge and opened the doors to the balcony.

'How's your yiayia?' she asked.

'She'll be okay. Just has to take it easy. She'll be home in a few days.'

They settled themselves on the rattan chairs overlooking the pool and the hotel grounds that glimmered in the evening sun. An air of expectation surrounded them, as though they were going through the motions of polite conversation before they picked up where they'd left off the other night.

'Ereni came and said goodbye yesterday.'

'She said.' Adonis curled his hand in hers. 'I wish you didn't have to go.'

Harlow nodded and bit her lip, uncertain how she was going to get through the next couple of days without becoming an emotional mess.

'It feels like we're just beginning to get to know each other and it's all over.' His voice was filled with emotion.

It was all so final and Harlow hated it. To spend the night with him, wouldn't that make leaving all the harder? Unless of course she made a different choice...

Tyler and Olivia were walking up the path hand in hand. Harlow's heart faltered. The briefest stab of jealousy evaporated the moment she glanced at Adonis. She smiled and turned back, watching Tyler and Olivia settle themselves on a pair of sun loungers. Olivia stripped down to a bikini and dived into the pool. Tyler watched her and whistled as she backstroked past him. He glanced up and caught Harlow's eye. Without meaning to, she squeezed Adonis's hand tighter. Tyler shaded his eyes and gave her a wave.

'Are things okay between you two?' Adonis asked.

'Things are fine,' she replied truthfully.

Harlow and Tyler hadn't discussed their relationship since their Friday night argument, but her being here with Adonis, and Tyler looking relaxed and happy with Olivia spoke volumes. She'd moved on from Tyler; she had a long time ago, she just hadn't allowed herself to let go of him until now. Somehow they'd find a way of remaining friends, that side of their relationship she couldn't give up. There was too much history and too many good things threaded through the negative, to chuck it all away, but a new start was what she needed.

Harlow switched her focus from Tyler back to Adonis. He was gazing out at the view she'd enjoyed over the last few weeks, looking as handsome as the first time she'd laid eyes on him.

'If you could have, say, six months away from here, where would you go?' she asked.

'I can't.'

'But *if* you could. What would you do? If you didn't have to worry about this place or your dad? Would you travel or work somewhere?'

'There's a woodworking course in Norway. It's run by a guy I've been talking to on Instagram. A residential course for six months.'

'It's expensive?'

'It's not the money that's the problem. It's the time away.'

She could hear the tension in his voice. The last thing she wanted to do was upset him. She took the nearly empty bottle of beer off him and put it on the table. Now was not the time for talking.

Taking his hand, Harlow walked backwards, leading him into her room. His grin widened.

'I thought we should continue where we left off the other night...' She peeled off her top and dropped it on the floor.

'Oh really,' Adonis said and silenced any more talk with a kiss.

Adonis's T-shirt was off a moment later, her skirt and his shorts swiftly following until a trail of clothes led across the tiles to the bed. She pulled him down with her and enveloped him in her arms. They kissed deeply.

'You want to pick up exactly where we left off?' His voice was full of mischief as he gently tugged at her knickers.

'I wouldn't mind.'

A tingling warmth flooded through her as she gripped his firm shoulders and he traced her curves with his lips until she was utterly lost.

There was no one to disturb them this time; no family emergency, just the two of them and the whole night stretching ahead. As the sun retreated, they moved together on the bed, making up for lost time. What a way to end it, as Manda had predicted, in Adonis's arms. The sun set on her time in Skopelos.

* * *

It was late and dark as they lay together, their hot skin cooled by the air con, the sound of the sea floating in through the open balcony doors along with peals of laughter and distant voices.

Harlow traced her fingers across Adonis's smooth, toned chest, taking in every contour, every piece of him. This couldn't be where it ended; both her time on Skopelos and her relationship with Adonis. Somehow it felt different with him to anyone else she'd been with. She felt complete. And leaving... that didn't bear thinking about. She knew in her heart what she wanted to do.

She kissed the side of his face and then his lips. He turned towards her with smiling eyes.

'You could go,' she said, stroking his beard along his jawline and down to his chest. 'You could travel for six months, enjoy time to yourself and have that freedom you've always craved.'

'Why are we talking about this now, Harlow? I really can't. I can't leave Baba, not after the scare with Yiayia...' His voice faltered with emotion and his hand tensed on her hips.

'What if your dad took on an apprentice?'

'We've thought of that before. It has never worked out. Young people on this island want to either work with tourists or leave.'

'What if it could be someone who would give 100 per cent,

someone who was passionate about working and learning about a place like The Olive Grove.'

Adonis laughed. 'If you could only find someone like that.'

'I can.'

'Who?'

'Me.'

32

After spending the night together, they went to The Olive Grove the next morning and sat down with Stephanos on the empty terrace overlooking the olive trees. The heat haze had yet to glimmer on the horizon. There were only the three of them and the birds swooping between the trees, a butterfly fluttering by the wall and Sam lying in the shade by their feet. Harlow made herself focus on the beauty surrounding her and less on her pounding heart as Adonis, clutching her hand, spoke to his baba in Greek about what Harlow had suggested the night before.

Harlow wasn't sure what to make of Stephanos's reaction; his weather-beaten forehead was in a permanent frown and his occasional grunts gave nothing away.

Adonis squeezed her hand. 'He wants to talk to you alone.' He kissed her forehead and disappeared into the olive grove with Sam padding after him.

Harlow swallowed hard. Sweat pooled in the small of her back. Stephanos watched her intently; she was hardly surprised at his mistrust, she knew how crazy the suggestion of her staying and Adonis leaving was.

'You like him?' Stephanos eventually asked. 'My son.'

'Very much.'

'You want to learn about all this?' He swept his arm towards the olive grove.

'Yes.'

'Why?'

'Because I'm fed up of working in an industry it was assumed I'd go into, one I didn't choose. I love the outdoors and the way of life in the country. My grandparents are farmers.'

'You can learn there, no?'

'Yes, I could, and I did when I was younger. I spent many happy summers mucking out stables, feeding the animals, riding on the tractor with my grandad. But I like your son and I think he likes me. I also like this island. I want to stay. I want to help. I want to learn.'

Stephanos grunted. 'You can learn with Adonis here. He don't need to leave for you to learn things.'

'True, but I know what it's like to spend years doing something you don't want to do. Adonis needs some freedom; he needs to get away. You'll end up losing him if you don't give a little. He needs to leave this island even for a short time. Let it be his choice to come back.'

'And if he doesn't? What will you do?'

'I don't know.'

'What will I do?'

'I don't know that either. But you have to let him do this or he'll resent you and it'll turn into anger – more anger than he already has. It's not good or healthy for either of you.'

Somehow Stephanos begrudgingly agreed, perhaps he had a glimmer of hope about what the future could hold, something Harlow dared not focus on yet. This was just the beginning. She had to finish the *One Greek Summer* shoot and sort out her life in the

UK before she could think about moving to Skopelos, whether for six months or longer, only time would tell.

* * *

The flight to the UK was the longest and most depressing journey Harlow had ever made. It didn't feel as though she was heading home, not when a piece of her heart had been left behind. What she'd suggested to Adonis was completely mad, but it also felt so right. A way of helping herself and him. She knew without a doubt that she wasn't ready to walk away from Adonis, put it down to a summer romance and a good memory. She wanted more; she wanted him. She knew he wanted more too, but she wasn't certain they could have a future without him first experiencing the freedom he'd always craved.

* * *

Four weeks later, *One Greek Summer* was wrapped. Her mum would be involved in the post-production, but she was heading back to LA for a couple of weeks first. Harlow wasn't sure what was happening with her and Jim and she didn't ask; it was for her mum to figure out. The last thing Harlow was going to do after berating her for interfering in her own life was to weigh in on hers.

Tyler had a movie filming in Cornwall lined up for later in the year and Joe, fully recovered from his broken leg, would be joining him on the shoot. Manda had a couple of weeks off to spend with her family and then she'd be working on a costume drama in London – an easy commute from home. Things were falling into place for everyone.

For Harlow, her time on *One Greek Summer* had come to an end. In a few short weeks, her life had been turned on its head. She felt like a different person to the one who'd arrived late on Skopelos. She was happier, more confident, sure of what she wanted from life. She'd stood up to her mum and opened up old wounds, but together and finally talking to each other, Harlow had hope that they'd find a way to heal at long last. She planned to spend what was left of her time in the UK with her dad and family in Norfolk before paying a long-overdue visit to her grandparents in Yorkshire.

Harlow leaned on the shiny copper bar and gazed out at the cast and crew celebrating. The wrap party was in full swing. With mustard-yellow lounge seating along one wall, glimmering bronze brickwork and a dance floor leading to an outside terrace, it was the sort of stylish venue her mum loved. So different to the hotel beach bar with its sand-sprinkled floor, wooden tables and sea breeze. Would Harlow miss this? Getting dressed up, rubbing shoulders with stars, free booze... Maybe, a little. But she knew what waited for her on Skopelos would make her happier. Her only regret about leaving would be seeing less of her dad, Gina and the girls, but they were happy she was following her heart, plus the girls were hugely excited that they'd get to visit Skopelos – if Harlow stayed long enough. And it wasn't as if she wouldn't come back and visit.

Tyler caught her eye and joined her up at the bar.

'You want another?' he asked, motioning to her nearly empty glass.

She nodded and he ordered her another gin and tonic and a beer for himself.

They perched on stools and looked out over the sea of friends and colleagues dancing, chatting and laughing together. It was as hot in the dimly lit bar as it had been at the beach bar on Skopelos, yet it was missing the backdrop of endless sea and sky, and the gentle swoosh of waves on to pebbles. Somehow it felt as though she and Tyler had come full circle, ending the shoot by having a drink together. There was certainly less anger simmering off him than during their first drink on the island. They chatted easily about their plans.

Olivia waved at him from a table.

'What's happening with you two?' Harlow asked, nodding to Olivia and the other production assistants.

'I'm pretty sure it'll fizzle out with me in Cornwall and her in London, but we'll see. I'm keeping an open mind. I'd better go join her.' He kissed Harlow's cheek and leaned close to her ear. 'Do what makes you happy. Forget about everyone else. And I'm sorry for the way I've treated you and what I said two years ago. I do love you and I'll always be here if you ever need me. Friends, remember.' He squeezed her arm. 'I'll see you around.'

She watched him until he was swallowed up by the crowd of cast and crew.

'Everything okay between you two?' Manda joined her at the bar.

'Yeah, I think it is.'

'Are you okay?'

Harlow laughed. 'I think so.'

Manda clinked her glass against Harlow's. 'It's brave what you're doing and I admire you for taking control of your life.'

'Admiration is better than believing I'm crazy, which is what most people think.'

'Meaning your mum...?'

'Exactly.'

'You're definitely not crazy, although you are taking a risk. What if, with his few months of freedom, Adonis doesn't want to come back? What if he meets someone else on his travels?'

'I know the risks, but I also know we wouldn't work unless he has this opportunity. I've missed him every single day I've been here, so I know it feels right taking a chance on what might be.'

* * *

Three days later, Harlow got a taxi with her mum to Heathrow. They would be heading in different directions – her mum to her home in the Hollywood Hills, and Harlow via Athens to an olive grove on a hillside of a Greek island. As long as they were both truly happy, did it really matter if they lived vastly different lives? Harlow was hoping to find her place somewhere between the expectations, hopes and dreams of her parents. A Greek island had beauty and glamour, while an olive grove counteracted that with nature and hard work. In her mind, it was the best of both; she just needed to follow her heart and hope it worked out for the best.

After going through to Departures, they had a coffee together. Harlow couldn't help but notice the looks her mum received – the double takes as people walked past. A group of twenty-somethings a couple of tables away pointed and whispered together. The attention seemed to fly right over her mum's head; after three decades in the limelight, she was used to it, but Harlow felt it was something she'd never want to get used to.

They'd been talking about the Skopelos shoot and her mum's return to LA, and the conversation naturally wound back round to their conversation at the villa after her mum had ended up in hospital.

'I've only ever wanted what's best for you, Harlow, and what makes you happy. Perhaps I've assumed – wrongly – that what has made me happy, professionally at least, would be the same for you. You're an enigma, shying away from fame and this industry that's given me so many opportunities and a life I once dreamed about. I thought that meant you weren't driven or had no desire to succeed, but you do, just in a different way. I'm sorry I didn't understand that.'

'I want to find my own way, that's all. But the last thing I want to be is a disappointment to you or Dad.'

Maeve reached across the table and took Harlow's hands. 'You're not. God, Harlow, don't ever think that. I'm proud of the kind, wonderful, grounded woman you've become, despite what you've been through and having me for a mother.' She sniffed and took a deep breath.

'Don't go mushy on me, Mum. It's so not your style.'

Maeve laughed and glanced up at the flight information board. 'You're sure about this, going back to Skopelos?'

'I'm certain.'

'Even without Adonis being there?'

'He'll be there for the first week.'

Maeve raised her eyebrows. 'You'd better make the most of that then.'

'I'm doing this for me. I like Adonis; I *really* like him, but if anything more is going to happen, we both have to figure out what we want first.'

'And you think working in an olive grove, feeding goats and picking fruit is going to answer that?'

'Yeah, I do.'

'Harlow Sands...' Maeve sighed. 'And we gave you such a film star name.'

'*You* gave me a film star name. Harlow wasn't Dad's first choice, was it?'

'No, it wasn't. He wanted to call you Sophie. But I think Harlow and Adonis make for a pretty special-sounding couple.' She glanced at her Cartier watch and stood up. 'Right, Jim will be waiting for me.'

Harlow stood too, a grin beaming across her face. Knowing that Jim was heading back to LA with her mum made her happier than she thought possible.

'I'm going to miss you, Mum,' she said.

Maeve hugged her tightly. She smelt of deliciously expensive perfume. She planted a red-lipped kiss on Harlow's cheek. 'Love you, Harlow Sands.' She walked away from the coffee shop towards the first-class lounge without a backwards glance.

With a lightness in her heart, Harlow gathered her luggage and walked the other way to the gate and the plane that would take her back to Greece and Adonis.

EPILOGUE

TWO YEARS LATER

The uplifting beat of 'Dancing Queen' floated across The Olive Grove. Greek and English mingled together along with laughter. Harlow walked the long way back from the villa. The orchard was shrouded in darkness with only the half-moon glinting through the branches. Beyond it, the restaurant terrace twinkled with hundreds of fairy lights, and lanterns, glowing cerise, tangerine and mauve, hung in the olive trees, casting a trail of colour like a fairy path down the hillside. Gazing down on the place she now called home, catching sight of her mum with her trademark red lips chatting to Ereni and hearing her youngest sister Flo's unmistakable giggle was the best feeling. It was everything she'd dreamed of and more.

'What are you doing hiding away up here?' Harlow's dad slipped his arm into hers.

'I'm not hiding; just taking everything in.'

'It's been a magical day.'

'It really has, and the night is yet young.'

Together they watched as her sisters twirled around on the terrace with Ereni's grandchildren, huge grins beaming across their flushed faces. Everyone was smiling; the combination of plenty of wine, food and celebrating to a backdrop of music at a location as beautiful as The Olive Grove was like a happiness pill.

Derek squeezed Harlow's arm. 'I'm so proud of you, you know. Making your dreams come true.'

'Thanks, Dad.'

'It took guts to follow your heart, particularly when it involved moving countries and defying your mum.'

Harlow snorted. 'She seems happy enough about it now.'

'Honestly, I've never seen her look so content. You talking to her, standing up for yourself and making her see sense was the best thing you could ever have done.'

'Yeah.' Harlow nodded. 'Coming to Skopelos changed my life.'

'Come on,' he said, leading them on to the grassy path that led to the restaurant. 'Let's find that new husband of yours.'

* * *

Harlow's arrival back on Skopelos a little over two years earlier had been the best decision she'd ever made, even if she hadn't realised it at the time. She was well aware of what it had looked like to everyone else, to give up her film career and her life in London for the unglamorous work on an olive farm on a Greek island miles and miles from home, but Harlow had been determined, even while being uncertain about how it would play out.

Harlow and Adonis had spent every minute of their one week together, building on their fledgling relationship. By the time Adonis had got on the ferry to Skiathos to start his long journey to Norway and his six-month woodworking course, Harlow had fallen for him hard.

Harlow's first autumn and winter on the island had been a vastly different experience to her Greek summer. She missed Adonis, she missed her dad, Gina, her sisters, her friends back home, even her mother, but she loved spending her days outdoors, learning about the olive farm and looking after the animals with Stephanos. She became an expert at making feta and filo in the farmhouse kitchen with Adonis's yiayia, and picked up a smattering of Greek along the way. Harlow had slowly begun to get used to Stephanos's gruffness which hid a soft and caring side, and she sensed how much he missed his son. Letting him go was as hard for him as it had been for Adonis making the decision to leave. Harlow carried the responsibility of it working out for everyone. Her own happiness and future were depending on it.

Harlow's homesickness had been offset by the eventual arrival of the olive harvest and long but enjoyable days spent in the olive grove, with local help brought in to pick and crate the olives. Harlow was in her element working outside throughout the winter, heading back at dusk to the farmhouse with Stephanos and Sam, who followed her about like a shadow, for a home-cooked meal before enjoying a soak in the bath. The only thing missing was Adonis, but they'd messaged or had spoken to each other every day, his happiness and enthusiasm for what he was doing infectious. They'd talked for hours, sharing their experiences and ideas.

As the weeks and months went by, Harlow's understanding of Adonis's need to build on what Stephanos had created at The Olive Grove grew. The restaurant was a small part of that, but there was the potential to do so much more. Adonis's idea of inviting tourists to help with the olive harvest appealed to Harlow and she could see how it would work. The place was too beautiful to keep hidden; she'd fallen in love with it almost as much as she had with Adonis.

Stephanos's fears of his son never coming home were quashed when he returned six months later. Harlow's worry had been eased too and after a big family get-together, reminiscent of the joyful evening Harlow had first spent with Adonis and his family to celebrate Ereni's birthday, Harlow and Adonis had tumbled into bed together. Adonis's bedroom had become hers too over the six months he'd been away, but it felt amazing with him back in her arms. They'd made up for lost time, getting little sleep and emerging bleary-eyed but immensely happy for breakfast the next morning, Stephanos grunting at their lateness, Yiayia smiling at them with a twinkle in her eye.

Whether it was because Adonis had fallen in love with Harlow or the time away had enabled him to rediscover his passion and find himself – or a combination of the two – he returned to Skopelos happier and with a real desire to stay. All he'd ever wanted was to escape for a little while, to travel, to experience new things and to do something for himself. Harlow had allowed him to do just that, while supporting his baba and yiayia. And all Harlow had ever truly wanted was to find her place in the world and share it with her soulmate. The last thing she'd expected to find when she'd arrived late to the island on that hot summer's day was love.

The summer after Adonis returned, Harlow went back to the UK on her own to stay with her dad, Gina and her sisters for a couple of weeks. It coincided with the Leicester Square premiere of *One Greek Summer*, a glamorous red-carpet affair attended by A-list stars galore. Maeve was in her element, and her risk of filming on location paid off with another blockbuster on her hands and decent reviews, plus the film picked up Golden Globes for Best Picture – Musical/Comedy and Best Actress for Crystal's performance. Maeve also became even more of a voice for women in the industry, receiving a standing ovation after her moving and passionate acceptance speech. Only Harlow knew that it was her mum's way of trying to make up for the past, but she couldn't have been prouder. Harlow enjoyed her brief return to the film world but was eager to get back to the tranquillity of the farm and into Adonis's arms.

Not long after Harlow had returned to Skopelos, on a picnic blanket in the olive grove beneath the stars and twinkling lights,

Adonis had proposed. The moment had been magical and romantic, unexpected but hopeful. Saying yes had been the easiest decision of her life.

* * *

Adonis, with a smile that could light up a room and wearing a white linen shirt that revealed a hint of his tanned and toned chest, was standing on the restaurant terrace chatting to Gina, Harlow's grandparents and his friend Jack. As Harlow and her dad stepped up from the path to join them, a cheer went up.

Adonis's smiling eyes widened at the sight of Ereni winding her way through the throng of friends and family towards Harlow.

'*To kalamatianó*!' Ereni cried, taking Harlow's hand and turning to her with a grin. 'The bride's dance!'

Harlow had been warned about this, but she'd thought she'd got away with it after the meal had finished and the *Mamma Mia!* soundtrack had been played.

Ereni had a wicked grin as the music switched from 'Voulez Vous' to the traditional, equally toe-tapping Greek music, which enveloped the olive grove in a seductive beat.

Led by Ereni, Harlow found herself in the middle of a group of women, the now familiar faces of Adonis's family, but she noticed others being dragged into the circle, like Manda, and Maeve with a bemused look on her face. The laughter and happiness surrounding her was infectious as she attempted what she felt were Greek dance steps. Adonis was standing on a chair clapping alongside his friends and her dad. Gina was drawn into the dance, and she grinned at Harlow as she was twirled around by Ereni. And then Abi, Ellie and Flo were in the circle, flinging their arms around Harlow's waist, the four of them hugging and laughing together as the music sped up, getting louder and more upbeat.

The dance ended with cheers and more laughter. Harlow headed for the nearest empty chair, her heart still thumping, her cheeks aching from smiling. She smoothed down the front of her ivory empire-line wedding dress and caught her breath. Adonis's uncle Kostas had now taken to the makeshift olive grove dance floor with a few of the other Greeks.

'Oh my goodness, that reminded me of the wedding scene in *Mamma Mia!*' Manda, still breathless and laughing, flopped down next to Harlow.

'The one where the ground splits open and water shoots everywhere?' Harlow laughed.

'The vibrations felt like the earth was going to crack open beneath us.' She sighed. 'I just love this, Harlow. I love how happy you are and how perfect your life is. I'm made up for you, I truly am.'

'I'm so pleased you were able to make it.'

'Wouldn't have missed it for the world. And you do realise, you'll have no trouble enticing anyone out here to visit.'

'We're taking bookings already.' Harlow winked. 'I don't think my sisters are going to want to leave.'

'I can't blame them. Rob and I certainly don't want to.' She gazed across the terrace to where her husband was talking to Adonis, Tyler and Jim. She glanced back at Harlow. 'And things are honestly okay between you and Tyler? I mean, he's here at your wedding talking to your husband...'

'How could I not invite him?' Harlow watched the three men who, in their various ways, had become such fixtures in her life. 'We've had our ups and downs and he's been a complete dick at times, but at the end of the day we're friends. Not only was the shoot on Skopelos the best thing because I met Adonis, but it allowed me the time to truly work out my feelings about Tyler, something I should have done a long time ago. And he's here with his girlfriend too.' She looked beyond the Greek dancing to where a slender woman with dark, curly hair was chatting to Gina. Harlow had been happy to invite her as Tyler's plus-one, the estate agent who'd sold him his London flat. They'd been dating for about a year and she seemed to have grounded him. 'We've both moved on. I'm genuinely happy for him and I hope he feels the same way about me. And Adonis is amazing – he's completely cool about Tyler, which he totally didn't have to be.'

She'd explained to him about her past and how Tyler had saved her. Adonis had a new respect for Tyler and she had hope that a friendship could eventually blossom between them.

'Well, Tyler ain't a patch on the Greek God. There's no competition.' She grinned at Harlow.

'No, there's not, but there's more to him than just good looks.'

'Oh, you don't need to tell me that. He's the whole package. As I've said to you many times before, you're one lucky, lucky lady.' Manda nodded. 'Look lively; your mum's on her way over.' Manda planted a kiss on Harlow's cheek and escaped to her husband.

Maeve was wearing a flattering blue and light grey patterned dress with a deep V-neck that showed just the right amount of cleavage. She was clutching two glasses of champagne and heading straight for Harlow, while doing her best to avoid being pulled into the dance.

Harlow got to her feet.

'I thought you could do with this after all that dancing.' Maeve handed her one of the glasses. 'I know I certainly can.' She raised an eyebrow. 'I wish we'd had a scene like this in *One Greek Summer*.' She gestured around them. 'It's a magical assault on the senses – the colours, the music, all that food, the surroundings.' She turned back to Harlow. 'If I'm being truthful—'

'When aren't you, Mum?' Harlow laughed.

Maeve smiled. 'I had my concerns when you said the wedding

party was going to be held in the olive grove. But it's so you. It's perfect.' She clinked her champagne against Harlow's.

They stood for a moment and watched the scene playing out in front of them. Kostas was leading the circle, the beat of the Greek song quickening, the footwork getting faster as the group of mainly Greeks with their arms across each other's shoulders sidestepped in unison. Even Stephanos was among them, his usual seriousness replaced with the quiet contentment that Harlow had seen grow since Adonis's return. The happy, glowing faces of her friends and family were visible in every direction. She caught Adonis's eye. His smile still made her heart melt. She blew him a kiss and turned back to her mum.

'I don't think I've ever thanked you for getting me the assistant location manager job.'

'Harlow Sands.' Maeve held her at arm's length. 'Are you actually telling me you're grateful for something I did for you?'

'Don't get used to it.' Harlow grinned. 'But yes. Coming here changed my life.'

'That really didn't have anything to do with me.' She sipped her champagne.

'Maybe not, but if you hadn't made me take the job, I'd have never met Adonis. We wouldn't be here now and we probably wouldn't have sorted out our differences. I think summer on Skopelos changed things for you too.' Harlow nodded towards Jim.

Maeve folded her free arm across her chest but a smile glimmered, lighting up her face. 'You were right; he's good for me. I couldn't imagine being here at your wedding without him.'

Her openness about a relationship and the tenderness threading through her words spoke volumes. It made Harlow even happier to see her mum happy. Jim and Maeve still lived separately, both keeping their independence – Harlow was certain her mum would never get hitched again – but they were publicly together and had been for longer than Harlow had ever known her mum to be in a relationship with someone, other than her dad of course. And although she was still very much focused on her career, there seemed to be more balance in her life – a stability with Jim and an openness with Harlow that meant they talked more. It was good for everyone.

Maeve downed the rest of her champagne and hooked her arm in Harlow's. 'Enough about me. This is your day. I'm so happy for you. I had my doubts you coming back here – well, we all did, even your dad, but you proved us wrong. You're about to begin a new and exciting time in your life. Despite my marriage ending, there were good moments within it, you being the main one. I suspect your marriage to Adonis will be far happier.' She squeezed Harlow's arm. 'Your dad's desperate to be a grandparent, you know.'

Harlow laughed and looked over to where Ellie and Flo were trying to teach him the steps to the Greek dance. Abi, now a full-blown teenager, was looking on and shaking her head.

'He'll be brilliant at it,' Maeve continued. 'You take things at your own pace though. I hated that at my own wedding, relatives who I hardly knew asking when there'd be the "pitter-patter of tiny feet", as if it was anyone else's business apart from our own. And don't get me started on them asking when baby number two would come along when I'd literally just given birth to you.'

'Oh, I already get the sense from Adonis's family that they're hoping for a baby, but we won't be rushing things – there's too much to do here first. So much potential and Adonis wants to focus on his woodworking—'

'Talking of Adonis...'

He was striding towards them, his focus on Harlow as he side-stepped away from his uncle. He reached them and looked from Harlow to Maeve with a grin. 'Can I borrow my wife for a moment?'

'You certainly can.' Maeve waggled her empty glass. 'I need a refill anyway.' And she was off, across the grass and enveloped into the colour and commotion of the wedding party.

Harlow looked up at him. 'Everything okay?'

'Yes, just wanted a moment with you.' Adonis took her hand. 'Walk with me.'

They slipped away from the light and laughter spilling from the terrace. The 'boop boop' call of the Scops owl took over from the music the further they walked. Everywhere was familiar, with so many places meaning something to Harlow: the spot where she'd first laid eyes on Adonis; the olive tree where the *One Greek Summer* scene had been filmed; the area in the orchard they'd set aside for romantic picnics; the outdoor kitchen by the workshop with a wood-fired oven where they cooked pizzas after harvesting olives in the winter months. Adonis's dream for The Olive Grove had come alive. While Stephanos had mellowed, Adonis had embraced his life on the island, and Harlow had bridged the gap between the two of them, opening up a line of communication that had been missing for years.

Harlow hitched up her dress and Adonis helped her over the low stone wall into the orchard. She knew exactly where he was taking her. Her heart flipped, the emotion of the day and her love for him flooding through her as they reached the wooden bench.

They sat down together and Adonis ran his hand across the smooth wood of the seat he'd carved in memory of his mama. He took Harlow's hand in his. The meadow was dark and starlit, the pine forest behind them like a protective hug. Music and laughter drifted on the night air, the colourful lights glinting through the branches of the ancient olive trees. ABBA had taken over again and Harlow imagined the Greek dancing easing for a moment as drinks were topped up and the kids took to the makeshift dance floor to jump around to 'Lay All Your Love On Me'.

'It seemed right to have Mama's favourite song playing at our wedding. She would have loved today.' Adonis clutched Harlow's hand tighter and she wiped away the tear slipping down his face. 'She'd have loved you too, almost as much as I love you.' He broke into a smile that made Harlow's heart soar.

'Oh Adoni, how I wish she could have been a part of today.'

He kissed her gently, his hand relaxing in hers. 'She is, in spirit at least. She's a part of this place and she's here too.' He pressed his free hand to his heart. 'The Olive Grove is filled with memories. It's my past, and it's our future too.'

'Always,' Harlow said as she put her hand on top of his and gazed across the moon-dappled olive grove.

ACKNOWLEDGMENTS

Writing a novel involves a lot of time staring at a blank screen before the characters and story slowly come to life on the page. And despite spending many hours alone making stuff up, it's also a collaboration. This book has been no different.

Thank you Illtud Llyr Dunsford, an ex-location scout who specialised in location shoots in Wales, who was generous with his time and helped me to figure out the logistics of my fictional *One Greek Summer* shoot. Thank you Heather Parsons, author of *Skopelos Trails*, whose knowledge of the island, its wildlife and walks was invaluable to help bring the book to life. My thanks also to the owners of The Olive Farm, Crete, and Antoniou Family Olive Oil on Skopelos. Any inaccuracies, or where creative licence has been used, are completely down to me. Thank you to my husband Nik and his aunt Soula for help with the Greek!

Thank you Judith van Dijkhuizen, always the first person to read my novels and whose suggestions are, without fail, spot on. Thank you to my family and friends, Mum, Nik and Leo in particular, who have got me through a challenging year.

Last but certainly not least, a huge thank you to Caroline Ridding for not only approaching me in the first place and for being enthusiastic about my ideas, but for making my dream come true with a book deal. Your insightful edits and suggestions have made *One Greek Summer* shine, so thank you. It's a joy to work with you and the rest of Team Boldwood.

MORE FROM KATE FROST

We hope you enjoyed reading *One Greek Summer*. If you did, please leave a review.

If you'd like to gift a copy, this book is also available as an ebook, digital audio download and audiobook CD.

Sign up to Kate Frost's mailing list for news, competitions and updates on future books.

https://bit.ly/KateFrostNewsletter

ABOUT THE AUTHOR

Kate Frost is the author of several bestselling romantic escape novels including *The Greek Heart* and *The Love Island Bookshop*. She lives in Bristol and is the Director of Storytale Festival, a book festival for children and teens she co-founded in 2019.

Visit Kate's website: http://kate-frost.co.uk/

Follow Kate on social media:

facebook.com/katefrostauthor
twitter.com/katefrostauthor
instagram.com/katefrostauthor
bookbub.com/authors/kate-frost

ABOUT BOLDWOOD BOOKS

Boldwood Books is a fiction publishing company seeking out the best stories from around the world.

Find out more at www.boldwoodbooks.com

Sign up to the Book and Tonic newsletter for news, offers and competitions from Boldwood Books!

http://www.bit.ly/bookandtonic

We'd love to hear from you, follow us on social media:

facebook.com/BookandTonic
twitter.com/BoldwoodBooks
instagram.com/BookandTonic

Printed in Great Britain
by Amazon